REQUIEM FOR
MARY MAC

A SUPERNATURAL MYSTERY

DOUGLAS COCKELL

Requiem For Mary Mac

A Supernatural Mystery

By Douglas Cockell

dunhillclare@gmail.com

First Edition

Edited by Jody Freeman

Published in Ontario, Canada

Hardcover ISBN: 978-1-990469-06-0

Paperback ISBN: 978-1-990469-07-7

Ebook ISBN: 978-1-990469-08-4

Library and Archives Canada Cataloguing in Publications

***Requiem For Mary Mac* is the third book in the Requiem Series.**

The previous series titles are:

Requiem For Thursday (Book 1) and ***Requiem For Noah*** (Book 2).

CHAPTER ONE

Twenty children moved through the shadows in the old one-room schoolhouse. They belonged to a time when the teacher mixed the ink for the inkwells in a copper pitcher with a long spout and banged a ruler for attention. A time when maps unrolled from the wall and a flag tipped out beside the chalkboard.

Time had ceased to pass for them, so all the ebb and flow outside their classroom—the summer sun, the sound of birds chirping, the dust disturbed by the wind—these were things no longer happening for the children. Timelessness was the only meaningful quality of their existence.

Of course, Cecil Warden, the new owner of the schoolhouse, didn't know any of this.

He couldn't see the children moving in the shafts of sunlight that made such a steep angle with the floor. Cecil couldn't see their scuffed shoes on the fly-specked linoleum tiles or their homespun tunics as they hid, timid and unblinking, behind the stacked wrought-iron desks with their angled wooden tops.

There was nothing he could have seen in the old cloakroom cluttered with boxes of books and foolscap paper turned brown with age except for a threadbare woman's apron, long forgotten, its floral pattern bleached by time, nothing in the two grimy washrooms, last renovated in the fifties, except perhaps a deep sense of a building dying from neglect. The girls' washroom was too small to echo, but there might have been a ringing near the edge of human awareness that was the jumbled sum of a century of giggles and horseplay. The one small mirror, a grudging concession to the sin of vanity, was starred where the silvering was peeling off the back, and it reflected the solemn shadows poorly.

The school children whose forgotten shades flitted behind the sunlight had all died here in the space of a month in 1918. People used the word "succumbed" a lot back then to refer to the thousands who died in the path of the Spanish Influenza: old people; strong, young farm labourers; veterans of the great war—some of them preordained to die by their gas-scarred lungs—and yes, children, undernourished by modern standards and unprotected by an overstretched medical system whose disorganized efforts barely deserved the term.

Back then, the school itself had become a makeshift isolation hospital, the desks moved aside to be replaced with striped mattresses stuffed with shredded wood wool, which in the parlance of the day they charmingly called "excelsior." There were no beds. The caregivers arranged the mattresses on the floor in a rough grid pattern, leaving enough space for them to move about.

The weakest children, which is to say the sweet and the innocent and the guileless, died there fighting with congested lungs for their last breath while volunteers cowered behind their homemade cotton masks and prayed.

Miss Burt's mixed-grade class had numbered twenty, but even when the children chanted together, swaying and clapping hands in a nearby wafer of time, one removed from his own,

Cecil Warden couldn't hear a thing in the high-ceilinged schoolroom.

Although…

Maybe it was because later that afternoon Cecil Warden would be fighting for his own last breath on that very floor, on a space where a mattress filled with excelsior had once lain. Right now, it was just a cleared space on the grey-green floor tiles. But in a way, Cece Warden and a fourth-grade girl would die together there, separated by that least substantial of things: time; a bit more than a hundred years of it.

That afternoon—the afternoon occupied only by Cece Warden and his helper—there was silence in the large room.

Then Cece said, "Does this mean anything to you?" He was looking at that same patch of flooring with a puzzled frown, almost as though he could see the fevered little girl or his own death.

Keith Blair, a tall young man of twenty-two wearing a three-button golf shirt, turned from his broom and gave a slow blink. "I'm sorry?"

"It's a song. I think." Cece, skinny and slightly stooped with age, seemed to beat time with his right hand, completely unaware he was staring down at his own death struggles on that coffin-sized stretch of flooring—anticipating them by little more than a hundred *minutes*. Cece closed his eyes and started to sing, in a reedy, tuneless way: "All dressed in black, black, black." He thought some more and then, "Silver buttons up and down her back, back, back." His foot tapped listlessly, raising a little dust.

The young man laid his broom against the old Franklin stove, tugged off a canvas glove, and wiped his hand across his brow. He narrowed his eyes in thought for a moment, and then brightened. "Oh, yeah. Silver buttons… Sure. It's an old rock song. A fifties classic, 'Walkin' the Dog.'" Blair chanted and did what he thought was a funky Motown move, shuffling with his arms and hips. Not knowing any more words, he hummed for a few seconds, then shrugged. "Something like that."

Cece looked at him, a skeptical eyebrow raised at the dance moves. He frowned and nodded at the floor tiles. "Huh. Well, whatever it is, I can't seem to get the words out of my head and I don't even remember hearing the damn song."

Strangely, there was an undercurrent of urgency about Cece's question, even though the old man wasn't aware that the rhythm in his head was counting out the remaining minutes of his life in handclaps.

In his youth, Cece had sported the physique of a long-distance runner, long-limbed and narrow chested, but in his late seventies, he stooped into an angular scarecrow who got about with a walking stick. It wasn't actually a walking stick—it was a blue hiking pole marked with a "Trail Buddy" logo because that drew less attention to Cece Warden's advancing years. The pole was nearby, leaning against the large maple teacher's desk.

Being a teacher himself, Cece found it easy to hire a young helper for the cleanup, choosing from a class full of business students who needed the money. There were eager young undergrads who would have helped their professor for free just to pad their resumés with his esteemed name.

Cece was a full professor of Economics. Although his first calling was teaching, he had the habit of accumulating wealth and he knew how it worked; even though being wealthy, he had lost sight of the point of it all. Buying the schoolhouse seemed a clever move, and shrewd acquisitions had become a habit hard to break.

"Try to sweep from the corners towards the middle of the floor, then we can bag all this sawdust stuff," Cece grumped, being a little annoyed with himself; what had possessed him, taking on this dusty old building?

Young Keith Blair, helping Cece for a modest wage, was still taking courses himself; a part-time student barely supporting himself with government loans and whatever work he could find. This job with Professor Warden was number three. It wasn't so much that Cece had an affection for the student—the kid was too taciturn and introverted for that—but the young man always seemed to be around, politely interested in Cece's lectures. He was a little odd, sullen and withdrawn, but the word had gotten back to Cece that the young man was good with his hands.

Blair took a cheap flip phone out of his pocket and looked at it. "I told my girlfriend that I'd be done by four. She'll be waiting."

Cece rubbed his grey stubble. "We can't leave the floor like this. You should always finish what you set out to do."

Blair fought to keep his expression neutral. The rich old geezer was lecturing him as though it was part of his MBA program. The old man had forgotten what it was to be poor and desperate.

"Come on, Blair. Another twenty minutes should do it."

The schoolhouse, Cece's newly purchased investment property, stood at the corner of two country roads amid a scruffy carpet of bush and weeds. It still had much of its last coat of paint, a sun-bleached wooden building with eight tall windows to a side, and a shingled bell tower perched near the front of the main roof. There was a slightly skewed weather vane topping off the tower, the rusted shape of a rooster creaking to face down the breeze.

Beneath this, a smaller wooden extension built onto the front of the main building had a lower peaked roof and a stepped porch. The iron railings screwed into the planks of the steps were a rust colour, shedding a few remaining flakes of black paint. The extension housed the cloakroom and the washrooms.

The schoolhouse had been the location of dozens of community events over the years, and for Cece, this particular venture into real estate had begun at a county flea market sale while looking over boxes of old schoolbooks and collectables, most dating as far back as the turn of the twentieth century. Cece had always been interested in old books, but that afternoon in one of the boxes he had found an edition of *Blackstone's Commentaries on the Laws of England* that went all the way back to 1832. The cover had the frayed patina of an old saddle. Cece was intrigued by antiques, mostly because he enjoyed the idea of things becoming more valuable with age—not like people.

It was as he was stroking the crumbling leather of the binding that day, weeks ago, that he looked around him at the vaulted ceiling and stacked desks pushed against the walls. The tattered book made him think about age, something he had always respected, but it occurred to Cece at that moment that the school desks alone with their iron filigree work and ink-stained wooden tops would be worth something online. Cece had an eye for value, and he was quick with figures.

The idea of buying the whole schoolhouse property seemed to just follow along into his head. The location of the wooden building was promising from a real estate point of view. The structure was old but simple, cured by time, with the lines of an old rural church. In place of a steeple, there was that covered bell tower. The building would be easy to demolish, being essentially a wooden box, but it might also be worth renovating. There were people with money who would find it cute to refurbish an old gem like this. All those TV reno shows put ideas into people's heads.

So, Cece went ahead with his plan to invest in the old structure, and one way or the other, to resell it. The building had been used for many purposes, but mostly for temporary events: bake sales and flea markets. Nobody had taken the trouble to toss the heavy furniture, the desks, fixtures, or that big old wood stove with its long, black stovepipe piercing the slope of the ceiling.

It was a Halton County rural school, circa 1910 with a tragic past, but Cece didn't know about the devastating flu of 1918 that had taken most of the students. To him, it was just a clever investment, and making money was something he did instinctively.

Laying his broom aside, Cece lifted one of the four circular plates off the top of the old Franklin stove using a hooked iron handle cast for just that purpose and peered into the dark belly of the stove. He sniffed rust and damp charcoal, wrinkling his nose in distaste.

"This has been used fairly recently. Good to know it's still usable. I might be able to sell the stove as is." He clanged the plate back in place and rubbed his hands together.

"Truth is," he groused to the young man, "I'm an academic first, not a businessman. I can hardly believe I bought the old place. It's gonna be more trouble than it's worth, I bet."

"So, why *did* you decide to buy it?" Blair asked, a trace of irritation in his voice.

Lately, he had been feeling sorry for himself and there was plenty of dust and trash in the room to remind him of his career prospects. He couldn't relate to someone having enough money to speculatively buy real estate. He could barely afford to pay rent to his parents while he attended his classes.

"I don't know." Cece sighed. "I guess I've got an eye for hidden value. Still, I don't know what got into me. The place seemed to speak to me. Lord knows I haven't bought any property this old before."

The young man groaned inwardly at Warden's self-importance and wondered just how much property the old-timer *had* turned over, making bags of money each time. A tinge of jealousy made him clench his gloved hand. Warden could also have afforded a professional cleanup team to stabilize the place instead of paying an undergrad with real carpentry skills a pittance to play janitor for him. For all his money and ivy league degrees, Warden was just plain cheap.

For his part, Cece Warden didn't want to put too much money into the enterprise, so it made sense to hire the student handyman to come on weekends. In a way, it was a stalling tactic while Cece tried to decide what the next step would be for the property.

Cece frowned at the way the boy leaned against one of the old desks. "Main thing is, protect the furnishings. That teacher desk up on the dais alone—that'll bring three or four hundred. I can get at least a hundred a piece for the student desks. Hell, it'd be worth it just for the wrought iron on those things. You could repurpose the scrollwork."

Blair thought about what he could do with three or four hundred dollars.

Cece brightened at the thought of his own cleverness and muttered his tuneless refrain, "Miss Mary Mac, Mac, Mac. Silver buttons up'n down 'er back, back, back..." He picked up a broom, hoping Blair would get the message. "The location will attract people working as far away as the west side of Toronto or in Port Credit," he said as though lecturing the young man on real estate. "Gothic revival, quaint bell tower, surrounded by pristine farm-land, gently rolling hills. Yeah," he assured himself. "She'll sell."

Out the tall windows, you could see the distant escarpment and the roads nearby, paved in single lanes, were quiet. It wouldn't be long before the sprawl of Oakville north of the QEW highway would be lapping at this quiet rural corner.

Burlington was expanding from the west, too, and the 407 Highway, built with public money and sold to finance the Conservative election campaign, had rolled nearby to the north. It all meant Cece's land would keep getting more valuable.

His first thought was to get the crumbling old building knocked down so he could have a big new house built on the land, but Cece had enough taste and reverence for the past to recognize that it was an imposing structure with a million-dollar nostalgia angle. By restoring the facade and reinforcing the framing, he could avoid endless rezoning applications. The place was a century-old building now, so he might swing a historic designation, which would allow him to repurpose the interior as a dwelling—if he kept the exterior intact and recognizable as what it had been: a rural school.

Of course, he was a teacher himself, a professor at the Ron Joyce School of Business in Oakville, so the old schoolhouse was a sentimental fit.

It started to rain, a brief sun shower. As it swept the roof, the rain took on a rhythmical quality that didn't sound quite right. It was a steady pulse, like clapping hands that Cece found irritating. Blair thought about his girlfriend sitting out in her car, wondering what was keeping him.

"You hear that?" Cece said. "The way the rain comes and goes?"

"Comes and goes?" Blair tugged at his damp shirt. "You mean because of the wind gusts?"

"Huh? Yeah. Wind gusts. I guess that's it."

Eventually, as they worked, dragging piles of desks and cardboard boxes aside so they could sweep to the walls, the rain quit and the sun came out again. It was hot work, and the rain did nothing to lessen the humidity.

Cece stood in the cleared space, while the shafted sunlight swam with dust motes, and he stared at the slightly raised platform that fronted the end wall and afforded a sort of focal point to the room.

"Back then, the teacher sat up there above the students. It was a less egalitarian age," Cece said.

The young man gave a bitter laugh. "Now they put the students on a pedestal—in theory, at least."

Cece nodded, loosening his shirt collar. "The teacher was probably an unmarried woman in those days."

Blair stood on his toes, trying to see through the window if his girlfriend was still there waiting. It would be stifling in the car, and hot in the sun. "Why unmarried?" he mumbled.

"Because when women married, they were forced to quit their jobs. Married women weren't allowed to teach."

The young man hauled a black garbage bag closer. "Was that to preserve jobs for men?"

"Maybe. There were a lot of young men just back from the war, but I think there was a suspicion that a married woman was too experienced to teach innocent children. It's a Protestant thing."

"And yet they'd let a man teach."

Cece smirked. "It was a prudish age. Full of hypocrisy."

"You're talking about what, early 1900s? Thirties maybe?"

"More the twenties."

"You know your history."

"Huh."

Cece gave a self-deprecating smile and poked a fly-specked line of dust out of a nearly inaccessible corner. There were still stacks of plywood tables left over from the flea market days. As he swept, Cece didn't look closely enough to see the excelsior that had spilled like straw from a striped mattress a hundred years ago, even though there were degraded traces of the shredded wood in every dusty crevice of the schoolhouse.

"History's a perfect fit with economics," Cece said. "You have to know about historic movements to understand the way the markets changed over the decades."

As though seeing some deep importance in the thought, Keith Blair narrowed his eyes without taking them off Professor Warden's back. Cece, who had been stooped over his task, backed up with his broom and straightened, and when he turned around, he found himself face to face with the young man. A little unsteady on his feet, Cece stumbled. When he steadied himself, he found that the long wooden shafts of their broomsticks were crossed between them, and for a moment, the two men stood there—medieval peasants with quarter-staves about to do battle.

The shades of the twenty children suddenly became still, their eyes shrinking back into the shadows.

CHAPTER TWO

Ten years later…

Indy, a tan-coloured Labrador, stood looking up at the door of A.L. Rouhl's office, uncertain whether to pay attention to the laughter behind him in the living room or to the voices on the other side of the office door.

The muttering from his late master's office meant nothing to him. There was no hostility in it—just the ramblings of people with eternity on their hands. One of the voices he recognized, the voice he had heard most often in his life. The other voice was soft, affectionate, and definitely that of a woman.

At last, he turned his handsome profile from the office door as the two women following behind him from the living room walked up to his side. One was tall and slender with generous pale lips, the other shorter and striking because of her coiling blond hair and large green eyes. Now *their* conversation was different: full of laughter and conspiratorial snickers. The shorter woman, who at times seemed a giggle incarnate, a petite blond with owlish glasses, reached down and ruffled Indy's fur.

"Isn't this exciting, Indy? I, Harriet Blaine, am about to enter the room where a great author actually wrote his books. A few years ago, I was reading him at school, and now, look at me! I'm about to see where those books were actually *written*."

Carly Rouhl, cooler and more jaded, chuckled at the young woman's enthusiasm. Carly had grown up with the great author, her father, but she knew enough about the cult of A.L. Rouhl to accept the hero worship. Her father's greatness was the profound mystery at the core of her life.

"What was it?" Carly asked. "What book did you study in school?"

"*Meridian*," Harriet said.

"Figures. A mid-career book. His last couple of books were too dark for high school. Too many brooding murderers and treacherous lovers. Too much cynicism. His sales suffered a bit towards the end."

"I've read them all. To me, he seemed to get more insightful and deep as he got older."

"Actually, the critics tend to agree with you, but the public thought his stuff was getting too heavy." Carly shook her head, letting her dark hair swing. "Come on, Indy, step aside. I've got a literary groupie here who thinks this creepy room is historic. Let's let her down easy."

Carly turned the knob and swung the door of the office in.

There was no one inside.

It had been her house since the death of her father last winter. Now, another winter was approaching and still, she seldom came to A.L. Rouhl's office, preferring to do her own writing at the dining room table or in the kitchen where she could pop in a coffee pod any time she felt the urge.

The office still made her uncomfortable. Her father had taken his own life here, and the crazy woman responsible for his final illness and decline died here, too, right in front of Carly's eyes. The story of Marcella Cole's mysterious death by gunshot had made the room notorious in the press, and if anything, A.L.'s cult following had grown. Nothing like a spectacular murder-suicide to enhance a writer's mystique.

If Carly were to throw the little office open to the public, crowds would shuffle morbidly down the corridor to stare at the carpet where Marcella Cole bled out into her stiff bodice. On a trip to Savannah, Carly had stood in the room where Jim Williams shot his gay lover with a Luger in *Midnight in the Garden,* and, yes, she had tried to visualize the body on the carpet. She got it.

There was nothing of that in Harriet's bubbly enthusiasm, though. Her eyes, usually made even larger by her green framed glasses, were now almost squeezed shut by her delighted grin. Carly noticed for the first time that Harriet's lipstick was applied generously, but just short of the corners of her mouth, giving her lips an old-fashioned rosebud effect. Sometimes her friend and office manager seemed all eyes and red lips to Carly, but the effect was charming.

Indy led the way into the centre of the little room. Harriet stood gaping in the doorway, taking in the genial clutter she had seen so many times in pictures. Indy did a ritual circle and began to settle on his usual spot near the centre of the braided rug.

"Funny about Indy," Carly said, stepping in. "He was in the room when my father passed away, and I suspect he saw Peggy Goss being murdered at the magazine offices, too. If any dog deserves psychiatric counselling, it's Indy. I watched him for a couple of weeks after all the violence was all over, and he was subdued and wary for a while. When I think about it, he got over it all much faster than I did. Look at him. I think he still feels comfortable here."

While Indy stretched, Harriet took tiny, reverent steps onto the oval rug. "I bet Indy spent many happy years sitting by his master's side while those books were being written—the later ones, I mean."

"A few. He was still basically a puppy then."

The lab raised his head and looked around. Another second and he was on his feet—alert, as though distracted by something. Then he was trotting as purposefully as though tugged by his collar.

Carly watched Indy's antics curiously. "Look at him, sniffing around. You'd think all those mementos on the shelves were his instead of Dad's."

Indy was making a sniffing tour, searching as if he hadn't memorized the scents by now.

Carly couldn't resist sniffing the air herself. There was no lingering scent of the man—no whiff of Scotch or aftershave, and no cordite from the two fatal shots fired here—just the mustiness of books and old leather: the chair, the desk pad, the rows of bric-a-brac.

Harriet, wide-eyed, approached the writer's desk.

"Well," Carly sighed, "you said you wanted to see the great man's hidey-hole. Sorry. Nothing special. Not any more. Only an ageing memorial to a fine storyteller. I have someone come in and dust now and then. I imagine that's a nightmare job with all these umbrellas and cigarette cases and whatnot. There's dozens of meaningless pieces of junk around the room, but, of course, I can't get rid of any of it because of Rouhl fans who see it all as priceless relics."

Harriet went on grinning without taking her eyes off the low-backed leather chair. "They're all important pieces because each one is related to one of A.L.'s stories, everything collected on his travels."

"That's the myth anyway," Carly said. "I don't know how much of that is true. Except for this, of course." She picked a black vinyl book from the shelves facing the desk and immediately put it down as though it felt unclean. "Marcella Cole's diary."

Harriet spun around. "What? The woman who died here? The serial killer?"

Carly nodded, and Harriet tore herself away from the empty chair to peer down at the diary. The sudden movement made her almost trip over Indy in the cramped space, and she swung her arms to regain her balance. Indy ignored her, working the room intently, beginning to focus his attention on a low shelf.

"Whoa! What's up with Indy? Is he always so intense? He reminds me of one of those hunting dogs pointing to a rabbit hole."

"Nah. He's usually pretty cool. I don't know what's got into him. Sometimes he seems to get all excited over nothing. Like now. Something's bothering him."

Carly stepped around Harriet, close enough to smell her warm fragrance. "What are you looking at, Indy? Found a rabbit in the old man's office, have you? Come on, mister. You've seen all this junk before."

Indy was sitting up now, his head to one side, one ear cocked at the lower shelf doing the "his master's voice" routine.

Carly followed his snout. "What? What is it, boy? This?"

She drew out a largish object about the size and shape of a box of printing paper protruding from a shelf of books. It was a mottled tan colour, worn at the edges and with a burnished sheen of wear from handling. If it was leather, it was stiff and hard from age. She cleared a spot at the front of the shelf and put the box down again—flat this time. Harriet looked on in horror as though a boorish tourist had just rearranged the paintbrushes in Giacometti's studio.

Carly gave the box a cursory shove without lifting it off the shelf again. "Is it because it's leather, Indy? You've got chew toys. You can't have this."

Harriet moved closer, tilting her head to one side and wrinkling her nose. Carly picked up on the faint scent, too; perspiration or seaweed. Carly sniffed at the box, and snatching it up, handed it immediately to Harriet. "Maybe we should take this out of here. The room's smelling a little musty."

Startled, Harriet turned the box in her hands, feeling its considerable weight. "That has to be it. Indy smells the leather." Harriet sniffed again, closer this time. "Leather and...the sea? What is this thing anyway?"

"I think it's a book," Carly said. "It's in a sort of case, but you can see the gap of the spine along this edge. It looks really old. Definitely antique."

Harriet tugged at the leather spine. "I can't get the book out. It seems to be stuck—I mean, if it *is* a book."

Carly nodded. "I should get Evan to look at this. It might actually be worth something."

Harriet had met Evan, Carly's movie-star handsome boyfriend, who often looked in on her at the magazine around quitting time. She turned and watched Carly rub her fingers against her slacks. Harriet gave a half frown, one eyebrow rising like a Chinese brush stroke on her winter pale skin.

"It's funny the way you touch things in here, Car," Harriet said. "You drop them as if they're hot."

Carly shook her head. "What's funny is *you* don't pick up on how *creepy* all this stuff on the shelves is. Dad would go around borrowing, trash diving, and just plain stealing stuff for his stories. He actually believed that he got a kind of stimulus for his imagination from things his characters owned and handled. I remember him sitting there turning an old tobacco pouch or something over in his hands as if it was going to write the next page for him."

"You told me that story. What you never explained is how he stumbled on so much drama that way. If I stole someone's toothbrush or their stapler or something, I'd pick up on a whole lot of boring yard work and grocery shopping—if I got anything at all. What drew A.L. to the serial killers, creeps and eccentrics he profiled in his books? Now *that's* a gift."

Carly rolled her eyes. "You're forgetting that I don't believe all that stuff about him getting insights from inanimate objects. I mean, I've read the testament he left on his laptop—how he believed in psychometry and prophecy and all that, but I don't think he was being literal. I think he was mostly just romanticizing the creative process. There's no way of knowing how much of what he wrote about is true, anyway. The bottom line is he was a great writer; an inventor."

"But you said yourself you'd had 'experiences.' You even called them visions. There was that time you kept seeing pineapples, and it turned out that pineapples were a design theme at the Moreland House."

"I shouldn't have told you that. I've had wild imaginative waking dreams that scared the shit out of me, yes; but that's neurosis, not clairvoyance."

"But there was that time you called 911 to get help for your detective friend Weiss, and it turned out he and his partner *did* need help. How did you know?"

"I *didn't* know. Don't you see? Oh, sure; I knew Detective Weiss and his partner were going to interview Noah Goodwin's family that day at Moreland House, and I was worried that they'd get in some kind of trouble. I got this irrational fear based on what I knew about Noah Goodwin. Remember I wrote that story about him for the magazine? I still can't believe I had the gall to call out an ambulance on so little evidence. All I actually knew was that Noah Goodwyn was a creepy guy. It was a complete stab in the dark. I'm glad I had the presence of mind to give a false name to the dispatcher."

"You told me that at the time, you were handling a carving Goodwyn had given you—that it made you imagine things."

"What I said was, the carving *helped* me to imagine things. There's a difference. I can see how stuff—this old book, for instance—can stimulate a writer's mind. It's rich, textured, it has a scent and a patina. It's evocative. That doesn't mean that the stories that flow from it are real, rooted in reality. They're just stories."

"But your father was right about Marcella Cole. She *was* a murderer. Maybe he got that from holding her diary."

"There were a lot of people who thought Cole was guilty of murder, even though she had been acquitted in court, including the police. I know they were right because she actually drew a gun and was prepared to shoot Evan and me right here in this office. But Dad? He had no proof."

Carly's head was swivelling slightly as if she was arguing with herself. "What I'm saying is, he was right about her, but so were a lot of other people at the time."

Then Carly held up her hands, conceding a point. "Look, I know there was a lot of strange stuff in the Moreland House incident and Marcella Cole's death. And it's true I've seen things I can't explain—things that keep me up at night—but I have to believe there's an explanation for everything. If I don't cling to that, I think I might begin to lose touch with reality."

"You're afraid of going mad?"

"Hey, easy, girl. Nowadays, we talk about our 'mental health.'"

"Is that why you're so ambivalent about writing fiction yourself? You're worried about your mental health?"

"Maybe."

Harriet touched Carly's arm. "That's a pity. You're hard on yourself, but if you ask me, I think you may have inherited your father's gift." Harriet returned her attention to the box, turning it over in her hands, sighting along the apparent spine. "Do you mind if I pull on this a bit more? I'll be careful."

"Sure. A.L.'s adoring fans will never know. Go ahead."

Harriet pursed her plum-red lips and frowned. She made a

breathy, grunting sound, and suddenly, her shoulders jerked as the contents of the box began to slide out. "It *is* a book, see?"

"Go on, pull it all the way out. That's it..."

There was a stunned silence as Harriet carefully exposed the book's internal cover, a worn leather surface almost black with age. Compelled by curiosity, Harriet laid the book on A.L.'s desk and slowly opened the cover. They both gave a quiet gasp.

The title page, the frontispiece, seemed to glow in the light let in by the window. Coiled dragons and tortuous vines in an intricate filigree surrounded a stylized letter "x."

Carly was wide-eyed. "My God, it's beautiful."

The single page that formed a frontispiece for the book was inscribed in gold leaf and a vermilion ink that still had a rich, blood-red lustre to it. Carly could see at a glance that it wasn't a printed book. The lettering was calligraphic and artful.

"They call that illumination," she said. "It's glorious. I'll have to have that dated, but it looks middle Christian. It's in Latin. The illuminations that I'm familiar with are from the Middle English period, but this could be later. Show me the next page."

Harriet turned to the second page. The back of the title page was blank, which Carly thought was curious. The facing leaf, after the wonderful opening page, was disappointingly drab: neat, calligraphic words separated by an almost imperceptible space, the sentences themselves spaced but unpunctuated.

"Yup. It's Latin." Carly said. "I recognize some words from the Vulgate. That would mean it's a later type of manuscript; medieval, not classical."

Harriet leafed carefully through the first few pages. There were crude woodblock prints spaced through the text: angels with oval halos and saints being gruesomely tortured, hung upside down and sawed.

"Nice," she said, her lip curled in disgust.

"Nice, but not spectacular." Carly had her hands behind her back, craning close, but not too close. "My first impression is that the book was for regular use. Not the sort of thing you'd chain in your library as a holy relic. A book of prayers maybe. Sermons..."

Carly bent further over the pages, angling her head. "Hey, I think I get it—these pages are vellum, animal skin. A kind of scraped leather. That's why the box was hard to open. The inside pages must have gotten swollen with moisture; the skins bulked up and jammed inside the wooden box."

Closing the book up, Harriet pushed it carefully into its case. "What are you going to do with it?"

"Well, I'll see what Evan says. He knows a lot about books. He just doesn't care to read them."

"What?"

"I'm just being snide. He's sort of an expert on things like graphology and QDE. It's a sore point between us that he sees books and texts as things to be analyzed and categorized. I don't think he's read a novel or a play since college. Still, he'd know what to do with this."

Harriet shook her head as though dusting off cobwebs. "Whoa! Back up. I get the graphology; that's the handwriting analysis he does on his TV shows and for the police, right? But QDE? I've never heard of that."

"Sorry." Carly wrinkled her nose in disgust. "It stands for—give me strength!—'Questioned Document Examination' or something. I think it has to do with assessing documents in court. I tell him he's one of the bean counters of literature."

"I bet he didn't appreciate that. Speaking of which, I haven't seen you with Evan for weeks now. Is he in town?"

"I can be hard on poor Evan. He keeps calling, but..." Carly shrugged.

Harriet picked up on Carly's ambivalence about her hunky TV personality boyfriend and casually turned away from her friend. But at the same time, Harriet's hidden reaction was curious: a mixture of surprise and—satisfaction.

CHAPTER THREE

Parry Sound is a tourist town, winding uphill from a natural harbour on Georgian Bay. Its population, inflated by summer people from the nearby Muskoka Lakes, is made up of locals, indigenous people, and wealthy retirees from the greater Toronto area looking for a quieter life. It's a quaint place to retire if you don't mind the pollution wafting up on the prevailing winds from faraway American cities.

It was a three-hour drive from Burlington, up Highway 400, with a coffee stop along the way at an en route food court. With an early start, Detective Eilert Weiss managed to show up on a scenic bluff outside the Bayview Retirement Home around noon. It was a Saturday, the sky over the great freshwater sound a complex impasto of wind-smeared cloud.

The glass entry doors whispered apart for him and Weiss walked into the lobby. Its dominant features were the two wedge-shaped windows that jutted like a ship's prow towards Georgian Bay. There was a marble theme to the benches and pillars. The couches were red velour and inviting. Or they would have been if they weren't already filled with senior citizens, some steepling their fingers over cane handles, some cradling silent cell phones.

There was nothing pitiable about these people, though. They may have shrunk within their shirt collars and pearl necklaces, but the collars were expensive linen and they had the air of hotel guests who were paying their way and expecting service. The women were dressed in ten-year-old fashions, but their slacks and blouses were expensive-looking, their fingers warm with gold.

Weiss paused on the snow mat, looking around at the slow-moving groupings of men and women before noticing the reception desk. A beefy concierge moved towards him, ready to head him off if he tried to go directly to the double elevator doors. Getting the idea, Weiss identified himself, and the attractive young woman behind the reception desk glanced at her computer screen. Without looking up, she said, "Gordon, get Mr. Clendenning, will you?"

Gordon, the uniformed concierge, didn't have far to go. A big bear of a man was rising slowly from an armchair. No cane, no walker—just a slow, bow-legged shuffle.

The receptionist waved. "Mr. Clendenning? Detective Weiss. I believe you were expecting him."

Clendenning, a retired detective himself, reminded Weiss of many of his own colleagues in Halton: smart men and women who had nevertheless worked their way up from the street. He looked tough and his rheumy eyes were remorselessly appraising. Weiss shook Clendenning's big meaty hand.

"Thank you for seeing me."

"Name's Harry. Been waiting for you down here in the lobby. Thank God there's a view." He tipped his head towards the big sky over the bay, and then glanced around the lobby. "And there's women. You said you wanted to talk to me about my consulting work."

"If you don't mind. 'Consulting'—that's unusual, isn't it?

Moving around from county to county, helping local police? How do you even *get* work like that? Last consulting detective I heard about was a Belgian named Poirot."

Clendenning's laughter came from a deeply congested chest and ended with a cough. "You don't get it formally, that's for sure. The paperwork would kill you. It was all word of mouth and favours exchanged by superintendents and local politicians."

"And all driven by your gift for unravelling dead-end cases of a certain type."

Clendenning smirked. "A certain type, you say. I'm guessing that's why you're here. You've got a case 'of a certain type' you want help with."

"Actually, no. I don't have anything current that calls for your particular type of experience." Weiss flexed his shoulders as though his shirt was too tight. "Although, my last two cases have left me...uncomfortable."

Clendenning grasped Weiss's bicep in a move that might have been friendly. "You're kinda thin, Weiss. Did you ever have to take down a violent perp?"

"Once or twice, but you're right. It didn't go well. These days, I'm more inclined to step back and call for backup."

"Uh-huh." Clendenning shrugged and indicated the elevators. Let's go up. I've ordered a flask of coffee and I've got shortbread."

All the apartments, including Clendenning's rooms, were bayside, and he had a small balcony that looked down on the narrow public parking lot and the vista that drew tourists from all over Ontario. By rising on his toes, Weiss could make out his car at one of the meters. Well, not *his* car.

Clendenning was unscrewing the top of a large chrome carafe and pouring steaming black coffee into mugs emblazoned with the building's logo. "I was a consultant, yes, but you think I didn't have to deal with thugs? You have to stand up to people, Weiss—criminals and angry families alike. But it's a hell of a lot easier if you have something *on* them, if you know what I mean. Information, evidence. Oh, and a gun."

Weiss raised his eyebrows. "That's not what I expected to hear from you. From what I understand, you brought comfort and closure to people the regular cops couldn't help."

"Comfort. Yeah. Sure. I did that." There was something sour about the way he said it. "I gave people closure by giving them an explanation of what happened to them or their loved ones, but I seldom got a conviction. Best I could do was, uh, confront the guilty," he waved his hand dismissively, "and exonerate the innocent, of course."

Harry Clendenning was thoughtful for a second, then he grinned and handed Weiss a mug. He gestured to the cream and sugar on the tray and shuffled to the window. Weiss watched the broad shoulders and thick arms that stretched Clendenning's jacket taut, thought about the old man's pug nose and boxer's ears, then joined him at the marble sill.

There was a narrow balcony with two wicker chairs and a table on the other side of the glass, and beyond the railing was the high bluff on which the retirement community was built. The window gave them a grand view of Georgian Bay with its scatter of islands fading into the distance.

Weiss nodded approvingly. "They call it the Thirty Thousand Islands, don't they?"

"I've never bothered to count them." With a twist of the waist that pained him, Clendenning looked down towards the curving roadway that had brought Weiss up the hill. "There's a school down that way," Clendenning said, gesturing. "You must have passed it. It has a big playground and soccer field." He thought for a moment. "That's the way it is, isn't it? You go to school, you get educated, you try out for the team." He paused. "You live your life, making compromises and taking names. You have a career." He laughed bitterly. "And then... You know what happens at the end, Weiss?"

Weiss looked at Clendenning's flattened profile and shook his head.

"Why, you climb the hill, of course." And he spread his arms at the windy heights outside his window.

"Is that a metaphor?" Weiss smiled, ruffling his moustache.

Looking puzzled, Clendenning went on. "If you say so. What I'm saying is, from up here, it becomes clearer, you see; the way you came, the choices you made, the mistakes. From up here, it's all spread out below you. Your whole life."

"And your conclusion?"

Clendenning was suddenly wary. "What are we talking about here, Weiss? Why did you come all this way?"

"My partner told me about you—how you consulted around the province on difficult cases."

Clendenning gave a humourless laugh. "Is that what your partner called them? Difficult cases?"

"No, he called them 'weird shit,' actually."

Clendenning smiled. "That's more to the point."

"My partner, Prem, told me about another cop over in Orillia, name of Macklin. I looked him up too, but turns out he passed away a few years ago."

"Yeah, I knew Mac. Respected cop, but..."

"Go on."

"Soft is the word that comes to mind. Sentimental. He was always thinking about the families and friends—all the people whose lives were tore up because of violent crime. He had a box of files he kept. He showed them to me. The 'dead files' he called them."

"And how about you, Harry? Did you have your dead files? Who were *you* helping?"

Clendenning's head was bald and shiny, but he rubbed the

stiff grey bristles on his cheek and looked at Weiss defensively. "I'm more like you, Weiss."

"Excuse me?"

"I was interested in how I could write it all up, how I could find closure for the department on a few outstanding cases. That's how it all started, this consulting business. I was officially with my department in Peterborough, but over the years, I was able to help out a few districts down your way. Wentworth, Halton—"

"Where did you get that idea about me?"

"After you called, I read up on your splashy cases. Can't be bothered much with the internet anymore, but there's a kid who works here who'll do the occasional search for me. You were stuck with that fire at the old Moreland House. I read about that fiasco. Although," he shrugged, "with my experience, I was in a position to read between the lines a little."

"And the A.L. Rouhl suicide? You must have heard about that one," Weiss offered.

"See, that's your first problem, Weiss. All this high-profile stuff. You're attracting *way* too much attention. I mean, honestly? A.L. Rouhl? Even *I've* read some of his stuff. Still, I got to hand it to you—you found a way of closing the book on Marcella Cole without sending some poor bugger up for her murder. As for rich bitch Ruth Moreland and her shady doctor, well, it's a wonder that you got your people to buy into *that* outcome—everyone walking free, I mean. But you did it. And that's why you're here. It still bothers you. Am I right?"

Weiss turned away. "I'm wondering if I should quit. I'm not sure what I'm doing anymore. Instead of revealing the truth, I seem to be in the business of disguising it. I tell myself that I'm making higher moral judgements, being as fair as I can be, but then I think, 'who the hell am I to take that on myself?' Didn't you ever feel that way?"

Clendenning's face darkened. "Moral judgements? Hah! Do

you know what they called me behind my back? The Sweeper. Now, there's an image for you, Weiss. Me with my wet broom, sweeping up the shit no one else could handle."

Weiss didn't want to look at Clendenning; he followed the rug pattern, shifting his weight. "How did you stay sane?"

Clendenning's voice was low and there was an unpleasant chuckle bubbling just below the surface. "Never had a problem with that."

"Look, Harry; I don't have much time here with you, so I'm going to be plain: you believe the cases you consulted on had supernatural elements, like the Rouhl case and Noah Goodwin —the ones I drew. That's what they said about you. That's what they were whispering: 'Harry knows how to resolve the weird cases,' and your colleagues were happy to shift those cases to your desk because... Hell, I don't know; because you were willing to take them on. And you worked with them."

"I'll be plain too, Weiss. You're here because you've had a couple of cases you couldn't close without, well, having an open mind."

Weiss winced. "I can't tell you how often I've heard that phrase lately; 'an open mind.'"

"I hope you didn't come here expecting me to tell you what to do about those cases of that sort. From what I've read, you found your own way to satisfy your superiors. Man, if you ask me, you got the gift. Of course, you had to satisfy the damn media too, because you were dealing with the rich and famous. I tried to stay away from publicity."

Weiss felt the cold glass of the window against his knuckles and let his eyes range across the washed-out grey of the sound. "I'm here because I'm on the verge of quitting the force. I mean, all of us have this fragile stick to lean on: the idea that we're serving justice. In homicide, you tell yourself that you're avenging the victim who can't get justice for himself. But twice now, I've found myself thwarting due process—suppressing evidence, lying to my colleagues, if only by omission—and all because I had to write up cases that defied rational explanation."

"So you broke a few rules."

"I'm guessing there's a big difference between you and me, Harry. You believe in this…other reality, so you invited these cases, made it your mission, or whatever. You helped a lot of people. I'm ready to believe that. But I—"

"Okay, stop right there, Weiss. First of all, I didn't go looking for these impossible cases. They found *me*, just as they're finding you."

"Because you're prepared to believe? Or maybe you somehow see what other people can't."

"And you don't?"

"Okay, at Moreland House, I saw something I would have called impossible," Weiss said quietly, choosing his words carefully. "But it wasn't just me. A half-dozen people saw it. Thank God we were all smart enough to keep our mouths shut. If we hadn't, we would have been ridiculed and disbelieved. I found myself helping to explain it all away with nonsense about flash fires. It left me humiliated."

Clendenning seemed surprised. "So you're saying you *don't* have the gift? You don't see what others can't?"

"That…that's all—Look, I'm sorry, Harry. I don't mean to disrespect you or question your motives. I'm sure you believe in what you do, and that you've used your instincts to help people."

"Instincts? That's what you believe in?" Clendenning sniffed. "That's what you think I relied on?"

"Harry, I don't believe in visions or prophecy or any of that. What I saw—that looming projection of a dying man's personality—had some kind of reality, it had a reality that other people besides me could see. But this business of personal extrasensory gifts, I don't buy it, and I have never personally experienced it."

Clendenning was looking at Weiss, but his eyes lost focus for a moment and then he nodded slowly.

"Aa-h," he breathed. "But you know someone who *has*."

Weiss jerked his head around and returned Clendenning's stare.

The old cop smiled. "Yes, I thought so. Do you have a relationship with this person? It's a woman, isn't it?" Clendenning went on searching Weiss's face. "Yes. I can see it is. I said that these cases found me. Well, maybe I was wrong about you, Weiss. These cases are finding *her*."

Despite himself, Weiss's mind was suddenly full of Carly Rouhl's face—her wide lips pressed in intense thought, her deep brown eyes narrowed in suspicion. "But she had nothing to do with the Moreland House case, not directly."

Clendenning sipped his coffee and went back to a survey of the cloud jam along the horizon. "I'm not going to bother trying to explain these things to you, but for me, there were times I felt like a lightning rod. I was handed insights into people's lives that I couldn't rationally explain. I think maybe in your case," he shot a sideways glance at Weiss, "*she's* the lightning rod. As long as you care about her, you're going to be drawn in. Drawn to the cases cops shun."

"You're asking me to believe in this woman's…insights?"

"And you do, don't you, Weiss? *That's* exactly why this is happening to you. Don't you see? You're in her orbit."

For a moment, Weiss was caught in a confusion of surprise and denial. "That's nonsense. Okay, I trust her instincts, but she's just someone I know—someone I… We were thrown together by the Rouhl case, you see—by her father's death."

"And again by the Moreland House case, I suppose. Don't you see, Weiss? This isn't over."

Weiss was looking down at his coffee mug, but there was an expression on his face that was hard to read. Fear maybe? Guilt?

Clendenning glanced across his shoulder. "Don't look so sad, Detective. Maybe she's good for you." He turned, put his coffee on the sill and crossed his arms. "She may even be saving you. It's all a matter of point of view."

"What are you talking about? You can't know anything about us—about our...relationship."

"So tell me some more about what you saw at Moreland House. Sounds interesting. None of that was on the web."

Weiss tried to deflect the question. "I'm willing to believe that a strong human personality can make an impression that lingers in the mind..."

And Weiss went on that way for a few minutes, Clendenning listening skeptically, but it was obvious Weiss was trying desperately to rationalize something rather than confront it. He was trying to transform a looming monster that had turned a cable car into a rotten framework of dissolving wood into some pseudo-scientific phenomena, so the conversation petered out.

Weiss knew he had to leave. He hadn't gotten sympathy, reassurance, or clarity from the old detective, but there was someone down in the car who, in his mind, represented all of those things. Weiss shook Clendenning's hand at the door, expressing his thanks. The handshake went on too long, Clendenning clinging to Weiss's hand and looking at him oddly as though reading something in his face. Weiss broke free politely and the old man watched him head for the elevator.

Weiss walked back to the car against a cold wind from the open water and got into the passenger side of the late model GMC Terrain.

"Looks like a nice place," the driver said.

"Yeah, it must cost a fortune to live there. Guess I'd better boost my savings for my retirement."

"Did it help?" Detective Antonia Beal leaned back against the driver's side window so she could watch Weiss's face. Her long hair was fastened behind her head with an amber pin that Weiss could see reflected in the window glass.

"Hell no. It was a waste of time."

"But it shook you up though."

"Clendenning explained nothing. He just spewed some Victorian melodrama about seeing what other people can't see."

"Why wouldn't you let me go up and meet this Clendenning character? I did drive you all the way up from Burlington, and it wasn't your promise of a nice dinner down by the harbour that sold me."

"I thought he'd open up if it was just me."

"You mean you could open up to him if I wasn't there? You're afraid I'll think you're crazy."

"I wouldn't be here if I wasn't worried about going crazy. I don't know why you humour me, Toni. I've never brought you anything but grief."

"That's not true." Toni frowned, straightening her eyeglasses with strained patience. "But I'm damned if I'm going to stroke your ego by explaining what I mean."

Weiss stared at the drooping hydrangea bushes that obscured their view of the vast lake. "He tried to blame what's happening to me on Carly Rouhl."

Toni raised an eyebrow. "Did he now? She does seem to be a common thread in your career lately. She's also a smart, attractive woman, and she likes you. That's what Prem says, anyway. Seems unfair, her having money, brains, *and* dimples."

"Come on, Toni. You're making it into a Hallmark movie. I've got fifteen years on her."

"Ah. So you've worked it out. Fine, but she's no child, Eilert. Of course, she does have an advantage over me, I suppose. She's not married."

"Toni, I've told you before. I love you. If things were different, if you didn't have your family to think about, I'd have begged to marry you. I hardly *know* Carly Rouhl."

"It's all right, Eilert. One way or another, you have to make a life for yourself. And I'm here because I want to stay a part of it. And because your car would have lost its transmission before we got as far as Barrie. And because we told everyone at the district we were following a lead. Stop me. I'm rambling."

Weiss shook his head wearily. "About that dinner. Can you find your way down to the harbour—where we saw the cruise boat and the floatplanes? There's a nice restaurant with a view of the bay. We could kill some time on the main street, then have an early dinner there."

Toni smirked. "Kill some time; I like that. So what does that mean, anyway? You're going shopping with me? Is that what this is?"

"Sounds funny when you put it that way. But they have a great secondhand bookstore in town and a nice German bakery. You could take strudel home to your kids."

Toni looked at him in annoyance. "My girls are in their twenties! See, that's your problem, Eilert; you have no kids to remind you how bloody old you are."

Tugging his jacket closed, Weiss thought about that. "I get it. We're colleagues. You're a Halton detective, just like me, and you're married. We're not dating or anything. I'm just..."

Toni waited. "Go on. This'll be interesting."

"I'm just going to fraternize the hell out of you."

Slapping the wheel, Detective Antonia Beal laughed. "That sounds good, actually. Evasive, but good. So, okay, but I want to know what that old guy told you."

"I'll give it to you word for word—how I maintained my dignity and kept my professional objectivity in the face of pure Fruitopia from retired Detective Harry Clendenning."

CHAPTER FOUR

Carly sat on Evan Favaro's leather couch, trying not to think about how it had felt on her bare buttocks two weeks earlier. Evan was holding the old manuscript open on his knees. Carly felt awkward seeking Evan's help. She'd turned down enough of Evan's invitations to make him wonder if she was trying to cool down their relationship, and now here she was, a friend asking for free advice.

If Evan was offended, he didn't show it. This new distance between them was all her doing, and Carly knew it.

Evan was doing his best to ignore the tension, peering at the old book through the narrow reading glasses he only wore when he was doing what Carly thought of as serious work. His appearances on daytime television were little better than celebrity fluff in Carly's eyes and she'd let him know it, maybe a couple of times too often.

"It's vellum all right," Evan said at last. "And, near as I can tell, authentic to the sixteenth century. It's a common book of hours: a book of religious devotions. I can't actually read it, but I noticed the word 'Lincolnshire' in the dedication. That might be where it's from. At the very least, it pegs it as English."

"Do you read any Latin?"

"No way. My education was in bibliography and information management. That means I was exposed to some early manuscripts and incunabula."

"Incunabula?"

"Early printed books. Hand-lettered manuscript making went on in the monasteries long after the first books were printed. Hand copying eventually died out completely, of course, but if you wanted a simple book of hours in those days, you would have one made by clerics. The labour force was there and it was Godly work that kept the monks' minds on the hereafter. I think that's what this is—a hand-copied book of prayers and hymns for their own use."

"Is it worth a lot of money?"

"Well, that's problematic. A book of hours from this period with proper provenance could bring a couple of thousand dollars, I'm guessing. It's that incredible frontispiece that changes everything. I mean, that's art. Collectors would go crazy trying to get that so it could be shown in a glass case—just that one page. So, maybe tens of thousands? I'm not an expert, but that would be my guess.

"But before you go calling up your university friends for a real appraisal, you should know... That frontispiece doesn't make sense. It's too damn fine for the rest of the book. I think maybe it's been added. That would help explain why the book jammed so easily, by the way. Vellum, especially cheap vellum, is coarser than paper and the bulk of the frontispiece made the original book fractionally thicker. In fact, I've got a theory —the smell gave me the idea—that the book had been immersed in water. Saltwater. That would have swollen the pages."

"My God. I know what you're going to say. One of the copies of the Lindisfarne Bible was lost off a ship in the Middle Ages. It washed ashore and when they found it, the text had been saved from the seawater because the vellum swelled up and sealed the pages in the box it was in. Kept the inks dry."

"Very good. It's a great story, and fairly well known among bibliophiles."

"You think that's what happened to this manuscript? It fell in the sea?"

Evan scoffed at the idea. "Nah. I don't buy it. It's just a commonplace book. Why would it even *be* on a ship? But if somebody was trying to hook in a potential buyer, they might have tried to simulate something similar. Nothing like glamorous provenance to draw in a collector. A story to boast to your friends about."

"So you think this manuscript was made to deceive?"

"Well, not exactly. The script looks authentic enough, to me at least. A book of hours would be a relatively common relic of the period—and therefore not all that valuable. That illuminated front page? That's something else again, which is why I'm suspicious that it was added."

"But I don't get it. If the illumination has all the value, why bother sewing it into an old manuscript?"

"To give the illumination authenticity. The value would have been in the period illumination, Car—but I think the illumination is fake."

Carly gaped. "But it's so beautiful."

"Yes, but as a stand-alone page, it's within the powers of a talented craftsman to create. What I'm suggesting is, some fine artisan drew this page on artificially aged vellum and married it to an authentic but commonplace manuscript. That would be enough to get it past most amateur collectors. Now, here's where I remind you that I'm no expert. I'm just a guy who has some forensic experience and a few relevant college courses."

Carly made a dainty show of clapping her hands. "Pretty damned impressive, though. And you always say you're not into literature."

"I'm really not. While you were reading Chaucer, I was boning up on the Dewey Decimal System. My background is all about information management. Books just happen to be one of those systems. So go find your expert, but if I'm right, this book isn't worth more than a couple of thousand—after you've paid to get the bogus illumination removed. Then I suppose you could sell the illumination. A modern work of this quality? You might get a few hundred for it as a piece of contemporary art. I don't know anything about the art market."

Evan handed the book to her. Carly was momentarily confused, slipping the book down on Evan's coffee table.

"What's the matter? You're afraid to touch the thing."

"I felt when I brought it to you it was tainted somehow. Just a feeling, of course. Do me a favour and just put it back in the box. I can slip it back in my bag."

Evan gave her a comic glare, then pressed the manuscript into its worn box. When Carly was getting her shoulder purse ready, he became serious. "Car, there's something I want to discuss with you. A production group has offered me an afternoon TV show. Not *my* show exactly, but I'd be a kind of anchor. It's not what I was expecting, not a direction I was planning for, but it's a huge opportunity. I'd be a—I'd be known. They'd be placing it on their news channel, but it's still a step up."

"Wow! Of course. That's amazing, Evan. You'd be a natural."

"I wouldn't be doing that handwriting analysis act. I'd be doing interviews and human interest segments. You know, celebrities and cooking bits in front of a studio audience. No more fake psychic stuff. That'd please you, right?"

Carly remained cheerful, but to her, it felt forced. "The audience would be mostly women, I take it?"

Evan made a helpless gesture. "Well, I suppose."

"That's why they're giving you this, you know. Women love you."

"Damn it, Car. That's so unfair."

Carly knew she had crossed a line, belittling Evan's talent, but something made her stubborn; jealousy maybe. "Evan, I understand about what you do. I know it's entertainment. You don't have to be defensive about it."

"But you've always hated it. I know you do."

"I don't hate it. It's just—"

"It embarrasses you. Look, there's one other thing. I… It's being produced at their Agincourt Studios, just off the 401, five days a week."

"Over in Scarborough?"

"Right."

"So, that's what? An hour away by car?"

"With the traffic these days, maybe longer. I don't think I'd be able to see you as often if I took it. Anyway, it isn't a direction I expected to take, so…"

"What are you saying? Evan, you *have* to take it. They're going to make you a celebrity. Who knows where that would lead? Your career would be heading to a new level. Just think of the fame, the people you'd meet."

"But doesn't it bother you that I wouldn't be here?"

Something grim and resentful stirred in Carly's chest. When she spoke, it sounded cool and dismissive. "Evan, my life is changing, too. I've begun to write. Just indie stuff so far, but it's starting to take off. I'm thinking of stepping back from editing the magazine. I think I've got someone who can run it for me. But I've got Dad's house now, and it's practically a historic site. I can't see myself selling it, and it's perfect for me as a writer."

Evan slumped back against a cushion. "I get it. Your roots are here in Burlington, but you still think I should say yes." Watching her downturned face, he said, "I mean, who knows. It might only last a few months."

Carly was looking at the floor, unable to meet the disappointment in Evan's eyes. "You know that's not going to happen.

You've got the looks and you've got the charisma. You'll be a success."

There was a silence then, long and uncomfortable. At last, Evan said, "All right then. Agincourt."

He held out the worn old box with the book back inside. She opened her purse and held it up. He got the idea and slid in the box.

Carly felt she'd been judged; wronged. She was only being sensible. Her annoyance must have shown as she stood.

"Thanks for this, Evan. I'll get the manuscript professionally appraised, but I expect you're right about...everything."

Falling back on a kind of polite dignity, Evan shrugged. "Do you know how your father got hold of the manuscript?"

"You know how it is with his mementos. He begged, borrowed, stole. Anything for his 'creative process.' Maybe he even bought it if he thought there was a yarn in it. I've been thinking I should reread a couple of his books—see if the thing figures into any of his stories."

"But he didn't necessarily mention his trophies in his stories. Not directly."

"No, but maybe I'll be able to identify the source, a collector or even an artist capable of faking an illuminated vellum page. I've got someone who'd be glad to help me search his stories."

Evan straightened, wondering if this explained Carly's coldness. "Someone I know?"

"Harriet. You've met her. She's been terrific these last few months. You know, since Peggy Goss was killed at the office."

"Oh. Harriet."

Evan walked her to the elevator, and when the door slid open, he let her step inside while he leaned against the frame. He was looking at Carly's face as the door closed. She wanted to smile, but she couldn't even give him that.

Carly knew she'd said something wrong, or rather that Evan saw it that way. What was she to say? That she felt him drifting away from her, and she was ready to let that happen? Maybe she'd taken Evan for granted, but she'd never been able to commit to the idea of him as a life partner. He adored her; she got that. But he didn't *get* her.

She'd expected him to ride down with her, maybe even take her to her car. Instead, as the elevator sank downward, she found herself staring at some fire emergency instructions and gripping the guardrail so hard her hand hurt. There was a keyhole there on the panel and she tried to think about a fireman with muscles rippling under his yellow slicker, his jaw set behind a smoke mask, showing up for a raging high rise fire with a little round key to the bloody elevator.

CHAPTER FIVE

It was close to two weeks before Carly got the official analysis back from the Information Technology people at York University. It was a faculty that had long ago engulfed the old Library Sciences, though they occupied the same sixties-era building on the Steeles Road campus. She'd wanted someone from the University of Toronto, where she still knew some people in Language and Literature, to look at the manuscript. Instead, an old U of T professor she trusted directed her to a scholar at York University who did learned appraisals for book dealers—for a fee.

The scholar was Esther Rollings, an assistant professor and a beautiful woman with magazine cover cheekbones. Her long hair was gathered in pigtails, pinned up to form a crown on the top of her head. She was abundantly pregnant, her belly proudly displayed by the spreading curves of a black coat with a designer notched collar. Carly noticed a large diamond on the woman's ring finger and was reminded that there was a lot of money to be made in trading old books.

Rollings had the manuscript and its box arrayed on a green felt sheet in a room behind the desk of the Humanities library.

"Lots of wormholes, nicely patinated surface," Rollings said, running a lighted glass cup over the surface of the illumination. "Very clever. It almost got me, but I'm satisfied that your friend is right. The book is period, but the illumination is a fake, intended to deceive. The first clue is that the illumination is on a not particularly high-quality vellum. You can see a small organic hole in the original skin—here near the edge.

"The period is right for the sheet of vellum the illumination is drawn on, but the whole leaf has been razor cut, presumably from the binding of an authentically old book. It's quite an elaborate deception. The person who did this was a craftsman with endless patience. There are signs that the frontispiece was clamped at each corner to a drawing board during the modern inking process. The artist is quite talented of course—not a genius, but meticulous—and he was careful about using inks made from gall and other period-specific tints.

"He only made one crucial mistake, but I caught it. I got the chemical signature of an aniline dye not quite covered by the gold leaf, which means it was definitely created in the twentieth or even the twenty-first century. Can't be more specific about that."

"And this doctored page was then stitched into the authentic book of hours?" Carly asked.

"The so-called illumination is referred to as a leaf—two pages front and back, unquestionably added to the genuine pages. By the way, I'm afraid you won't get much for the rest of the book. It *is* sixteenth century, more or less, but not very good. Not very remarkable."

Rollings picked up a jewelled pointer, its tip possibly ivory. She followed Carly's curious gaze and explained. "This thing? It's an aestal—an affectation on my part, but not back in those days. Medieval orthography was difficult because modern conventions of paragraphing and punctuation didn't exist; reading was more difficult, and the men who inscribed and checked these pages would have used a pointing aid similar to this to read their way through the text. I'm sure their pointers weren't as fancy as mine, of course. I got this one in Geneva at an estate sale."

She returned to the text using the ivory pointer to pick out ink drawings and marginalia. "The illustrations—they call them decorations—are crude, and the calligraphy around them uneven. Woodblock illustrations were used in early printing, but they could be applied by hand, too. Interesting thing; the hand calligraphy shows signs of imitating the conventions of printed books of the era. That shows us that the monks who made this also had printed books in their libraries and were influenced by them.

"The work is of many hands; you'd expect that, of course. These things were cobbled together in monasteries mostly, but it's a little more complicated than that. I suspect your book of hours was actually compiled from a number of other deteriorating books, possibly as late as the eighteenth century. Some of the pages have been trimmed to fit the others. See? You can tell by the way the width of the margins varies. Somebody trying to make a decent book out of a number of damaged and discarded ones, I'd imagine."

"So, in a sense, the whole book is a fake."

"You could say that, though the parts are certainly sixteenth century. No later additions, I could see. Except for your bogus illumination, of course. My advice is to have that lovely frontispiece professionally removed. Put the remaining book on the market and see what you can get for it. As a sixteenth-century manuscript compiled and stitched together in the eighteenth, it might bring four figures, but without the glamour of the illumination, not a lot."

"And the illumination?"

"Well, of course, technically you can't call it an illumination at all. It's a piece of contemporary art, carefully aged with heat, tannin, and chemicals. If I were you, I'd approach a gallery. They'll find a buyer for you, but you won't get much after their commission. A few hundred dollars, I'd guess. You'd have to be very careful not to suggest it's as old as it looks. That would be fraud. Call it a simulation or a reproduction."

"You said it was contemporary. Are you saying the fake illumination could have been done recently?"

"I can't give you a year, but it's modern all right."

"The manuscript has been in my father's office for..." In her mind's eye, she had a picture of her father's little room with its shelves of books and mementos. She had no memory of the manuscript's arrival, but her father's long illness had turned him into a recluse incapable of adding to his collection, so... "We've had it for at least two, three years. Probably longer."

"I'm sorry I can't help you beyond that."

"Yes, of course. One other thing about the manuscript and the box: what about the story of the Lindisfarne Gospel? You know, the story about it being lost at sea and recovered?"

"Ah, yes. You were saying you thought that the box might have been immersed in saltwater. That would be ingenious of your faker. And yes, there is evidence that the whole box has been briefly submerged in brine. Maybe you're right. Perhaps the artisan knew the old story of the Lindisfarne Gospel and thought he could intrigue collectors who were familiar with the myth. This faker must have been quite learned in his own way. 'A little learning is a dangerous thing,' as they say."

Carly nodded. "'Drink deep, or taste not the Pierian spring.' Alexander Pope."

"Hmm? Ah, well. My own learning is very specialized, you see. Anyway, I received your cash transfer and I wish you luck unravelling this untidy business. Quite a mess you inherited."

Carly held out her bag. At first, Rollings was puzzled, but she caught on to what Carly wanted, and picked up the box, sliding it into Carly's open bag.

She watched Carly's avoidance as if she thought the box was infected with something. Rollings chuckled. "It's quite all right to handle it, you know. It's not a Gutenberg Bible."

Carly gave an embarrassed smile, slipped the bag over her shoulder, and offered her hand. Rollings switched the pointer to her left and shook Carly's hand, her fingers feeling long and cool.

Carly walked out of Rollings's office space, crossed through the library, and headed for the stairs to the main floor of the Humanities complex. Her shoulder bag moved against her ribs, and one of the shaggy, nose-ringed undergrads who hurried by on all sides might have seen her slip the bag down to her hand and rub her side uncomfortably. She took the handrail and chugged down the main stairs to the atrium, but it felt awkward because the bag was almost grazing the steps and she had to hike it up. Eventually, she folded the fabric of the bag and carried the doubled strap clutched uncomfortably in her fist.

Walking across the campus to her car, she had a moment of surprising detachment, wondering at all the fuss and bother she was taking over this shrivelled box of leather. Was this her way of connecting with her father again? Did it bother her that she would never be privy to the dozens of stories hidden in plain view on her father's shelves?

CHAPTER SIX

Harriet watched the little groupings of happy people around her, hunched over tables full of colourful food, and gave a contented sigh.

The sigh was misleading. Her mood was more one of excitement. She felt a warmth that made her almost giddy as she looked across the table at Carly Rouhl. She had the feeling of having come a long way from the obscurity and irrelevance of a suburban community in North Bay to be captured by some miraculous fluke of gravity into a near orbit of the Rouhl family. A.L. Rouhl had been a bright light on the curriculum of her high school English classes, as distant and otherworldly as Shakespeare and Arthur Miller, and now there was Carly Rouhl, the great man's daughter, incandescent in her own way, smiling at her in a lovely restaurant, her hand only inches from Harriet's own. If her classmates could see her now.

The two women made easy conversation about fashion and politics, Harriet's intensity seeming to flicker like the tea light on the table. Carly took advantage of a brief pause in the banter.

"You've read all the A.L. Rouhl stories, Harriet. Did you ever come across a sort of artisan in the books—one who would have been capable of pulling together something of the order of that old boxed manuscript? I've had it assessed, and it's a carefully assembled fake, made up of some genuine period pages. It would have been easy compiling it because a book of hours is mostly short individual hymns and prayers each confined to its own page."

"I remember you were looking into it." Harriet thought for a moment, her eyes almost closed. "Hmm. Something's niggling at the back of my memory. Let me think about it."

Carly's attention was caught by the bracelet hanging loosely from Harriet's wrist, mere inches from her own. Carly herself didn't go in much for jewelry. There was a small pearl ring on her right hand that had been her mother's, and she occasionally wore a heart-shaped locket around her neck on a gold chain as thin as a filament. So, the chunky silver chain around Harriet's wrist with its clinking charms, each a piece of minor sculpture, made her curious.

"Do the charms all mean something?" Carly asked, pointing.

"Oh, yes. Gifts mostly. Sixteenth birthday, graduation, mementos of holidays." She flicked the individual charms over, turning them in the light.

"What's that one that looks like a little house?"

It was figured silver, the tiny roof tiles suggested by droplets of red enamel inlay.

"I actually lived with someone for a while when I was in college. Just a rooming house, but it was my first home away from home, so it's still kind of special. We broke up, of course. That was a long time ago." She said this with firmness, almost as though she was trying to assure Carly of something.

Carly smiled, thinking of her own college infatuations, then clasped her fingers together, and with a firm nod, it was time for business. "Harriet, I wanted us to have some time to talk.

This is an important crossroads for me—and for you, too. I've been thinking things over for months now. Ever since Dad died, I've been reassessing my goals, thinking about the future."

Harriet watched, lips pursed, her large eyes smouldering in the crystalline light of the halogens above.

"And I've decided," Carly said, "to step back from the magazine. It's doing well now, and it's established its niche in the market. The business plan is sound and we just need to keep doing what we're doing. I'm comfortable enough financially with Dad's inheritance that I can take a shot at writing what I want. I've had enough success at placing some short fiction, and I think I can build on that. And if I fail, well, I can always follow my interests in other ways. Independent journalism maybe, where I don't have to flatter local celebrities and boost local businesses.

"Of course, I wouldn't be able to do any of this if I didn't think there was someone who could replace me at the magazine. Harriet, I want you to step up as editor. Run the whole thing—the *Escarpment Magazine*. We'll adjust the pay scale accordingly."

Carly watched for Harriet's reaction and was puzzled at what she saw. Harriet seemed to subside in her chair, a cloud passing over her face. She had been so exuberant, thrilled by the atmosphere of the restaurant, which was a regular advertiser in the *Escarpment Magazine*, but that faded now to non-committal neutrality.

"Oh. Ah. Wow," Harriet stammered. "I didn't... Does that mean you won't be coming into the office every day?"

Carly thought that was an oddly tangential question. "Well, I'll be writing at home most of the time. At least, that's what I envision. But I'll be checking in, of course, making sure the transition is going smoothly."

"I see." Harriet sagged back in her chair, seeming somehow crestfallen.

"I don't mean that I doubt you. Not for a minute." Carly waited, but Harriet's smile was forced and her eyes roamed the faces of nearby diners. "Harriet, what's wrong? I thought you'd be thrilled. This is a huge promotion for you. You'd be more than just an editor. You'd be an entrepreneur. A force in the community. You've already established relationships with dozens of businesses and cultural centres—that's why you'd be a natural to continue our program. Don't say you're not interested."

"No, of course not. I'm honoured." She straightened and affected good humour. "I just didn't see tonight going this way."

"Tonight? I don't understand."

"No, please forget I said that. I'm just stunned by the thought of all that responsibility. I'll be fine. Thank you for your...for your trust."

The next half hour was pleasant, but subdued somehow.

Harriet loved the food and kept looking around at the little outbursts of hilarity at neighbouring tables. Carly wondered briefly if she'd made a mistake in judging Harriet's readiness, but she had seen the way that Harriet comfortably took charge in the office—even all the times when Carly was there in body but not in spirit. No, she couldn't be wrong about Harriet's abilities.

Their wine glasses touched for the second time and Carly saw the charm bracelet slip up Harriet's forearm. Her eyes followed it and then lingered on Harriet's necklace and earrings. She noticed, as if for the first time, Harriet's lovely white dress with gold-flecked accents.

Harriet had dressed up for this. She looked lovelier than ever. Lip liner, eye makeup—but it seemed to hood a kind of sadness now, a sadness imperfectly disguised by a bright red smile framing perfect teeth. The eyeglasses were different, too. As green as the ones she wore around the office, but more stylish, as though she kept a pair for hot dates. This pair had tiny sapphire accents that glistened above their size.

Carly wondered if the mention of Harriet's lost love was at play here. "Do you miss him?"

"What? Who?"

"You know—the little house. The one you shared?"

It took Harriet a second to recompose herself and think of an answer. "Oh. 'Him.' No, not at all. I'm just grateful for what I learned, for my independence. It gave me the courage to move down here to the Golden Horseshoe and pursue my dreams."

"You are special, you know. I could tell when I first hired you. You're meant for great things."

It seemed natural enough for Carly to touch the little charm that dangled so close from Harriet's wrist. She did have an affection for this young woman with an effervescent personality and quirky cuteness. Harriet didn't draw away. Instead, she turned her hand so that it brushed Carly's own wrist.

Nothing much happened, but as Carly's fingertips grazed the little silver house with its delicate red roof, in her mind, a silence as profound as congenital deafness smothered the commotion of the restaurant. The gaudy fabrics and cluttered vignettes of the restaurant walls seemed to disappear, and Carly felt as though she was suddenly standing bolt upright six inches above the floor, looking down.

And there, in Carly's mind, was Harriet. Much younger, breathlessly pretty with long blond hair down her back.

In Carly's vexed imagination, Harriet was holding hands with a tall, thin, redhead; athletic and barebacked. The girl wore a sweatband around her short hair, and her long fingers were knuckled sweetly against Harriet's cheek. Then the two girls kissed, and it was a long, sensuous embrace that brought Carly crashing back to her seat and the present moment, her vision filled once again by her wine glass bobbling precariously from her hand. She stirred in confusion.

"Car! What's wrong? Are you okay?"

Now it was Carly's turn to dart her eyes about and clutch at her napkin. At last, she said, "Omigod, Harriet. I'm so sorry. I mean, did I spill any of the wine? I had…I had a dizzy spell. The heat and the wine, I guess."

"Breathe in and out. You'll be fine."

"Harriet. I…I shouldn't have set the evening up this way. I took you by surprise. I see that now. Please take all the time you want to think things over. I assumed you'd be delighted, but, well, there's more to life than a job, and a career, isn't there? People can be so ignorant about those around them. I mean, what do I know about your hopes and dreams? I'm being an insensitive stuffed shirt. God! I'm getting out of this business just in time. But you'll be better than me. You'll find a balance, love, happiness. Not like me. I'm a frightened basket case. A freak."

Carly stopped and took a sip of wine, aware that she was babbling.

"Car, what are you talking about? You're brilliant and you've got your talent…Evan…"

It took a minute and the arrival of their desserts, but they both seemed to step back from a brink of sorts and relax.

When they had finished dessert and Carly handled the cheque, they walked out into the night over black pavements glistening with recent rain. They talked freely and easily about friends in common, and staff Harriet could count on for help and encouragement, but Carly was conscious of their hands now, dangling close between them, the click of Harriet's high heels, so inappropriate for a business dinner, and their breath visible in the nighttime cold.

Carly was dealing with a deep shame about the evening, as though she should have known, as though she should have picked up on Harriet's little shows of affection. At the same time, she knew she couldn't give Harriet the kind of love she really wanted, hoping that some part of their growing friendship could survive this night.

What a bloody fool she'd been. What a mess she'd made of it.

CHAPTER SEVEN

When she got home, Carly didn't hang her coat in the hall cupboard. Instead, she calmed Indy with a belly rub and clipped the spring-wound leash to his collar. They stepped out into a chilly night and crossed to the lakeside park. She allowed herself to be dragged from the glass pavilion beside Spencer's Restaurant, down the ramp to the lakeside lawns. Indy led the way towards the curve of the downtown pier. They passed the children's playground with its plastic ship and yellow nylon rigging.

Seeing the swings, she thought of Eilert Weiss, the strangely sympathetic detective with his long crew cut and bristling moustache. It was odd associating him with this park, this symbol of innocence; but they had met here twice, and each time they had cautiously let their guard down, circling closer to the truth of what they knew and what they believed. It was a bonding experience, though neither of them knew it at the time, and she wondered if she would ever see him again. It didn't seem likely. Their worlds didn't naturally intersect.

When they got home, Carly's face was glowing with the cold, flushed as if blushing. She took off her boots; they padded into the kitchen together, and she topped up Indy's food bowl. Opening the fridge, she went through the motions of getting a glass of milk but stopped before she poured. She didn't want to eat or drink. What she wanted was to stop thinking about that bungled dinner with Harriet.

Closing the fridge, she went into the living room where her eye was caught by her shoulder bag, which was still there where she'd dropped it on the dining table after getting home from York University. The worn cover of the manuscript box was half out of the bag. Recognizing the distraction she needed, Carly swept the manuscript box back into the bag and carried it down the corridor to her father's office where it belonged. She put it on the shelf near where it had been originally and sat down on her father's desk chair.

She was there, fidgeting with a pencil, doing nothing for five minutes; but if she expected the room to give up any more of its secrets, she was to be disappointed. It might be different if she had the manuscript open in front of her, but she just wasn't ready.

The following morning was a Sunday and the chilled sunlight caught a crystal hanging on a filament against the kitchen window, sprinkling tiny rainbows across the walls. Carly spent the time after breakfast writing. She had in mind a story that would somehow incorporate the boxed manuscript—a tale of deceit and revenge perhaps, but her mind kept wandering back to last evening's dinner.

How had she and Harriet left things? Could she still count on Harriet to take on the management of the magazine? In this sense, at least, was she going to be a free woman?

It was silly to let things just slide. Harriet was a friend.

They'd talk this out between them. Retrieving her phone from its charging station on the mantle, Carly called Harriet.

"I'm at the magazine offices," Harriet said, her voice sounding a little hollow in the silent space.

"On a Sunday?"

"I want the team to know—I want the team to *think* I'm on top of everything on Monday."

"You know I'm going to be there to help as long as you need me. I'm not going to just throw you into the deep end."

"I appreciate that. I'm just excited to be taking over. You're a huge presence around here and you'll be missed."

"Thanks for saying that, but the truth is, you've been running things for months already. Listen, is there any way you could come over here to the house tonight for a couple of hours? I wanted to talk about that manuscript. Now that I've had it professionally evaluated, I'm wondering what to do next."

Harriet came over a little after seven that evening, her pale cheeks as red as harvest apples. She fussed with Indy for a bit, and then Carly steered her down the corridor to A.L.'s office.

Once inside the room, Carly turned until she was facing her father's old desk. She straightened, feeling the latent power of the little office all around her. No wonder she tended to avoid the place. In the evenings, her father's stories and his brooding spirit hung in the air and almost spilled from the shelves full of memories: an old lamp-style flashlight, a hand-wound tape measure, a brass harness decoration, a bar of medals, and on and on.

She picked the manuscript box off its place on the shelf. It was still in her shoulder bag, and she carefully let the box slide out of her bag so that it was at the centre of the desk blotter. Its burnished cover almost matching the colour of the blotter's four leather corners. A.L.'s old laptop was there too, closed, and off to one side. Seated on a dining room chair that Carly had dragged in for her, Harriet watched the carry-on with amusement.

"Are you afraid of catching something?"

"I explained this to you; there have been a couple of instances where I got too carried away by my imagination. I remember how Dad would sit at this desk, turning an old belt buckle in his hands. He'd get all dreamy and far away, and eventually, he'd come out of it and start to write. I think those memories have made me wary. I want you here so that if I start getting glazed and speaking in tongues, you'll step over and slap my face. This manuscript is just a goddamned book and I know next to nothing about it. If I fondle it and start having wild imaginings, I want you to remind me of that. Okay?"

"Okay. I get it. Your mental health."

"Exactly—my mental health."

Carly pushed the bag aside and picked up the old box. Her eyes darted from side to side for a moment. Then, with renewed determination, she began to tug at the binding. Almost immediately, the bound book popped out an inch from its box.

"We seem to have loosened it up a bit."

She applied more pressure, and the book started to slip out of its box with a sucking sound. Then it broke free, and the box clumped flat on the desk pad.

Carly centred the book and swung open the cover. "And there it is. Wow. It is beautiful. And it looks authentic to my untrained eye."

"What does vellum feel like?"

"Like...skin. Because that's what it is." Carly realized it was a trick question. Harriet had pushed her to lay her fingertips right on the page. "I should probably be wearing white cotton gloves."

"It's a fake, remember?"

"Yeah. The frontispiece, anyway. I read they age this stuff

with tea." Carly was running her fingers over the edges of the heavy page. It was worn and stained, but now that she looked more closely, she could see that the inking and gilding were a little too bright against the vellum. And she waited.

Harriet raised an eyebrow that seemed to pop up above her glasses, but she didn't say anything.

Carly let her index finger trace the lovely curves of the gold leaf lettering. She recognized the swooping "x" that constituted the Greek letter *Chi*—the first letter in *Christu,* Christ—and she found herself admiring the workmanship and trying to read the smaller letters.

"This isn't what's supposed to happen," she said. "I'm just taking in what I see."

"What's supposed to happen?"

"Well, you know. I'm a Rouhl. I'm supposed to get inspired and start creating. Storytelling. That's what my dad was all about, for all his fantasies about premonition and clairvoyance. He'd touch one of his precious artefacts and the ideas would just flow from it."

"And you're not getting anything?"

Carly's gaze ranged from side to side. "Nope."

"So are you disappointed?"

Carly closed her eyes. "Well, *yeah*. I didn't expect fireworks, but I figured I was good for a daydream or two. But, nothing. Well, this is embarrassing. I thought you might have had to drag me from this chair waving my arms about and muttering in a fit of creative bliss."

"Slapping you would have been cool. A great story for the water cooler."

"I don't want this embarrassing fizzle to reach the water cooler either," Carly laughed. She thought for a moment. "Do we *have* a water cooler at the office? No, we have a sink, remember?"

"Right." Harriet drooped her head. "I've only worked there

close to five years."

"Anyway, I owe you a drink for babysitting me while I tried. Maybe I can get you drunk and convince you this never happened."

Harriet did that thing where she seemed to sparkle. "Okay. I hear you're a sucker for hard cider."

"Agh, cider! Have you heard this one?" Carly stared at the ceiling and recited: "There was a young lady from Ryde—"

"Is this dirty?"

"All limericks aren't dirty." With an air of affront, she resumed. "Who ate some green apples and died. The apples fermented inside the lamented...And made cider inside her inside."

Harriet chuckled. "God, that's morbid."

"*Now* who's got an active imagination?"

Harriet went home, driving her Prius back along Lakeshore against a wet and dismal wind. Carly watched her go, feeling a little foolish. Indy stood beside her at the living room window.

She looked down at him. "Imagine—asking a friend over to watch me fondle a book. Does that make me more or less crazy?"

Carly wasn't sure. All she knew was that since her father's death, she had experienced a few of what she thought of as night terrors, except that one of them had hit her in the early morning while she stood beside the fireplace. She'd done an excellent job of rationalizing them away. After all, she was a creative person; a writer, and wild imaginings could be said to be a professional hazard.

Funny thing is, in the years before her father's death, Carly had been one of those heroines in a romance: practical, organized, reliable, a solid businesswoman. Not at all like the old man who sat long hours at his desk sipping whisky and tapping away at his laptop, spilling his rich imagination into every pixel. After his illness, the whisky became port and the wild dreams began to fade as if it had been the alcohol all along.

Back then, a super-efficient manager was what her magazine desperately needed, and she had been a competent editor. There were plenty of feature writers and freelancers producing the civic boosterism she needed for the quarterly's glossy pages.

Losing her father and inheriting his estate had upset her world. She made herself financially independent before he passed away, but now she was... What was the slang term? Flush? It meant that she didn't need to be solid for everyone. Not any more. She could be...not herself, but the self of her fantasies: a creator and an original. Just maybe she had, at the same time as his estate and residuals, inherited her father's creative mantle.

After all, there wasn't anybody else; no older brother or baby sister. It was all on her. She was the repository of the Rouhl genes. If A.L. Rouhl's legacy was to live on, it had to be through her, and she wasn't going to sit back content to manage his literary properties and film rights.

Sitting there in her father's office with her hand on that old book, she had expected her newfound gift for imagination to come roaring back. Of late, she had taken heart that she too could craft a story out of next to nothing. The short story she had written based on the Goodwyn family was polished, worthy of comparison with one of A.L.'s profiles. Maybe all she needed was a starting point—an object she could hold in her hands, something richly evocative. That's what she had seen her father do countless times in that very office. And yet this time—nothing. No woozy visions, no emotional rush. Was it because Harriet had been here, watching her?

She turned from the window and discovered Indy was still staring up at her. "What's your problem?" Indy shot a quick glance out at the empty street where Harriet's car had been parked, then looked sheepishly back at her. It was an unsettlingly human gesture. Carly put her hands on her hips. "It's not like that, Indy. Harriet and I are just friends. I think she understands that now. I can't be what she wants me to be."

Indy shifted a little, but he kept eyeing her, skeptically, she thought.

"Oh, give me a break." She turned from the window, settling into her favourite armchair by the fire, and dragged a woollen throw across her legs. At least she could read herself into someone else's imaginings. Carly had always been happy with that, and she loved reading for the release it gave her from her mundane life. "Come on, Indy. You know the routine; slump down there and keep my feet warm."

Carly's hand groped the side table where she had abandoned the latest on her reading list, a mystery novel steeped in the southern sun and sleepy bayous. But it wasn't there—or rather it was covered up by a burnished old box. Carly didn't remember bringing the manuscript out of the office with her, but then she'd been deep in that sort of competitive banter she and Harriet enjoyed. Yes, she would have tossed it there carelessly as the two of them made their way to the front door.

The manuscript seemed benign now. The worn box had lost its aura of danger—had proven to be inert and ordinary. Carly would have dumped it there as she would an expired discount coupon from Burger King.

Indy got up from her feet and casually sniffed the box. Carly laughed. "You're not going to be happy until I let you chew this thing, are you?" She picked up the box and flopped it protectively on her lap, pointing at the rug. "Indy! Feet. Warm. Stay focussed." Indy seemed happy enough to comply, and Carly let her head sink back in comfort. "There we go."

She had forgotten all about the boxed manuscript resting on the warmth of the throw, her hand splayed across it; her mind relaxed, empty, receptive. And then unbidden, it began to happen.

Her waking dream seemed to settle out of the warm glow of the fireplace to cover the furniture, Indy, and her own languid body. But when the imaginary sheet settled, it was draped over some other place—a place that slowly took form and texture as though shrink wrap was shaping itself around pork chops. The dominant colour was a pervasive blue that smothered the warmth of the room in a chill.

Carly struggled to make sense of the daydream. It wasn't a type of room she was familiar with: it was large, high and mostly empty, although there were vague shapes piled against the walls. Tall windows let in a joyless light.

There was a soundtrack to this daydream: *Miss Mary Mac, Mac, Mac. Silver buttons up and down her back, back, back...* in a childish chorus that was half-sung, half-chanted. And behind it, the steady rhythmic percussion of small hands clapping.

The imagined scene seemed pointless, centred on a patch of dusty flooring tiles made out of linoleum. Yeah, that's what they used to call them: lino tiles. There was nothing on the bare flooring, but Carly somehow knew that these tiles were imbued with suffering and death. She felt the emotions rush into her mind, and the dominant one was pity.

"Poor thing," she muttered to her empty living room. "To die so young. Without even her mother there to comfort her."

Carly felt her throat tighten and a sob spasm in her chest. The cold tear that trickled down her cheek was real enough. Suddenly angry, she had the sensation of spinning around, although part of her knew she was lying back in a soft chair, as still as everything else in her lakeshore home. Without making more than a low growl in her throat, she could imagine herself screaming out, "And you!" In her mind, she was spitting out the words. "How could you defile her resting place with your miserable, selfish violence?"

Who was she shouting at? The question seemed to conjure its own answer. A figure bathed in the light that angled down from tall windows—a heavyset man with broad shoulders, and on those shoulders a hideous black hood. This, she somehow knew, was the executioner, but the hood he wore wasn't a simple black bag with eyes slits. It had a sort of beak hanging down so that the man took on the appearance of a predatory bird.

Carly sat up so quickly that Indy bolted from his resting place. He circled, then stood nervously by the fireplace. But it was Carly who was panting.

"Whoa!" At first, she stared stupidly at Indy, who flopped back on his haunches, but after a moment her eyes fell to the manuscript gripped tightly in her fingers. She nodded slowly and breathed out. "Ah. It's okay, Indy. I'd just forgotten, you see?" She nodded. "You don't concentrate when you do this... You *let go*. I remember now. That's how it works."

CHAPTER EIGHT

The Cessna was deep in cloud cover, approaching Burlington Executive Airport from the southeast. Byron looked out the window and let his mind wander for a second. There was nothing whatsoever to see except for a grey void; maybe a little bit of streaking on the windshield from condensation.

It was okay for Byron to relax for a moment because Forrest was flying the plane, balancing a large GPS on the control yoke. They wouldn't see shit until they broke out of the cloud layer at less than two thousand feet, so this was a straightforward ILS approach. They'd been informed by the tower that the pilot-controlled runway lights system was out of service, but the airport was leaving the lights up at maximum because the late afternoon weather was so changeable. Rain had been sweeping the runway regularly, but it was relatively clear now, and the wind at ground level had died down for a bit.

"I'm interceptin' the localizer for runway thirteen. You ready with the folks on the tarmac?" Forrest said into his mic.

"Relax," Byron said. "They'll be there. Just get this shitbox on the ground."

"Ain't that easy. We're overloaded. I warned you. Damn

plane handles like a damp turd." Forrest cursed at the bank of instruments as he adjusted the power to follow the glide path. "Switchin' the Garmin to VLOC mode," he mumbled into the mic. There was a loud burst of static and he wiggled one ear of his headset. The automated weather update crackled in his ear, promising him a manageable sheer from the north, and he placed the plane on the geo-referenced approach plate. "It's just a damn video game from herein," he groused.

"You should be good at that then," Byron sneered.

"Cessna one-niner, stay at three thousand feet until final approach point," a woman's voice said into their headsets.

It was fine for Byron to daydream, but if Forrest took his eyes off his instruments for a second, he'd get disoriented in this soup and fly them into the treetops.

Time droned on with the single prop, and now it was time to descend, so Forrest adjusted his throttle to hold him steady on his glide scope and adjusted the flaps. The drone of the engine lowered in pitch and suddenly a washed-out, featureless landscape appeared. Runway lights, the painted bars of the runway, and the two rows of markers pointed up into the mist…

There was a bump as the ageing Cessna touched down and it wallowed a bit with its weight bouncing against the hydraulics. Forrest worked his rudder and brakes, looking for the first taxiway from the single runway.

"Where to now, genius?" he said. "I can't see much of anything."

Byron was alert and tense now, desperately trying to get his bearings. He was the one who knew the little airport. He was the one who had made the arrangement for transfer. "Here. Turn here and all the way to the chain-link fence. Okay?"

"Fine." Forrest goosed the engine a little and he felt the wheels skew and slip a little as he veered away from the administration building and tower into a tidy parking area half-filled with private planes. Their dorsal fins were sticking up out of the gloom, catching the muted light.

"All right," Byron barked. "When you kill the engine, we've got a narrow window to get the cargo out of the back and into their van. Those guys aren't gonna wait around if we trip over our feet."

The silence seemed cosmic after two hours of droning over upstate New York. The only sound was the scuffing of Byron's boots clearing the door and jamming the co-pilot's seat forward.

He shouted over at Forrest, who was working the panel. "Get over here and help me, goddamnit."

Forrest fudged his ground check and swung his legs out into the cold. He edged around the ticking engine and started taking the assault rifles from Byron one by one. A third person moved in beside them with a cart. Forrest took a second to take in the grey-haired man in his quilted Mountain Warehouse jacket.

"What are you looking at?" the man snarled. "Put the damn guns on the cart."

Forrest hefted one rifle after another onto the cart. They were protected by brand new plastic cases, so he could afford to hurry. As soon as the little four-wheeled cart was full, the grey-haired man muttered, "We'll be in touch," and rolled the cart towards a waiting minivan.

Just short of the van, he stopped and let the cart's telescoping handle drop. He was expecting his driver to be in the van with the motor running, but there was no exhaust, and the driver's door was open. Why couldn't the moron follow instructions?

The grey-haired man walked forward, but not directly towards the waiting van this time. He was hedging his bets, inching off towards the fence, getting ready to run if need be. His eyes were on the open back door of the van and the pale damp air around it when he heard a woman's voice from behind a gasoline tender drawn up beside a small aircraft. In the mist, the voice sounded very close.

"There are four of us, in case you're wondering," she said. "We've all got guns and enough evidence on the ground to shoot anyone who starts to run. You getting all this?"

The grey-haired man tensed, ready to leap behind one of the parked aircraft and draw his gun, but he was cursed by an active imagination. He found he was preoccupied with how it would feel having a police bullet rip through his guts. His courage failed him, and he let his hands fall to his sides, palms open. He cursed once and waited.

Detective Antonia Beal, gun in hand, stepped into the clear, spoke into the handset that hung from her collar, and immediately saw the lights of two police cruisers go on in the parking lot on the other side of the fence. The lights were fuzzy in the mist but the line of cops approaching the fence looked solid enough. They hooked a tubular ladder on the chain-link and began vaulting over.

Detective Tom Krosnow, Toni's partner, came out of the mist, leading Forrest and Byron past Toni, letting the uniforms take them into custody. For a minute, he watched all four of the weapon smugglers being herded in the direction of the tower, but then Tom became aware of Toni Beal standing alone by the tail of a high-winged private plane. Her hair, a sandy blond shade covering premature grey, glistened with microdroplets condensed from the mist.

"Toni?"

"Just taking a minute, Tom. Babysitting these bloody guns until the uniforms get back."

Tom looked at the pile of plastic cases with distaste. "I'm used to seeing these in crates, but on a plane, I suppose it's all about weight. You ever seen one of those beasts being used? Fully automatic. They'll cut some poor bugger in half."

Toni winced.

"Sorry." Tom waited, doing his usual stony-faced uncle routine. Then he breathed out noisily. "Hey, we've done some good here, Toni. We kept those things out of the hands of gangs and psychos. Saved lives."

Toni Beal nodded, glowering at the ground. "I know. I'll be fine. I was just thinking about the intel."

"The information we got was solid. The RCMP were tracking this shipment all the way from Albany."

Toni gave a bitter laugh. "It was the wife, you know. Byron's wife. We wouldn't have got them if it wasn't for her. She told us just enough so we could figure out the rest."

"She must have had a real grudge against old Byron. He deserved what he got."

"Sure he did, but the wife didn't hate him. She loved him. Putting him in a Canadian prison will probably save Byron's life." Toni's eyes glistened in the diffuse light. "Sometimes couples don't turn on each other," she said. "They just move apart, bit by bit. Leave the other behind."

Tom shifted uncomfortably. "What's this about, Toni?"

"Forget it, Tom. You hate this stuff. I know you do."

"I also hate seeing you miserable. Tell me. Maybe I can help."

Toni frowned at him. "You're a nice guy, Tom. People see you as tough, but I've seen you with the victims and the families."

"Toni."

Toni ran her hand over the nape of her neck. "I've been going home to an empty house, that's all. I forgot how important it was to have a warm place to hide after shit like this."

"But the girls...David..."

"The girls have been off to university since September, and my husband? It made sense for David to travel to Hilton Head with his buddies. I don't play golf, never have, never will. Thing is, I've been wondering if there's any point in him coming back —at least to the life we've been living. We haven't shared a common world together in months, maybe years. I don't know, Tom. It just happens, you see."

Tom looked at the shapes in the mist, then at his feet. "I guess it doesn't help that you're in love with someone else."

Toni turned and stared at him in shock. "Damn it, Tom. I thought you wanted to help."

"I do. Call it tough love. I've seen you when you're happy, and it's not at home. I'm sorry Toni, but I'm not blind."

Toni thought about a blustering denial, but it was no use; Tom was a detective, after all. She looked this way and that as if looking for a way out. In the end, all she could do was droop her head.

"I…I can't do anything about that."

"Maybe you can. I don't care what people see when they look at me. I know *you're* the tough one in the department. I've watched the way you take charge; I know how you just make things happen. And, if they don't go exactly the way you hope, I also know that you'll beat the pain."

"Okay, that's enough, Tom. I can handle your sweet side, but I'm not ready for goddamn wisdom."

They stayed for a while, watching an officer roll the assault rifles off the tarmac while another strung yellow plastic tape on the van and Forrest's plane. By the time the detectives felt they could leave, it was dark.

CHAPTER NINE

Carly showed up Monday morning at the offices of *Escarpment Magazine*. Walking over to Brant Street from her Lakeshore Road home was still a part of her routine, although she had been taking time off regularly, confident that Harriet would keep the writers, layout people, and advertising sales staff busy and on track for the next quarterly edition. She went in through the glass door, called her greetings to the staffers who were settling down to work, booted her workstation computer, and opened files in aimless curiosity.

She was painfully aware that she no longer had defined responsibilities. She was just putting in time at her old desk, noticing snail mail that she hadn't put there, and petty cash receipts that someone else had submitted and someone else would process. What did she expect? A brass plaque on her desk with the inscription, "This desk retired in commemoration of our founder?"

And then, at last, Harriet was free to join her. She made her way between the desks with that happy smile she always seemed to bring to Carly—a smile full of equal parts devotion and forbidden love.

Carly robbed a nearby work station, wheeling over a vacant task chair for Harriet, and started right in. "It happened," she grinned, miming an explosion around her head and making a puffy, booming sound. "I had one of those waking dream things. It was spooky as hell."

Harriet, a sucker for mysticism, sat forward and grinned back, her teeth a blaze of enthusiasm. "So spill!"

"Okay, well, I imagined a schoolhouse—one of those old one-room classrooms you see in sepia photographs."

"A schoolhouse?" Harriet's gaze dropped to one side as though snagged by a passing recollection. "Okay."

"There were pupil desks and an old stove and linoleum flooring tiles. I don't know where all the details came from. I must have seen an article somewhere. There was other stuff, sort of fuzzy in the background, but I felt riveted to this one patch of floor. It's weird, but a wave of emotion came over me and I got the idea that a murder had happened right there—there on that patch of floor. It's the damnedest thing. I even pictured the murderer."

Harriet seemed to have contracted, her hands clasped tightly on her green slacks. "What did he look like? It was a guy, right?"

Carly squinted, remembering. "Yeah, that's the way I saw him. He was big, heavyset, and he had," she gestured around her ears, "this hood thing on his head and it had," she made a claw-like gesture in front of her chin, "a sort of baby elephant trunk or a curved beak or something. Creative, huh? And I felt my revulsion and anger at him."

"You were angry at what he did. Did you see the victim? The person he killed?"

Carly shook her head and made a face. "You know, I haven't made up my mind about that. It's sort of muddled. At first, I got the idea he had murdered a little girl, but then... No, he killed someone else. I don't know where the girl fits into it, but I could feel pity for her all the same. Strange, huh?"

"Who was the someone else?"

"It was a daydream, not a summer blockbuster. I've no idea."

"Kinda thin on plot. Did you see anything else?"

"That's all I can remember. That's the way it is with dreams." Suddenly, Carly brightened. "Oh! There was a soundtrack. That's kind of unusual, eh?" Carly began the chant, clapping her hands in a muffled rhythm.

Herb Brenner, a layout guy at a large monitor nearby, turned at the sound.

"Miss Mary Mac, Mac, Mac," Carly sang quietly, tapping her hands in a subdued rhythm. "Silver buttons up and down her back, back, back."

"Great Big Sea," Brenner said.

"What?" Carly looked over at him.

"It's a Canadian Band. 'Mary Mac' is one of their songs."

Not content with booming out the melody, Brenner began to play an air guitar along with the rhythm. It was a spirited sea shanty.

Carly and Harriet both stared until Brenner stopped in embarrassment. "Seriously. They're a band from down east." He turned back to his screen, frowning and muttering. "Just trying to help."

"Thanks, Herb. Great Big Sea, huh?" For Harriet's ears only Carly whispered, "It didn't sound anything like him—not in the dream."

Harriet rolled her eyes. "Good. He's ruining the spooky mood." As she said this, a thought crossed her mind and she looked up at the fluorescent lighting. "Wait a minute!" She shot to her feet and did a little pacing thing, thinking. "Yeah. Schoolhouse. Murder. A manuscript in A.L. Rouhl's office..." Harriet flung her hands wide. "Carly! I think I've got this! I may know what you're remembering. Look, I've got to run home for a few minutes. If I'm right, I'll show you when I get back. Is that okay?"

Several staffers turned to watch, picking up on Harriet's effervescent enthusiasm.

"Sure," Carly said. "Go, go."

After Harriet blustered out the door in a twirl of scarf and coat, Carly waited impatiently, sauntering around, hovering, looking over shoulders and smiling supportively in a way that made the staff nervous, but Harriet was mercifully quick. Her condo was up Maple, not far from the lake and only a few minutes from the magazine. She burst into the office from the plaza parking lot, brandishing a hardcover book with a grey dust jacket.

"Underworld Tales!" she shouted. "I was right!"

Carly glanced around the office. The magazine staff were staring, but they would just have to get used to Harriet's spontaneity. It would be an adjustment after Carly's low-key demeanour.

Carly took the book and looked at the lettering: "A.L. Rouhl" in big red letters because that was what would sell the book. Then the title, smaller and in a gothic-looking font: *Underworld Tales*."

"I do kind of remember this. One of Dad's most obscure books." She looked at the copyright page. "Fairly late career. Written around the beginning of his decline. It didn't do well and it almost stopped his writing. I can't believe you have this."

"I've got them all. Everything he wrote. And..."

Harriet took the book back and Carly could see that Harriet had hastily bookmarked a page with a strip of tissue. "The schoolhouse murder thing rang a bell and, bingo!" She opened the book and presented it for Carly's inspection. "Read that."

Carly scanned a couple of paragraphs, her eyes wide. "That's so weird. You're right; I guess it's possible this is what I was thinking of when I had the daydream, but I'd completely forgotten about the book itself. At a subconscious level, I must have been putting the fake manuscript together with one of Dad's stories."

"You can relax. No mystical trances required. Your mental health is safe. There *was* a murder in a schoolhouse! It's right there in your dad's book."

CHAPTER TEN

That night, Carly took the old boxed manuscript, slipped it into her shoulder purse, and carried it down the hall to her father's office. She opened the door and walked onto the braided oval rug. Her father's leather chair was skewed to one side, and she remembered the last time she'd sat there, trying to force the manuscript to speak to her. She knew better now.

Feeling the weight of the leathery pages and wooden case in the purse, she turned and let the box slide onto its former place on the shelf, still partly inside the purse. The box, seemingly loosened now, let the manuscript slide out an inch with a gentle bump and it lay there in Carly's shadow, partially exposed. The room was well lit, but there were so many shelves and wall hangings that there were always pockets of shadow everywhere, and one covered her outstretched hand.

Okay, so last night, alone and vacant, she'd touched the damn thing, and she'd had the fireworks she was hoping for: she had her "vision." Touching it that second time had been a careless, distracted act, but her earlier wariness had been well-founded. Holding the manuscript and letting her mind roam freely was enough to ignite her imaginings—or if Harriet was right and she was recalling a passage from her dad's book, her memory.

Through that afternoon, Carly wondered what it all meant. It seemed she wasn't going to be able to control her dreams, asleep or waking, but then who could? Still, it bothered her, because she'd become used to her persona of efficiency and self-control; that's what Carly clung to in the shadow of her father's genius. Now this: A.L. was gone, and it seemed she was to be prey to vivid imaginings, just as *he* had been in his productive years.

Well, enough speculation. She spun abruptly and went out the door of the office, almost slamming it behind her. That was that, she thought, although she was annoyed by a lingering feeling she was running away from something.

There wasn't anything she was obliged to do, was there? Except maybe sell the damn manuscript. After all, it didn't mean anything to her personally. But first, there might just be another story to write.

She slumped back in her favourite reading chair by the fireplace. The days were getting shorter, the pall over the lake growing darker, so she turned on the reading lamp with a touch of her fingertip. The light caught the side table and on it Harriet's copy of *Underworld Tales*, her father's name big, bold, and red on the cover. Carly breathed a sigh and resumed her reading of the section Harriet had bookmarked. She had barely skimmed it before.

"There was a dark side to Wood's fascination with the past," A.L. Rouhl wrote, and Carly could picture the old man's wide mouth and long grey eyebrows—could hear his deep growling voice as she read the words.

> "Every now and then, he'd reconstruct a set of iron shackles copied from the Old Bailey, or a Spanish-style beaded garrotte he'd come across in his reading. If you caught him in a talkative

mood, and if he felt safe, Wood might tell you about his enthusiasm, letting his facade of middle-class blandness slip in the process. I could see the shy delight he took in discussing the monks of Medmenham Abbey, a cult of prominent upper-class degenerates in eighteenth-century England.

Sir Francis Dashwood, with his motto 'Do what thou wilt,' was almost a hero to Wood. He would chuckle, recounting the prank Dashwood pulled on his friends, having a monkey leap from a contrived altar to the devil. He smirked at the story of George Selwyn, a member of the British Parliament who paid the public executioner for the privilege of watching the heads of beheaded traitors being sewn back on for burial. The past, Wood believed, is so much richer than the everyday.

I learned in my travels, though, that history sifts the outrages of the past for us. There's plenty to be outraged at all around us today if we care to look.

It was in those moments when he let down his guard that you could glimpse the devious horror of a man that Wood really was. I'll go further: I think Wood had at least two personalities. Now, I don't mean that he was schizophrenic and unaware of his multiple personalities. He knew exactly what he was and what he was doing.

Some people have the knack, you might even call it a gift, of becoming someone else just for the pleasure of it. It simply occurs to them one day that you don't have to be yourself—consistent and knowable. You can be a saint or a monster and indulge in singular thoughts and experiences, so long as you are self-aware enough to slip back into the everyday persona you're obliged to present to the world.

In this way, a saint can walk among men; in this way, a monster can prey on us from the shadows.

The key is to keep the personalities isolated from one another. You can commit a crime, say, as long as you don't leave a trail of breadcrumbs back to your staid and stolid day-to-day self. I chose to call this person "Wood" because he can appear to be a quiet and unremarkable man, which is, of course, why people miss how feral he is.

His suburban home is as ordinary as he is because he guardedly keeps his horde of peculiar and telling artefacts in a single basement room. He likes to go down there and be surrounded by his collection, and when he does, he enters a state of otherness and lives in an era of his own choosing, washing his face in a ceramic bowl and toileting with a primitive privy.

His research isn't focussed and organized the way it would be with a true scholar; he might take an interest in the Middle Ages—anything from the late Anglo-Saxon period to the English Renaissance. At other times, his fancy could veer to Victorian spiritualism or even the quaint pornography of the post-war period. He has no exam to write or dissertation to submit, so his mind ranges free.

Wood has unquestionable artistic skills, and he has made set decorations for local film productions. He even has a mechanical turn of mind, having been a machinist for a while.

Our paths first crossed because of an old friend of mine. Wood had sold my friend a manuscript. It was supposedly sixteenth century, but Wood hadn't insisted on its authenticity. He merely shrugged and said things like, 'It looks convincing to me.' Then he emphasized the finer points of the manuscript with the air of a modest connoisseur. The object was convincingly ancient, a hand-lettered book in a leather-covered box, but Wood was careful to remain vague about the manuscript's provenance.

My friend, Gill Watters, sensing a bargain, bought it at a price that seemed reasonable given the shaky provenance, and, for a while, the boxed manuscript had a place of honour in Gill's home.

Of course, Gill couldn't resist showing off his latest

acquisition, and I found myself turning the leathery pages with increasing suspicion. I caught on to what Wood was doing: he had a business model based on this kind of vaguely fraudulent dealing, and I realized that, as a con artist, Wood could make a steady income—not a fortune, mind you, but enough to warrant his long hours sewing, inking, and gilding.

It all demanded a deceitful, shadowy existence for Wood. As near as I could tell, Wood had never had a committed relationship with a woman or man, but in his guise as a friendly neighbour, he could be charming. His front of normality was as artful as the little grotesque antiquities he would assemble."

Carly looked up from Harriet's copy of her father's book. Indy stirred and was watching her intently for no apparent reason. The dog actually broke eye contact when Carly returned his gaze. She smiled. It was such a human thing to do: "Who, me? I wasn't staring at you. I'm just over here minding my own business."

She returned to the hardcover on her lap, but before she read another word of A.L.'s spellbinding character study, her journalistic instincts made her twist her lips in skepticism. How the hell did A.L. know so much about Wood—where he lived, his sinister basement?

It was a familiar pattern with her father's writing, one that defined his style and set him apart from his contemporaries. A.L.'s gift was characterization, but as far as Carly could tell, his profiles of the odd and eccentric people he encountered were mostly a kind of fiction. Typically, A.L. would start with a real person, and using some artefact connected to that person he let his mind wander, turning the diary, cigarette lighter, or glove over and over in his hands.

Carly had seen him do it a hundred times, fidgeting away until it was time to write. He'd come up with details that he couldn't actually know. If Wood was as secretive as A.L. said, how would the author know about Wood's suburban home? Had Wood really let down his guard and talked to A.L. about his ghoulish interests, or was that just A.L. composing, drawing on his own eclectic reading?

Indy stole another glance at her, and Carly shook her head. "What aren't you telling me, Indy? You saw him writing even more than me. How did he do it, eh, boy?"

But Indy flopped down, again looking guilty, his head turned away. Ah, well, given what the poor dog had seen, including two murders, Indy had every right to be screwed up.

Carly returned to A.L.'s least successful book and read on:

> "When I convinced my friend that he'd been deliberately taken in by Wood, Gill was furious. He saw himself as a canny businessman, and his ego was stung. Wood had been prepared for this possibility. Following his tested game plan, Wood simply offered to take back the manuscript and return Gill's money, but this time, his fallback ploy didn't work. To Wood's amazement, Gill wasn't interested in restitution; he wanted Wood prosecuted. You see, Gill was that rare type of guy who liked to talk about honour and justice. He took Wood's low-key antique dealings very seriously and was determined to expose him as a fraud.
>
> Faced with this attitude, Wood, who had a bland and blameless standing in his community to protect, panicked.
>
> Wood had always been slippery in his antique dealings, making careful disclaimers and warnings about an old book or map, then shifting seamlessly to a hard sell. Wood never demanded huge sums for his quasi treasures, so the mark would fall for the old ploy that there were a couple of other buyers interested, and would take a chance.
>
> Usually, Wood's clients were hooked. It was a variation of what grifters used to call the long con: even if the mark found out his purchase was a fake, he or she would generally swallow

the loss out of embarrassment, and Wood never heard from them again.

Once before, Wood went too far and had been sued for fraud, but because there wasn't a lot of money involved, he'd been able to quickly settle out of court, and Wood was left with the impression that he wasn't taking a very big risk in his illegal dealings after all.

What he never anticipated was that he would one day sell to a man like Gill, for whom ethics were more important than money. Gill steadfastly refused to return the manuscript to Wood, seeing it as evidence, then, in a fit of indifference, Gill gave it to me—on the condition he never had to look at it again. Gill was determined that Wood be publicly exposed and that his antique business shut down as the criminal enterprise it was.

Of course, Wood saw Gill's anger as a terrible overreaction. The amount of money that had exchanged hands wasn't great: around two thousand dollars, but Wood had misjudged his mark this time. Gill was well off, but with his bow ties and sleeveless cardigans, he came across as a skinny, weak-jawed bookish type. Wood couldn't believe that this sort of fussy Norman Rockwell could work up such a steaming head of indignation.

What would exposure have meant to Wood? Well, he would have had to cut back his side business in antiques—and perhaps some of the collectors Wood had sold to would have taken notice and come around suing him. Most of his troubles would probably have been settled in small claims court, with no time to serve, but the thought of all the complications and distractions drove Wood a bit crazy. Just crazy enough for one quick, vicious act.

See, that was the problem with Wood. He didn't understand the depths of his own depravity and his fascination with cruelty. He had been too successful in compartmentalizing his baser personality. And so it was that he had sent out the version of Wood that loved the ghoulish and sordid side of humanity—sent him out on a mission.

The way I see it, Wood tracked Gill down to a place where he was alone and far from help—an old schoolhouse a few miles from Gill's Oakville home, a building Gill was renovating for resale.

Wood murdered Gill Watters there.

Carly's eyes drifted off the page. Earlier, cradling the old boxed manuscript box, she pictured a schoolhouse. Damn it. She had no memory of having read this passage before, but she must have; maybe some vestigial memory of her father's story had stuck in her subconscious, and she conjured it up in her imagination. It was possible.

She returned to the page in front of her:

"I have no proof of what happened in that old schoolhouse, and yet I catch glimpses of it in my imaginings. I see a version of Woods who is capable of violence, one that is at odds with the man his neighbours see.

I wish I could tell you how Wood murdered my friend. My guess is it would have been something medieval and brutal, a spiked mace of the kind they used to call a 'holy water sprinkle,' or a fine Italian stiletto perhaps—because that's the kind of thing Wood was drawn to in his reading and research, but the truth is, I don't *know* how it was done and the police weren't about to tell me what they had found out. To them, I was nothing but a writer looking for material for my next book.

Wood was never prosecuted for fraud, far less murder. Never even suspected in official circles. His connection to the man he supposedly killed was too tenuous. Imagine *my* horror though, knowing in my heart that this monster murdered my friend, and knowing, too, that I had nothing conclusive to take to the police. I had the manuscript, but couldn't tie it to Wood except by hearsay.

It all sounds damning for Wood the way I tell it, but the only thing I could prove was that Gill gave me a manuscript which he believed was a fake. I gave the police the name Gill had given me, but the man I call Wood had been clever, presenting a false face to the world, and the police never found a dealer in antiquities by that name. I'm not even sure they looked.

That's been a recurring theme in my life: to know things with little evidence. To bear witness only in the privileged confines of my books.

One thing I'm sure of—standing over the body, stunned by what he had just done, Wood must have been shaking with indecision. My guess is he was surprised by his own fierceness. He'd done such a good job of compartmentalizing his ghoulish side that he could hardly believe what he'd done. Back in the shoes of Wood, the small-time antiquities dealer, he knew he had to put distance between himself and his victim.

Wood wasn't plagued by guilt, mind you, just fear of exposure, and it wasn't long before he grasped the essentials of the situation. As far as Wood knew, no one could connect him to the little affair of the bogus manuscript, and who would believe someone would kill over such a trifle, anyway?

No, the problem was simple: scramble the scene as much as possible so as to impede investigators, and then get far away. Then he would resume his life of convenient obscurity and avoid any more high-risk sales for a while. He had no difficulty slipping back into the ordinariness of his day-to-day livelihood, but what had happened, of course, is that Wood had met his destiny, becoming the medieval monster of his dreams.

Carly put the book down. It wasn't shocking for her to read this stuff because her father's work was full of the gruesome and the macabre. If you thought about it, or if you were the great man's daughter, you would wonder again at how A.L. could make such damning accusations and get away with it. Sure, her father changed names in his books to protect himself; that was standard practice for him in writing his "creative nonfiction," but if he honestly believed these stories about fraud and murder, surely he would have pressured the police to investigate.

He'd answer by saying he had no proof—that the details about Wood's house and business practices were conjectures built on few real facts.

For example, if you read carefully, you would notice that Wood didn't seem to know that the famous writer, A.L. Rouhl, was on to him—that there was a third party who knew about his shady antique business and suspected him of murder. The story only made sense if Rouhl had gotten his information about Wood solely from his friend Gill—and had fabricated the rest, never having personally met Wood.

Of course, if all that stuff about bogus antiques was second-hand... "How do you justify accusing Wood of murder?" you'd say.

"They're not accusations—they're stories," her father would answer with that sort of diabolical scowl that was half smile and half frown. "That's what I do. I tell stories." Carly had attempted that kind of discussion with him before on other matters, and she knew the litany.

Carly groaned in exasperation to the empty living room. "Creative nonfiction."

Her father was a literary genre unto himself. *No wonder I'm such a basket case,* she thought. It was why the last year had been such a strain for Carly; she was still coming to grips with A.L. Rouhl's legacy: a slurry of facts, lies, lucky guesses, and intuition. Maybe that was what made A.L. a genius. He'd invented a new kind of storytelling, one that verged on fraud itself.

He'd undoubtedly guessed right about Marcella Cole, the

woman who he claimed was responsible for his own fatal decline. In the end, the police put together enough on Cole to lay charges. Only her death had saved Cole from prosecution.

So maybe A.L. was right about this Wood person, too. But there were the same old questions: how had he conjured up so much information about that basement-dwelling recluse? Who was the mysterious Gill Watters who died in the schoolhouse? Who else had A.L. spoken to about the murder? Was there any serious journalism involved, or was this just another colourful Rouhl profile, one of the many woven into his stories? Carly understood that this Wood character might not even exist.

"Travel writing," A.L.'s editor had called it. "There's a market for this"—and so, as it happened, there had been, and her father made a living crying wolf. One of the ongoing costs to him was that no one had thought to take his colourful parables seriously as fact.

The narrative on her lap ended there. The next chapter was about another mysterious character entirely, so she closed the grey hardcover and let it rest in her hand. She stroked the dust jacket, her love for her father in the gesture.

Suddenly, her eyes caught a movement by the fireplace.

Damn. There it was again. Indy was staring at her.

CHAPTER ELEVEN

Detective Eilert Weiss of the Halton District Police spotted Carly Rouhl standing under a tree on the far side of the street. A streetlight on that side was spilling well-defined shadows through its few remaining ruddy leaves onto the lawn and sidewalk where Carly stood. Even from this distance, mottled by shadow, she looked dignified and self-possessed, a long red scarf hanging to the hem of her coat.

The sun had set, but along with the streetlights, the upscale houses with their soffit pot lights and lawn-mounted floods made the early evening a lighted streetscape of warm brick and glowing kerbs. Behind Weiss, a police cruiser was raking its headlights through the legs of a half dozen officers, turning their dark trousers to the shade of blue jeans. The street was wet and the boulevard still green beneath Carly's tasselled boots.

Weiss shouldered Joshi. "Know who that is over there?"

Joshi looked at Weiss getting the sightline and swivelled his head until he was peering over his shoulder. "Is that…? It's your tame journalist, the Rouhl woman."

"Carly."

"What's she doing here? She's a crime reporter now?"

"No, but last I heard, she's still a magazine editor. She has the contacts to find out what's going on around town, and tonight it seems she's dispatched herself here. Question is why."

Joshi glanced up at the overcast, seeking strength. "You're going over there."

"Yes, I suppose I am."

Weiss put a reassuring hand on Joshi's shoulder and then stepped down into the road. As he got closer, Carly backed into the shadows, and Weiss realized she'd been using the streetlight to get noticed.

"Not really your beat, is it?" he said as he joined her in the leaf shadow.

Carly gave a polite smile that managed to convey sadness. "I heard a policeman had been hurt."

"That didn't happen here. It was at a gas station on Walker's Line. Couple of cops followed this guy, tried to arrest him at the pumps for being under the influence. He bolted into his car and backed up fast. Hit one of the cops with the open door."

"Is the policeman okay?"

"Dislocated shoulder. Massive bruising."

"Is that the car?" She nodded at the driveway across the street where the police were gathered.

"Yeah, that's it. We tracked him down to his house using the licence plate. Drunk as a skunk. They had to taser the guy. Prem and I were just trying to find out if the girlfriend was a passenger in the car. Not likely to end up in your society pages, I'm guessing."

"I'm not far from home. I came over hoping you might be here."

Weiss thought she sounded oddly shy. "What? You're here for me? You could have just called me."

Carly looked at Weiss's face with an amused smile. "I see you've grown a beard."

Weiss rubbed his chin. "I'm testing department policy. I expect somebody is going to walk up to me and tell me I have to shave it off. I'm curious who it'll be."

"Did you know that petitioners in ancient Greece were supposed to kneel at the feet of the king and grasp his beard? You know, kind of reaching up? I've seen pictures, and it looks kind of weird."

"Mine's too short to grab. I hope it wasn't the tradition for the king to kick the petitioner on his ass."

"Don't worry. I promise to leave your beard alone."

"Wait, so *I'm* the king? Wait till I tell Prem." Weiss scratched the fine greying beard. "But then that makes you the petitioner, doesn't it?"

"My point is, some things you have to ask for in person; you know, as you gaze into the ruler's eyes?"

Weiss laughed. "Ruler. Yeah. As if." He looked at her unflinchingly, not an easy thing for him to do with a beautiful woman. "If you'd called, I would have come," he said. He glanced back across the road. "Although, I wouldn't have told Prem. He frowns on me talking to the press. There are protocols."

Carly smiled. "You can tell your partner I'm no longer the press. I'm handing the magazine over to a new editor. Oh, and when you heard what I was asking, you might *not* have come."

"Tell me."

Carly looked across the street at the milling officers. "Is it okay? You're working..."

"Tell me."

She nodded her thanks and clutched at the strap of her shoulder bag. "During the Cole investigation, you read one of my father's books in which he described a serial killer. You and I, we know he was writing about Marcella Cole. He said as much in that Docx file he left me. You know; you've read that, too."

"Go on."

"Well, Dad was right, wasn't he? Cole was everything he said she was—a murderous sociopath."

Weiss let his moustache bristle. "Probably. There's no way we could establish Marcella Cole infected your father with the HIV that led to his decline. That much is still speculation, but... yes, we know she was capable of murder and she had the motive and means to carry it out."

Carly moved closer, the leaf shadows following the curves of her brow and cheekbones. Weiss noticed her skin was shining, damp from the rain. "So do *you* believe it?" she said, looking worried. "Do you believe Marcella Cole was a serial killer?"

"As a matter of fact, I do. But you know how picky my people are about evidence. Fortunately, Marcella Cole is dead, so the case is closed."

"Okay, so, I'm drawing on precedent here: what if there was another unpunished murderer in one of Dad's stories?"

Weiss held up his hand to stop her. "There are at least five I could name since our run-in with Cole, murders alluded to in your dad's books. I've read most of A.L. Rouhl's stuff now. There was the murder in South Carolina. What was his name; Beddoes? And the spy whose cover was blown in D.C., the kidnapper in Glasgow..."

"Yes, all right. I get what you're saying. You've basically got nothing to go on but the stories themselves, and the murders are not in your jurisdiction, anyway. But what if there *was* one close at hand? Right here in Halton? That would be yours, wouldn't it? What do they call them? Cold cases?"

"Okay, what have you got?"

"Well, I've got a name: 'Wood,' which is probably false. This Wood person murdered someone in an old schoolhouse. Judging from the date of publication of Dad's book, it would have happened sometime around the year 2010, somewhere around Oakville."

"A murder in a schoolhouse?"

"You know; one of those old one-room schoolhouses from the 1920s."

"I don't remember a case like that in my reading of his books."

"Neither did I. Harriet Blain came up with the connection. You remember Harriet from the office? Blond? Green glasses?"

"Ah yes. Unforgettable."

"The book is *Underworld Tales,* and it's an obscure late-career book that didn't sell well. I'd forgotten it myself."

"Guess I missed that one."

"So, in the book, there's a story about an antiquities forger named Wood who made, or put together, all sorts of fake antiquities. Wood murdered a rich guy who had an interest in history—a skinny man with a weak chin, name of Gill Watters, who threatened to expose him. All the names are probably fake; that was standard practice with A.L."

"This Wood guy was a convicted forger? That'd help."

"No. Not actually convicted. There was a case settled out of court, though. Seems he was a small timer with a gift for getting away with things; which means he's probably still out there, unnoticed. You see, this forger specializes in fabricated historical artefacts with weak provenance. He acknowledges the questionable authenticity and sells his wares at a discount. That was his cleverness—he kept his profile low by selling cheap. If the buyer found out he'd bought a fake, Wood could just apologize and say, 'I warned you.'"

"Huh. So a small-time crook. Can't see him getting rich that way."

"A.L. seems to suggest that Gill, the mark, was a friend of his and that Wood murdered Gill to avoid being exposed."

"The mark? Does your dad say what it was that Gill bought?"

"Yes, he says it was a 'boxed manuscript' and I found just such an object on my dad's shelves. That's why I think this may be a real case."

"What's it worth? Any idea?"

Carly hesitated, frowning at her boots. "A couple of thousand dollars. Maybe."

"Kind of unusual for a small-time huckster to up the ante to murder."

"But the case should be easy, shouldn't it? A murder in an old schoolhouse? Can't be many of those."

"How do you know it happened in Halton?"

"There's a reference in the story to Oakville and Dad usually used authentic locations in his work, but I can't be sure." A lock of Carly's hair stuck to her brow, and she drew it back with her fingers. "Look, let me say this before *you* have to say it: the police can't do P.I. work for members of the public. I know you can't waste taxpayers' money on something as flimsy as this, but what if there *was* a schoolhouse-related murder in your local records? Would that be enough to get you interested? I mean, you can look into a case that's actually in the record, right?"

Weiss thought about that for a moment. It probably wouldn't be enough. There had been a dozen unsolved murders over the last decade, but it was Carly asking, and he admitted to himself that seemed to matter.

"It would be interesting," he answered. "But if the original murder investigation didn't make a connection with this forger, I probably won't be able to either."

Carly swung her bag around on its shoulder strap and snapped it open. "Look, just take this book. It's Harriet's copy so I'll need it back, but read the bookmarked passage and see what you think. Would you do that?"

Carly realized that she had almost said, "Would you do that *for me*?" That's what she was asking, but it would have sounded too personal by half.

Weiss glanced up at the glistening leaves. "Carly, have you had any...premonitions about this?"

Carly looked away. She knew what he was asking; had she had any visions? “Premonitions? No. Not exactly.”

“Not exactly?”

“Do feelings count?”

“I’ve learned to take your feelings seriously.”

Carly started to describe her daydream and as she did so, two words popped into Weiss’s mind: “lightning rod.” And with them, Harry Clendenning’s beefy face.

CHAPTER TWELVE

After watching Weiss's meeting with the Rouhl woman under the tree, his partner, Prem Joshi, adopted a suspicious air. It was a reasonable posture; the daughter of A.L. Rouhl had managed to get mixed up in their investigations twice already.

Joshi also knew about the devastating suicide of Weiss's wife, which seemed, to him, relevant. It made Weiss bitter but vulnerable to women, and Carly Rouhl was a formidable personality. To his credit, it wasn't until they were alone in the car headed back to North Burlington and District Station Three on Constable Henshaw Boulevard that Joshi asked Weiss the obvious question.

"What did she want?"

"Carly?"

"Yeah, Carly—the woman who may or may not have been an accessory to Marcella Cole's murder."

"Come on, Prem. You don't believe that."

"Maybe not, but we didn't exactly wrap up Cole's and her father's murder with a neat bow."

"Life is messy."

"You type real neat, Eilert, but sometimes I think you've got a flair for politics. Don't get me wrong. You kept us out of a deal of shit on that case, but you've got me longing for some old-fashioned police work—a murder for profit, say, with a nice, straight chain of evidence."

"You may get your wish, Prem. Carly was asking about a murder in a schoolhouse. You know, the old rural schoolroom type of thing?"

"Oh, wow! A case ripped right out of today's headlines!"

"Actually, if it happened, it *would* be an inactive case, but not ancient. Maybe ten, eleven years ago? Maybe in Oakville. "

"So semi ancient, which is fine, because we have so little modern brutality and violence in Halton. You are getting my ironic tone here, I hope?"

"Blatant sarcasm noted. All the same, it won't take long to do a web search on schoolhouse murders. You can drink coffee and make culturally insensitive cracks while I work."

Joshi nodded. "I do enjoy that."

"There you go then."

Weiss's proposal held up quite well. Within minutes of their return to the second-floor office off Walker's Line, Weiss was tapping away at his laptop, getting results while Joshi scowled over a paper coffee cup he brought up from the downstairs cafeteria.

"Find anything?" Joshi said, curious despite himself.

"Actually, yeah. How's this? December 1954. Teacher shot in a one-room schoolhouse in Dalton, Ontario. That's up Sudbury way. It was a dispute over a homosexual relationship, it says here. But that doesn't work for me. Too long ago and not a Halton case."

"But thanks for sharing." Joshi wove his fingers around his cup and squinted at the ceiling fixture. "Why don't you talk directly to Oakville? Guy named Sutton, been in Homicide for decades. Do you remember? We met him and a bunch of his people at Shoeless Joe's last winter. There's the greenbelt north of Oakville, lots of farmland and rural roads. If an old schoolhouse still exists, that's probably where it would be."

Weiss raised an eyebrow. "You can't resist being a sweetie, even when you're pissed off. It's worth a call."

Joshi closed his eyes in long-suffering disgust and squeezed his cup into a deformed oval.

CHAPTER THIRTEEN

Weiss remembered meeting Darryl Sutton once before. They'd had a drink together. Back then, there had been a half dozen other people seemingly all talking at once, and Weiss hadn't singled Sutton out from the crowd at Shoeless Joe's. He might not have even recognized the big shaggy man who met him at the reception area of Twelve Division in Oakville. The voice came back to him though; boozy and brimming with easy humour.

"The question is," Sutton said before Weiss could get a word out, "will you be buying me a donut—or lunch?"

Weiss grinned. "I need to talk to you about the Cecil Warden case. You mentioned that name when I phoned asking about schoolhouses."

Sutton deflated a bit and twisted his mouth. "Oh, yeah. Cecil Warden. Donut then. That's an unsolved; interesting case, though. Tell you what. We'll compromise. How about a bagel? Did you see the place up Kerr Street? Called Schlagel's Bagels."

"You're kidding, right?"

"That's what *we* call it. It's something like that anyway, and their bagels are huge."

They took Weiss's car, the one he signed out from the Burlington pool, but they could easily have walked the wet pavement up Kerr.

"Schliemann's Bagels," Weiss read the raised logo fixed to the wall tiles. The letters formed an irregular circle with what might have been plastic cream cheese oozing from its edges.

Sutton shrugged. "Schlagel sounds better."

They stood at the counter, squinting at the chalkboard menu above them. Sutton knew what he wanted, but Weiss took a while, settling on an avocado and bacon on a sesame bagel. They sat at a red Formica table near the window where they could see metered parking and passing umbrellas.

"Schliemann," Weiss repeated. "Wasn't he the archaeologist who found the site of ancient Troy? Tied himself to the mast of a ship until he learned ancient Greek."

Sutton groaned. "I remember you now from Shoeless Joe's in Burlington. Where do you find time to read all those books?"

"That's easy. I have no social life. Speaking of books—that's why I'm here. Friend of mine thought there might be a parallel between something she read and a real schoolhouse murder. I should have asked you to bring the Cecil Warden file along with you."

"Not worth it. It's pretty thin, and I can tell you everything that's in it. Besides, I don't do paperwork at lunch."

"You remember all your cases?"

"No, but that one kind of sticks in my mind." Sutton grimaced at the memory. "Also, there's not much to the file. Some cases you need a whiteboard and coloured markers. Warden's case: no viable suspects, not a lot of interviews."

"Can you run it by me in outline?"

"Sure. Brenda Warden, the wife, calls in the missing persons. Body was found two days later in a ditch along Eighth Line by an employee of Chudleigh's Orchard. We brought the corpse to the coroner. Turns out Warden hadn't been dead long. A couple of days. Initial assessment: death by asphyxiation."

"He was smothered. You're talking about a body dump."

"That's what we concluded."

"So anything about a schoolhouse?"

"What happened was we found out Warden owned a nearby schoolhouse building he planned on reselling. We went with the hypothesis that he was actually murdered there in the schoolhouse and his body was dumped in the ditch to slow us down."

"Did you get anything from Forensics in the schoolhouse?"

"Not much, but that's not surprising. A bit of dust disturbed, so we figured old Cecil Warden was probably smothered there. Violently."

Weiss frowned. "How do you *do* that? A pillow?"

"Well now, excellent question. A big guy could smother a woman in bed with his bare hands, or a small child maybe. But Warden was a wiry old guy and there were no soft cushions or anything in the schoolroom. My first thought was that the killer had to be big and strong—maybe did it with an open palm. You know; pinch the nose with the thumb, cover the mouth with the palm of the hand. That would be hard to do with the vic bucking and twisting and all. Sorry, but the whole case was suppositions and theories because we had nothing else."

"Evidence of violence on the body?"

"Warden's body wasn't brutally beaten or anything, not even the face, so the murder had to be relatively fast and efficient. I kept thinking about how it could be done, and it creeped me out. What I did is, I got the coroner to black light the face and—we picked up traces of adhesive. So then I made a snap assumption: a gag, right?"

"What about the wrists, arms? Was Warden restrained? Ropes, anything?"

"No, but he must have been held down. Warden was fairly

tall but skinny, and what bruising we could find was on one forearm. His left."

"I'm having trouble picturing this."

"So did we. So my partner and I, we kind of acted it out. Must have looked bloody silly rolling around on an exercise mat. We kept coming back to the adhesive. Why gag someone if their hands are free? We looked more closely at the autopsy results and it turns out the adhesive wasn't just over the mouth. There were traces across the brow, temples, and chin. We tried to figure it out. At one point, I shoved a piece of paper on my partner's face—you know, regular eight and a half by eleven printing paper? The paper sorta lined up with the residual adhesive on Warden's face, so we went online and looked for adhesive sheets that were about that size. You follow?"

Weiss leaned forward, his eyes wide. "What did you come up with?"

"Are you ready for this? A fabric patch for repairing upholstery."

"Upholstery?"

"Big friggin' patch. Seriously. We found a product that had a strong adhesive on one side—a rectangular vinyl patch—and it was about the right size."

"The guy was murdered with a vinyl patch?"

"We tried modelling the attack using the paper. I got on top of the other guy and I pushed the sheet of paper against his face with my right hand." Sutton wiggled in his seat, raising one shoulder. "I used my left hand to pin my partner's right arm above his head."

Weiss raised his own arm awkwardly, splaying his fingers, visualizing. "Which would explain the victim's...*left* arm being bruised. It was free. He would have been hammering away at his attacker with it!" His enthusiasm drew some stares; people looked up from their lox and cream cheese.

"Exactly. The vic's left arm would have been free, beating at the attacker, tearing at the adhesive patch and the killer's fingers holding it. It would have been a brutal scene, but quiet. We worked on it a lot. The killer would've turned his head to the side to protect his eyes, so the vic's left arm would be limited to tearing away at the killer's hair or fingers."

"Was there any hair under Warden's fingernails?"

"No. If I'd been the victim, I'd have been scratching at the vinyl patch or the killer's fingers, trying to breathe. But there was nothing on the vic's fingers but a couple of black linen fibres."

"So maybe the killer wore gloves to protect his hand," Weiss offered. "Maybe even some kind of hood to protect his head. That would account for the fibres."

"That's what we figured. Everything points to premeditation. The murder was well thought out by someone who was confident he was bigger and stronger than Warden. You don't try something half-assed like that unless you know you've got an advantage in strength—or unless the victim is incapacitated in some way."

Weiss's eyes were narrowed, focussed absently on a woman's boots at the next table. "The killer was probably someone who knew Warden was weak, so it makes sense that it was probably someone that Warden knew."

"That brings us to motive," Sutton said, his cheek filled with bagel, "and that's where we run into a brick wall. There doesn't seem to be any money involved, and no one benefited directly from Warden's death. The widow got a reduced teacher's pension—two-thirds of what they were getting together—and some property, but that didn't lead us anywhere."

"You said the killing would have been quiet?"

"Well, think about it. The vic wouldn't have been able to cry out, and he would have been muffled with both the vinyl and the killer's glove. It would have been a struggle, but a relatively quiet one."

"And not much more than three minutes," Weiss said, wincing at the thought.

"Yeah. We thought of that, too. Rapid asphyxia, followed by brain death. It wouldn't have taken long."

Weiss sipped some tea from a paper cup printed with the cream cheese logo. "So, a premeditated, clever murder."

"But at the same time, a desperate act by a frightened amateur. We came to that conclusion, too. Maybe the killer had the idea of using the patch as a weapon, but it was still a messy, brutal affair. Not what you'd expect of a cool-headed professional. We went ahead on the possibility that the killer himself would have sustained injuries—a scratched face, a bloody ear, maybe even a dislocated finger. I mean, what would you do if you were the victim being smothered and you had one hand free? You'd scratch away at the assailant's fingers, wouldn't you? Rip out his hair?"

"Did you look for hair in the ditch or at the schoolhouse?"

"Yeah, we went back after the autopsy, but we didn't find anything. What we did find were a few traces of adhesive on the schoolhouse floor. No discernible shape this time. That made us crazy again, but then we figured, what if the killer came back to the schoolhouse with the adhesive patch he'd peeled off Warden's face, and what if he used it to pick up hair or any other evidence he saw?"

"You mean he brushed at the floor with the patch? Man. You're way out on a limb with that. Creative, though."

"Yeah. Anyway, we talked to a lot of people, mostly at the college where Warden worked."

"And you asked about the schoolhouse?"

"Of course. It was a real estate speculation by Warden. We thought we had a suspect. Warden used a student as a helper cleaning up the schoolhouse property. His name was Keith Blair and he would have been there with Warden at the schoolhouse the day the old guy was murdered. We examined the kid for injuries. Nothing. Checked his alibi. It was soft—Blair's girlfriend basically—but the thing is, his motivation was weak at best. He didn't stand to gain anything from his instructor's death. Besides, someone—anyone—could have come to the schoolhouse after Blair left. We had practically nothing else, so..."

"Unsolved."

"One of many. Don't you like your bagel? "

"No, it's good. Just too big. You could feed a family of four with this thing. I'm going to wrap it up and take it with me." Weiss coddled his teacup, and the conversation drifted to the gang they remembered from Shoeless Joe's.

Sutton laughed. "Who was that guy with the, uh, dark complexion? He did an impression of your super—a riot!"

Weiss smiled at the political correctness. "That would be Prem Joshi, my partner. I'll have to ask him how he remembers you."

"Hey, don't do that. I'd been drinking. I've been helpful, haven't I?"

"Yeah." Weiss laughed and finished his tea. "Look, I think I'm going to need that file. Can you encode it and email it to me?"

Sutton winced at the thought. "Damn. If I can remember how to do that."

When he got back to his office, Weiss found Prem Joshi studying a printout with his feet up on Weiss's chair.

"Kind of you," Weiss said.

Joshi sat up and took his rubber-soled shoes off Weiss's desk chair. "Mm?"

"I mean, it's kind of you to put a magazine on the chair before you put your feet on it. Shows you have the habit of civilization."

Joshi removed the magazine and sniffed. "Nice to be appreciated. How was Sutton?"

"Sort of entertaining. Can you picture Darryl Sutton rolling around on an exercise mat, trying to slap a piece of printer paper on another guy's face?"

"You'd better be prepared to explain that. I'm tired of your teasers. No, wait. Give me a second to relish the image." Joshi closed his eyes and then nodded. "Okay. Go."

"Well, as it happens, some guy called Cecil Warden was murdered with a sticky pad." Weiss took the printout Joshi had been looking at, balanced it on his fingertips and pointed. "The murder weapon!"

Joshi stared at the piece of paper, wide-eyed. "Touch me with that and I'll deck you."

"Come on, you have to be part of this. Go online and search 'fabric repair patches.'"

Slowly, with the air of a man wary of a practical joke, Joshi turned his chair to his own laptop and began tapping rapidly. He was faster at this than Weiss.

"Okay, great. Now find some of those patches that are this size." Weiss waved the paper at Joshi.

Joshi banged away a little more tentatively. "I'd use Siri, but someone might overhear me. I'm not sure I could live with the shame of it." He stopped and peered at his screen. "'Leather repair patch kit for couches, car seats, handbags… Dark brown?"

Tossing the printer paper gently so that it flopped on his fingertips, Weiss nodded. "Okay, I'm seeing it. Go on."

Joshi gave him a pitying look. "Fine. The murder investigation moves on apace," he said, then returned to his screen. "'High-quality PVC leather. Soft. High viscosity.'"

"What's the small print say?"

Joshi looked back at the paper balanced on Weiss's fingertips. "What it says is, 'peel back—and *stick*.'" Joshi quickly snatched the paper back from Weiss with a warning glower. "So, *this* is how Sutton works?"

"It may be how Keith Blair murdered Cecil Warden. He was the prime suspect. It would be a heck of a tricky thing, trying to keep your hand over someone's mouth and nose while the poor bugger was bucking and tearing at your hand. But with a pad like that to help you? High viscosity means the pad is as sticky as hell. And PVC leather—fake leather—would make an airtight seal on the victim's face."

Joshi creaked back in his chair with a look of horror. "Well," he looked at a loss, "what now? I could search crochet. Maybe Blair knitted Warden some socks."

"Come on, Prem. We've got to decode Sutton's file and see if there's anybody else in all this who would have the remotest reason to have large adhesive patches on hand. And," he added, holding up a commanding finger, "we've got to find the schoolhouse."

CHAPTER FOURTEEN

Weiss was driving along Ninth Line, quite enjoying the switchback ride over low hills. The road curved a lot, but there were few side roads or driveways, so it was tempting to speed. Joshi kept glancing down at the GPS, frowning.

"We're practically there. I can see the intersection up ahead and there's no schoolhouse. This is where Sutton said it was supposed to be. Damn GPS must be wrong."

"Go easy on our tech, will you?" Weiss leaned towards his window and shot a glance at the scudding clouds. "Did you know that our lowly service-issue GPS is designed to allow for time dilation? The satellites up in space are moving fast, so time passes more slowly for them. It's relativity—Einstein."

"You've got to work on your small talk, Eilert."

"Hey, you have to take time seriously. Timing is everything in detective work."

Since there were no other options nearby, Weiss pulled into a small parking lot on the northeast corner of the intersection. "And it appears *our* timing is off. My guess is the schoolhouse is long gone, demolished for this nice new local convenience."

Weiss parked, and they looked out at a mini plaza composed

of a convenience store, laundromat, and bakery. He sighed. "We could call it quits and head back?"

Joshi looked at the bakery. "Or…"

"Hmm. I think it has seating inside. We could interrogate the waitress or something."

Weiss killed the engine and followed Joshi.

The bakery was long and narrow with only three tables. A tall, sinuous girl with short purple hair and a nose ring came out from behind her counter to hand them single-page laminated menus. Their orders came and they sat contentedly with their coats draped over their chair backs.

Joshi leaned into the butcher block table. "This sandwich is excellent. We should come back here."

Weiss admired the shelves of exotic loaves and rolls that lined one of the long walls. "Yeah, nice. Kind of rustic. Not too big."

"A bit off the beaten path. The nearest house is up Milton way."

"They'll get a lot of through traffic from Oakville." Weiss chewed, admiring his sandwich. "You should have got the super seeded roll. Nice and crunchy."

Joshi wrinkled his nose. "Those are mostly sesame seeds. I hate sesame seeds."

"I thought all you guys liked sesame seeds. Hell, you make candies out of them."

"If by 'all you guys,' you mean every inhabitant of the Indian subcontinent, I'll dismiss that comment as the racist crap that it is."

"It's not racist. Sesame seeds aren't racist." Weiss thought for a moment. Stereotyping? Hmm, maybe. "Besides, you made that crack about my car being old."

"Your car is a disgrace. Broad consensus on that."

"Okay, but you implied that my having an old car was because I'm Scottish, and therefore cheap."

"If the shoe fits."

"See? Stereotype. Actually, that stereotype probably has something to do with Scottish Presbyterianism."

"So not just a stereotype then." Joshi bowed, gracious in victory.

"Besides," Weiss sighed, "I'm saving up to retire in Parry Sound. Bayview Mansions overlooking Georgian Bay." He stopped the aproned shop girl who was hurrying past with a metal tray dusted with flour, stocking the shelves. "Excuse me. Do you know how long this shop has been here?"

She stopped and fidgeted with her hairnet. "I'm not sure. I'm new. But it's been a few years, anyway."

"Is the owner here?"

"Yeah. She's in back."

"Could we talk to her? Halton Police."

"Omigod, okay. Maybe you should go back into the kitchen to talk to her."

Joshi glanced at his half-eaten sandwich. "No, it's okay, we're just making inquiries. She got something to hide?"

Weiss shook his head wearily. "Come on, Prem."

The girl looked confused for a second, then said, "Well, I guess I'll get her."

Joshi looked out the front window at the rolling fields of the greenbelt. "Are you sure we got the right intersection?"

"You're thinking I set the GPS to find bakeries?"

"I'd be okay with that."

The manager, a round-faced apple-cheeked woman lightly dusted with flour walked up to their table. Weiss started to rise.

"Please don't get up. In fact, do you mind if I..." She dragged a cane-backed chair over to their table.

"Very nice bread you have here." Weiss smiled. "Don't be alarmed; my partner and I were just wondering how long your business has been open."

"It...it'll be five years in the summer."

"The building looks relatively new."

"Yeah, we built it special. Architect and everything. Me and my daughter."

"Do you happen to remember what was on this site before you built?"

"Nothing. It was an empty lot. The real estate people called it a pad for building on."

Weiss looked at Joshi and slumped his shoulders.

The manager picked up on his disappointment. "You're not thinking about the old schoolhouse, are you?"

Weiss brightened. "So there *was* a schoolhouse on this road?"

"Never saw it myself, but some of the local customers remember it. One old guy even remembers attending when he was a kid. But it's been gone for a while."

"Any idea how long—or what happened to it? Demolished, I suppose."

"No, no. The old guy said it was taken away to a museum or something. Maybe ten years ago?"

"A museum?" Joshi looked skeptical. "So, like sitting there between the mummies and the dinosaurs?"

The manager seemed to share Joshi's doubts. "This customer is pretty old. Probably doesn't accept the idea of his childhood being demolished."

Weiss leaned forward in a little bow. "Well, thanks. You've been helpful."

Joshi watched her go. "You're not dragging me to the Royal Ontario Museum."

"Nah. They can't be talking about a big indoor museum. But it's not inconceivable that the building was preserved somehow. It's worth a shot. I'm going to call a couple of historical societies. We might get a lead on the damn place yet."

"Remind me why we're doing this?"

"A murder was committed in that building. Probably."

"And you think there's going to be evidence there after all

these years?" Joshi watched Weiss bite into his roll. "This has to do with *her*, doesn't it?"

Weiss looked up. "Carly Rouhl? Yeah. It does. She has... uncanny instincts; you know that."

"A vivid imagination, you mean."

"Okay, but with some people, there's no difference. It's all neurons, after all."

"Man, you're getting weird."

"Prem, when you find people in life that you feel you can trust—well, all I'm saying is it doesn't happen all that often."

"You've never said why you trust her."

Weiss shrugged. "She walked into my life and she seems to be staying there."

"Oh, hell, this is about your wife. I knew it. You couldn't trust your wife, and now here's this great-looking woman whose father was a national institution."

"Carly's smart without being pathologically cruel. I gotta say, that is refreshing after my wife."

"She's also way too young for you."

"Oh, come on, Prem. It's not like that."

"Didn't you see *When Harry Met Sally*? It's *always* like that."

"In that case, you'll just have to hope I'm not a stupid old fool. Does it make sense that you can befriend someone attractive without having any expectations?"

"So you do find her attractive?"

"God, who wouldn't? But here's the strange part, Prem. I think she's going to lead us to a killer."

Joshi shook his head slowly. "Whose turn is it to pay?"

CHAPTER FIFTEEN

The only viable suspect in Sutton's original investigation was a young man by the name of Keith Blair who, according to Sutton's file, had been helping with the cleanup of the schoolhouse. Weiss looked Blair up and found he was now working for a financial planning group in Burlington.

"So are we talking to this Blair guy?" Joshi wanted to know.

"Mmm, before we do that, I want some ammunition. Let's check out the man's alibi first, and that involves Blair's then-girlfriend."

Keith Blair's former girlfriend, Natalie Cowell, wasn't hard to find. She'd been working in a hair salon in the Burlington Centre mall for close to a decade, and the mall was ten minutes from the District Three Police Station in north Burlington. The shops were starting to get busy with the run-up to Christmas, and the detectives had a long walk from their car across a chilly parking lot. After a quick study of the store directory, they realized they'd pretty much parked at the wrong end of the concourse.

They walked through the crowds until they found the salon next door to a Home Outfitters. There were two stylists and three customers visible behind the big plate-glass facade. Joshi stopped out front of the shop and looked warily at the mirrors and capes inside.

"These people clearly have never heard of the term 'unisex.'" He touched Weiss's elbow as his partner reached for the door. "I'll stay outside—I can cover your retreat."

"My retreat? You mean if they try and frost my bangs or something?"

"Man up, Eilert. You can handle this alone."

Weiss grumbled. "First sign of trouble, he caves on me." He pulled open the door and stepped inside. There was a steady hum in the salon, and it smelled as though something heavily perfumed had died some hours before. Since all eyes were upon him, Weiss cleared his throat and said, "Could I speak to Natalie Cowell? I called earlier."

Natalie Cowell, a gaunt, twiggy woman with large, overly made-up eyes, was in the process of folding foil over a middle-aged matron's hair. "I can't leave this," she said. "You're uh, *Mister* Weiss, I take it."

Weiss got it. She wasn't keen on talking to the police in front of the ladies. "I saw a Starbucks," he said. "Could we talk there in, say, five…ten minutes?"

Natalie looked at the other stylist, who shrugged her approval. "Okay. Ten minutes," Natalie replied, and went back to painting a strand of hair.

Joshi dealt well with the prospect of wasting time in Starbucks, leading the way without having to consult the directory.

Finishing a biscotti dipped in calories, Joshi was the one to spot Natalie Cowell approaching from the concourse. She had removed her blue smock and wore a round-necked blouse, slacks, and laced white runners. Her collar bones stood out within the neckline of her top.

"I'm actually glad you didn't come to my apartment," she

explained. "I'd rather not talk about being the girlfriend of a murderer with my husband and child there."

Weiss stood, and Joshi wrestled briefly with his chair while Natalie sat. She placed a small iridescent purse on the table.

"A murderer? You think Keith murdered Cecil Warden?" Weiss said.

She took a few seconds to answer. "Not really. But from what I've read, who else could have? Keith was bitter enough, but he was more the sullen, brooding type. He would act hurt, but he wouldn't get all worked up. I don't know what to think."

Joshi raised his bushy eyebrows and held up his empty paper cup. "Can I get you a coffee, Ms. Cowell?" He gave a grudging glance at Weiss, who was still holding a half-empty cup. "Or tea?"

Natalie shook her head. "No, thanks. Let's just get this over with if you don't mind."

Joshi looked disappointed, but he had a question. "You picked Keith up at the schoolhouse when he was finished for the day. He called you, I guess."

"No, actually we had agreed on a time. All the same, I had to wait outside in the heat for a half-hour. It rained a bit and it was uncomfortably humid. I was in a bad mood when he finally came out and he was too, grousing at Warden for keeping him late. We had a fight about it, but it was mostly, you know, stony silence in the car on the way back to his parents' place. We broke up not long after that. There were a lot of things coming between us. Keith was in a bad place then, feeling sorry for himself, resentful of the kids who had rich parents or bigger student loans, or anything for that matter. Looking back, I think he was on the verge of clinical depression—overworked and not doing that well at school. It was tough, you know; at that level, one failed course could have derailed his career plans completely. All I knew was that I didn't want to be part of that."

Joshi smiled sympathetically. "Sure. It happens. Can you

think back, though: was he carrying anything when you dropped him off—a lunch bag, toolbox?"

"Nah. He was dressed to work; tight blue jeans and some kind of t-shirt—no, I guess you call them golf shirts, you know, with the three buttons and collar? He was all sweaty and dusty when he came out."

Weiss asked, "So, no jacket?" She pouted in thought, then shook her head. Weiss went on. "It says in the file that you heard somebody moving inside the schoolhouse when Keith got to the car."

"Did I say that? Yeah, I guess. I vaguely remember both of us looking back at the windows for a second."

"At the time, did Keith say anything about that? Presumably, it was Professor Warden inside, moving around. Did either of you speculate about what the noise was?"

"No, I don't think so." Natalie looked puzzled. "I'm not sure what you mean."

"Was it like someone moving furniture about, or was it a single sound—you know: something falling?"

"Uh, single sound. *Thump!* It was loud enough to get our attention for a second or two."

Weiss smiled reassuringly. "Okay, great. That morning, Keith had got a ride to the site with Professor Warden, right?"

"Yes. They met at the campus, drove from there. It was a Saturday."

"You were in Keith's parents' house a few times, I imagine."

"Sure," Natalie said. "They were nice people. They had a small bungalow on Spruce. Keith went to the campus by bus every day."

Joshi took a turn. "Keith told the original investigators he made end tables to sell—small pieces of furniture. Did he show you where he did that?"

"Detective Sutton never asked me about that before, but yeah, it was just a corner of his parent's basement. Unfinished, dusty. It smelled of glue or paint or something. His dad used it, too."

Joshi looked at Weiss, then, "Did he or his dad do any fabric repair? You know, seat cushions; that type of thing?"

"Fabric repair? Huh. Don't think so. If they did, I knew nothing about it."

"Has Keith ever contacted you since you broke up?" Joshi asked.

Natalie rushed to answer. "Absolutely not. Look, that was ten years ago. I wish people would let me forget all that."

Weiss looked at Joshi curiously for a moment, but when Joshi didn't follow up, he thanked Natalie. She got up quickly.

"This isn't going to flare up again, is it?" she said. "It's so unfair; I had nothing to do with that old guy's murder."

She was about to say more, but finally, she turned away with an exasperated sigh. Before the two detectives could sit down again, Natalie Cowell was lost among the passing shoppers.

"Kind of intense," Weiss said, picking up the cup of tea he had been sipping since they first sat down. It was cold. "I'll bet she's a hard worker. Just a feeling, but I'm guessing Keith Blair wasn't her last bad choice. Where were you going with that question about Blair contacting her since the breakup?"

Joshi peered balefully into his own empty cup. "I've learned not to compartmentalize. If Natalie had anything to do with Warden's death, that stuff about a noise from the building could be a fake alibi for her boyfriend. Sutton thought the noise was significant because it implied Warden was still alive, still moving around in there after Blair left. It's a detail that almost seems calculated."

Weiss nodded. "If it was a lie, then it was to divert suspicion from both of them. So here we are again; thin on suspects, thin on alibis, thin on motivation. Why, I keep wondering, did poor old Cecil have to die? Something to do with that fake manuscript—the one Carly is interested in? Blair was just a kid back then. I can't see him pulling off a sophisticated scam involving calligraphy on vellum."

Joshi snorted. "Keep that in perspective, will you? That manuscript business is from a book by a famous storyteller, handed to you by a fetching young woman with Julia Roberts lips."

"I'm painfully aware of that, but it's also the only new lead in an old case. In a way, we're seeing the whole file through that fresh lens. Otherwise, why go over ground that Sutton's team covered? Either young Blair was a lot more accomplished and complex than he seems, or his girlfriend was."

Joshi thought about that for a moment, then shook his head. "Or someone else was watching from a distance and came to the schoolhouse after the girlfriend's car left."

CHAPTER SIXTEEN

Prem Joshi was settling into his work station, prepared to start a new day. His right ankle was aching, a carry-over from his fall at Moreland House the previous spring. It got sensitive if he slept with his leg the wrong way. He gave it a quick rub, trying to soothe it. Over his shoulder, he caught a glimpse of Weiss's laptop, which was displaying an old black-and-white image of school desks and a chalkboard.

"Why bother with the schoolhouse?" he said to Weiss's back. "You don't think you're going to find evidence there after all this time, do you?"

"Probably not. It's just that a one-room schoolhouse is an abstraction for me; no more than a few photos from the web. The idea that the probable murder scene might still exist somewhere intrigues me, though. The whole business of moving a building around—I almost feel the schoolhouse is a missing suspect."

"Sure," Joshi said. "The damn place fled the scene. Let's track'er down and put her on the witness stand."

Weiss grinned. Sarcasm aside, Joshi was approving of his curiosity. "That's the spirit, Prem. I'll see what I can find out."

Joshi returned to his laptop, determined to clear the Walker's Line gas station file from his caseload.

Weiss spent the next hour calling around to various historical societies, surprised there were so many. He started with Oakville, then spoke to two Burlington preservation groups. One of these had successfully moved a railway station to a location on the north side of Plains Road, but they'd never heard anything about a schoolhouse. Weiss moved on to Hamilton.

Hamilton was promising because it was a favourite place for American movie shoots, particularly, fifties-era films. The postwar era was still there in the facades of buildings, stadiums, and statues, beneath a thin veneer of modernity. It was a man with a sandpaper voice handling the Hamilton Pump Station, an old restored industrial building that had been used in a Ryan Reynolds movie, who gave him the connection that he needed.

"Talk to the people at the Halton Street Railway Museum up in Milton," the man rasped. "I think they've got a schoolhouse."

Weiss found it a little difficult getting past the Halton Street Railway Museum's recorded P.R. facade: "Step back into the past—ride the rails into the forests of long ago on one of our authentic, completely restored streetcars." But he finally got the main desk in their visitors centre, and a woman was able to refer him to one of the volunteer managers. The woman on the desk was reluctant to give out the home number of the manager directly over the phone, but Weiss had her call a published police number to prove he was who he said he was.

Weiss was afraid that the runaround wasn't over, but apparently, someone had checked him out by phone because at last there was a voice on his cell—and it turned out to be the manager himself.

A deep, aristocratic voice said, "Are you Detective Weiss? I'm Aaron Sylvester. The desk clerk at the museum gave me a heads-up that you wanted to talk. What do the Halton police want with a railway museum?" The voice was genial and rotund, as though it were coming from a department store Santa Claus.

"I understand you have an old schoolhouse on your property?"

There was a pause on the other end, and the sound of a chair creaking. "Ye-es. We had it trucked here over six years ago. Why?"

"I was wondering if my partner and I could have a look at it. It's connected to an ongoing investigation we're conducting."

Once again a pause, as though Santa was conferring with his elves. "Does this have anything to do with the murder that was committed there?"

Weiss sat up in his chair in surprise. "You know about that?"

"Certainly. It's one of the reasons the building was donated to the museum. All we had to pay were removal costs. The owner just wanted to be rid of it. She didn't want to demolish it and couldn't sell it. I heard about the situation and went in with an offer to lift it off its foundations and bring it here. She got some kind of charity tax break on the deal."

"Is the building still intact? Could we take a look?"

The voice rumbled a little as though Sylvester wasn't sure what to do. "It's not restored yet. We haven't come up with the money to do anything with the building so far. We just tinker now and then, hoping we'll get enough funding to set it up for visitors someday. It's still pretty much as it was when we got it here—a bit of a mess, in fact."

"This is part of an official investigation. You wouldn't be held liable in any way. We just need to take a look."

A cough. More movement. The chair creaked again.

"Thing is, it's in the bush alongside the rail line. We haven't even built a platform at the site. The idea, long term, is to make it a stop along the main track, but these things can take years when you're dependent on corporate donations."

Weiss gave a small chuckle. "I know what you mean. I visited the fortress at Louisbourg once. A guide told me the reconstruction had taken longer than the original fortress stood on the site."

"Yes," Sylvester said, a little scornfully. "That's Canada for you: 'historical site under construction.' We're too cavalier about our past."

"So when can we come in?"

Sylvester gave a long sigh, then, "Okay. You want to come in this afternoon? Say three? I'll be there to guide you."

At three that afternoon, Weiss was singing. Sort of. It was breathy and low, and the rhythm was broken the way people mumble-sing when they're half distracted.

"Endless station stops on endless lines," he breathed. He sang the next line to the ceiling lights: "Deserted platforms..." An overly long pause while his fingers brushed the wooden panelled walls, "...with their lonely signs." A plaintive, not unpleasant tenor mutter: "But it's the thought of you that fills the time..." Then an amused finale for Prem Joshi's benefit, complete with spread arms and jazz hands. "My patient valentine!"

Joshi gave him a jaundiced look and scratched his jaw. "So now you're the singing detective. Give it a rest, Eilert. You're colourful enough."

Weiss feigned hurt. "Long forgotten song, but it seemed appropriate."

Joshi glanced around at the mid-twentieth century railway station house impatiently. Once a town railway stop, it had been restored and transformed into a visitors centre for The Halton Street Railway Museum. A dozen tourists were browsing posters and displays, taking pictures with their phones. A woman wearing a quilted hoodie had her nose within inches of some period postcards. They were quaintly displayed under the crisscrossing ribbons of a French display board. Joshi watched it all like a cow contemplating traffic.

"Anywhere I can get a coffee?"

"Probably. We'll ask somebody. They're all volunteers, you know. This whole place is a giant electric train set. They work here because they love it. They dress up and punch tickets and build platforms and whatever because they want to taste the past. I know the feeling. A lot of my illustration posters have that same quality—a little twinge of days long gone, most of them before I was born."

"I've got an ashtray from The Royal York Hotel," Joshi offered wistfully. "We had lunch there when I was a kid."

"There you go. We're all invested in the past. This whole park—it must be a hundred acres—is a memorial to an age long past when streetcars ground along rails in every major city. You ever ride a streetcar, Prem?"

Joshi snorted. "They still have them in Toronto."

"Yeah, sure, but they're all sleek and quiet and articulated. That old tram out there must be, what, 1940?" He gestured at the row of windows where a dozen people were visible outside, standing in wait on the platform.

Weiss stayed back until the young woman at the ticket counter was free of tourists before taking his turn at the beautifully restored cage window. The bars were the warm yellow of polished brass.

"I'm Weiss, Halton Police. I called ahead, spoke to an Aaron Sylvester about coming in. Do you know where I'd find him?"

"He's out on the streetcar. Talking to the conductor, I think."

Weiss followed her gaze to the tall windows. He might have been looking out at a super graphic of 1950 draped from the eavestroughs, were it not for the Nike windbreakers and Roots toques on the visitors. They were lining up along the riveted wooden side of a tram car circa 1940-something. It had a long roof-mounted armature that connected it to an overhead power cable, and there was a single hooded headlight mounted on the maroon and cream curved slab of its front end.

Weiss and Joshi went out into the weak daylight, a crisp autumn scent in the air. Blown leaves were being kicked about by urban couples and nostalgic seniors, tourists who had now begun boarding the carefully restored streetcar. Each, in turn, would step up on the cast-iron step, pull themselves up past the motorman with his bow tie and pillbox hat, showing their tickets to the conductor to be punched and cancelled. Weiss caught the eye of a man in the cab, leaning back in the narrow space behind the motorman. When the last of the tourists, twenty or so, were boarded and happily finding their benches, the man took his chance to step down to the platform.

Aaron Sylvester was a portly man, but he carried it fairly well on a square frame, jolting down to the platform with little effort. "I'll bet you're Detective Weiss." His tone was jovial, his cheeks as pink and perfect as a baby's bottom. "Glad you could make it. I'm dying to know how the Halton Street Railway Museum figures in all this. Anything scandalous?"

Weiss took a second, sizing the man up. He was fiftyish, a bit taller than average, stocky but soft. Balding with a shaggy fringe, he radiated a kind of amiable benevolence as though he were a host, eager to show off his toy collection. He was wearing a short, oil-stained apron over a heavy plaid work shirt and jeans.

"We talked on the phone about a building on the property—an old schoolhouse," Weiss said.

"Yes, yes. You said that you had an interest in it. I'm sorry if you had to wait. I was out on the line and everyone is a slave to schedules out here. I ride the rails as often as I can. These old carriages are why we're all here after all. We're enthusiasts. Time travellers, in a way. When I'm out on the rails, I'm in another world."

"How does the schoolhouse fit into a railway museum?"

"Just a recent acquisition. We have this vision, you see, of turning the site into a sort of pioneer village, only focussed on the early to mid-twentieth century. Nice thing about the past: it just keeps getting more precious. It's the way of the world, Detective Weiss. Someday, our descendants will be opening theme parks dedicated to remembering the second millennium. It's fun thinking about what they might feature—a gasoline-powered SUV, perhaps? A skateboard?"

Weiss recognized that he had sympathy for Sylvester's taste for the past. "So the schoolhouse will be restored to the early twentieth century when it was in use."

Sylvester hooked his thumbs in the shoulder straps of his apron. "We train enthusiasts are always looking for ways to decorate our layout. Think about it as if the whole setup was on a big tabletop. The only things we didn't need to bring in were the trees and part of the old line. Anyway, we've added a few old historic structures accurate for the period. We've got an old general store we use as a gift shop. Authentic billboards, track signals. All of it funded by donations, everything relocated by volunteers. We have a wonderful group of people who help us in dozens of ways, and most of us are still holding down day jobs. Thank heavens for the gig economy, by the way. People can work from home and set their own hours more than they could before. The irony is they come here to get away from that complicated world."

"You, too?"

"Yes, and fortunately I do piece work these days, so I'm my own boss and I can come here whenever I want. I do it frequently. It's my chance to live in a more appealing age. Some of us were born too late, so to speak."

"Could you tell us where to find the schoolhouse?"

"Oh, uh, well, you'll have to climb aboard." Sylvester gestured at the streetcar. "This party is leaving," he fumbled behind his apron for his antique pocket watch, perfect for the period, "in five minutes."

Weiss looked down at the tracks, following them until they disappeared into the nearby forest. "It's out there?"

"On the track, yes. Our main line is just a wide loop through the forest, of course, some of it leftover from an old railway that used to run from Guelph to Toronto, but we've added some trackside decorations to make the trip more authentic and interesting. There's the rural platform shelter where country folk would gather to wait for the train, an old reconstructed road crossing complete with warning lights, and the schoolhouse—all back there in the bush. The whole place is actually a hybrid; the focus is on the old rolling stock from Toronto street lines, but it also recalls an intercity railway that ran on some of these same tracks.

"We hope to add more sites as they become available. A mid-century country scape type of thing, with everything spread out and visible along the line. One day, you'll be able to get on board and glide through a bygone era—an exciting vision for nostalgia buffs like me. So, uh, what's your interest in the schoolhouse?"

"Oh, it figures in an investigation."

Sylvester raised a brow. "Ah, yes. The murder."

"You were saying you know about the murder."

"Well, that's why we have the building. Some people are leery about buying a murder scene, you see. The owner was killed, and the widow donated it on condition we pay to move it off her land. Most of the value of the property was in the land, anyway. Donations, volunteers—and presto! They managed to transport the whole building on a flatbed truck. It wasn't hard to lift; just a big wooden box, but it was tricky getting it back in the bush. Had to run the truck in along the trackbed; we did it slowly but surely."

Weiss looked at the windows of the streetcar and then at Joshi as though seeking assent and Joshi, glancing sideways at the steel coil suspension beneath the streetcar, gave Weiss a subtle lip curl. Weiss brightened to cover Joshi's lack of enthusiasm.

"We'll tag along then."

There was a sort of corporate pause—Sylvester still seemed reluctant as though he were reconsidering safety issues—then he gave a lop-sided smile and gestured to the tram door.

"Be our guest."

Weiss grabbed a vertical handrail and swung himself up. Joshi followed onto the iron-mesh step with a cold smile for Sylvester. Sylvester followed, resuming his standing position behind the driver.

The carriage was authentic WW2 vintage, from the overhead lights to the fabric seats. If anything, it was too clean, too polished for a working streetcar, the signs of loving restoration everywhere. Weiss and Joshi sat near the front so they could take in the view through the divided front windshield.

They were settling in when a bell rang and the motorman levered the folding doors shut. Seconds after that, a slight lurch and the long carriage began to rumble forward. There was a long, easy turn that brought them slowly back in the direction of the tree line.

Sylvester pointed. "That's the restoration and repair building. In the summer, it spills its work out onto those tracks that meet the mainline, but with the coming cold weather, the doors are all shut and the activity outside is sparse."

Besides Sylvester, the only person standing was the conductor. He clung to a chrome handrail with an easy smile on his face, a million miles away from the light speed matrix of the present day.

Then they were plunging into the forest. The whole enterprise had been partially carved out of an old farm plot, but mostly from the vast Ontario forest that had once been everywhere on these gently rolling plains.

The forest was a mix of evergreen and autumn leaves, most the colour of dark beer, but with a few boughs of emerging red. The sky was a dull grey avenue overhead. That was a constant because of the need to keep the electric power cable free from intrusive branches.

"Nice," Weiss said, leaning back and watching the foliage scroll past.

Joshi managed to convey a shrug without moving a muscle, which Weiss interpreted as pleasure. Joshi too was enjoying the idea of being paid to glide through a quiet landscape. Whatever sound there was in these shadowed bowers they brought with them. These streetcars had shouldered their way through fumes of leaded gasoline in their working lives, but now the carriage that city folk had once nicknamed the red rocket rolled smoothly through a leafy idyll. The crushed stone of the trackbed slid steadily beneath them with a gentle lurching that was restful and calming.

After long minutes of passing foliage and the rhythmic clicking of rail joints, Sylvester turned back to the two detectives. "We're coming up to the schoolhouse. It's off to the right of the line. I take it you're getting off?"

"Is that a problem?"

"No. No. Just remember, the building isn't open to the public yet, so the site is still rough. We have a lot of work to do before we can get it certified as safe. I warned you, it's a bit of a mess inside. I can't imagine what you hope to find, but as long as you understand this is all at your own risk…" Sylvester turned to the motorman. "Vern? Pull up here, will you?" He turned back to them. "Vern will be by again in an hour. If you wait by the track, he'll pick you up."

Weiss and Joshi got to their feet, hanging onto a horizontal handrail.

Sylvester pointed towards a widening gap in the trees. "We

found a nice level spot for the old place right there. Most of the clearing is natural, but we had to take out a few trees."

Weiss nudged Joshi. "Look, Prem."

The grey building emerged from the curtain of evergreens with the grace of a wooden church on a Christmas card. From this distance, you couldn't make out the ravages of age, so the tall windows and arched doorway seemed almost picturesque.

"I've worked on the interior myself," Sylvester said. "We strung a temporary line for the power tools, so there's a work light if you need it. Just remember to turn it off when you leave." Vern rolled the streetcar to a stop and pulled on the lever to fold open the doors. Sylvester gave the two detectives a slightly worried-looking smile and gestured to the doorway. "There's no platform yet, you'll have to jump down. It's not too high."

Weiss thanked the motorman and his conductor and stepped down into the cold, followed by Joshi and the curious stares of the other passengers. A woman in a quilted coat had gotten up and was asking the conductor why she couldn't get off, too.

The streetcar rumbled away from them into the forest and Joshi turned his attention to the ill-defined pathway leading up to the schoolhouse. The building was set back from the track by about a hundred yards.

Joshi tugged his coat collar closed over a patterned grey scarf. "What do we hope to find?"

Weiss answered with an exaggerated shrug. "Okay, you're right. This is probably a stupid waste of time. On the other hand, maybe it'll bring the case alive somehow. Like I said, 'rural schoolhouse' is kind of an abstraction for me."

"It's less than an abstraction to me," Joshi said. "We haven't officially told anyone we're following this case yet. And we don't know for sure that the murder took place here."

"'Course it did. Cecil wasn't the type to wander along the roadside on foot. The killer wouldn't risk being seen killing a man in the open by a road. Then there's the adhesive traces Sutton found on the schoolhouse floor tiles."

"Which could have been from any manner of duct tape."

Weiss bowed. "You keep me humble, Prem."

Joshi shook his head. It was hard to get a good argument going with Weiss.

They trudged up through the weeds and dead leaves and mounted the steps to the entrance platform.

Joshi looked at the weathered door. "What about the lock?"

"Sylvester didn't say anything about a lock. It's a construction site."

Weiss tried the doorknob. It turned, and as it swung open, the old door sagged a fraction of an inch as though it had been held in place by the catch. They pushed through, the door binding slightly on the uneven tiling of the floor, and then they were in the small annex that formed the front of the building: washrooms to the left, cloakroom to the right.

"They may have brought some of the old books and supplies separately and dumped them in here." Weiss indicated the stack of boxes in the cloakroom. "Watch the extension cord."

They skirted around a table saw and worksite FM radio until they could see into the main schoolroom.

In the light from the big windows, they saw where the floor of the main room had been swept, but now there was a fresh coat of dust everywhere. Joshi found a switched cord that ran up to the panelled ceiling and turned on the work light. A barely noticeable pool of warm light appeared on the floor and they walked carefully into the large schoolroom. Their footsteps sounded loud and crisp in the vaulted space.

Joshi went right to the cleared floor, his instincts identifying it as the probable murder scene, and began kneeling in the dust. Weiss searched the shadows, taking in the old desks piled up to three high against the window walls. He mounted the low platform that held the large teacher desk and drew a tentative finger across the blackboard. Then Weiss made a claw out of his hand and scratched it down the surface.

Joshi winced. "Cripes, Eilert. Do you mind?"

"Sorry. Always wanted to do that."

"No wonder you people like fucking bagpipes."

Weiss turned his head, doing a quick survey of the space. "So, let's see: Blair is working here with Warden. They have a fight. No, there was no evidence on Warden of a fight. Blair just jumps Warden suddenly, forces him to the ground..."

Joshi looked up. "The attacker would have had to have the patch stripped and ready to apply to Warden's face."

"Right, so the two men are standing, Blair strips off the protective layer, exposes the adhesive... Or, how about this? He comes up *behind* Warden and slaps the patch on his face. He drags Warden down to the floor from behind, still holding the patch, and scrambles on top of him."

Joshi stood up. "That's about the only way you could do it. Unless he did it from the front by tripping Warden somehow, but that would be awkward."

Weiss stared at the floor. "It was a real act of brutality, and that bothers me because I don't see Blair's motive being strong enough to drive him to violence. I'm not even sure I *see* a motive."

Joshi made a sweeping gesture at the big space. "He was a kid feeling sorry for himself, living with his parents, having trouble with his girl. Some kids—they get to higher education and realize they have no idea how to break into a career or even a decent job. It can be a low point in a person's life. So, you get clinical depression. I see him weeping to himself, despairing."

"Maybe," Weiss conceded. "Some kids are driven to consider suicide. But murder? That just makes things worse."

"Despair can lead to rage," Joshi suggested.

"Okay, but rage causes overt violence—strangulation or a

blow from a heavy object. This was premeditated. Offbeat, twisted, but planned. Choreographed even."

Joshi got the idea. "So you're still thinking *not* Blair then? What else have we got?"

"Well, we've got our old friend A.L. Rouhl. Carly's dad."

Joshi brushed off his knees and sighed. "You're talking about that book Carly Rouhl gave you."

"Old man Rouhl wrote about a dealer in antiques who tried to pass off a bogus manuscript on a friend, right?"

"Who may or may not have been Warden."

"It has to be Warden if you buy the passage in the book. Carly has the manuscript. Old man Rouhl links the schoolhouse and the manuscript in his book. The schoolhouse is the link to Warden."

"Rouhl had no proof that the antique dealer he wrote about committed the crime."

Weiss nodded. "No; we have to treat it as supposition, pure and simple. But it's a lead, isn't it?"

"*If* we could find this antiquities dealer. Sutton couldn't."

Weiss stepped down off the dais, past the big iron stove, and joined Joshi.

"It was probably here," Joshi said, indicating the open space on the floor. "Assuming Warden had wanted all those old desks pushed to the walls, this is the obvious open space for a struggle."

Weiss stared down at the large greenish tiles made of old-fashioned linoleum. "No adhesive traces?"

"Nothing that I could see. That was ten years ago."

Weiss took one last sweeping look at the appalling desolation of the place. "Okay. That's me, done. I can't think what the hell else to look for."

CHAPTER SEVENTEEN

Carly was back at her old desk in the magazine office. It felt peculiar that not one of the copywriters or layout people had come over to her with questions. She realized that she had been relinquishing control over the day-to-day running of the quarterly for some time now. Harriet's promotion had been an overdue formality.

Harriet was busy and looked happy enough, pointing at the screens of various staffers. When people started heading off to lunch in small groups, she came over and sat with Carly.

"So, you've read the passage in your dad's book—the one I marked?"

Carly nodded. "I can't believe you recalled the passage."

"I remember I had trouble hunting down *Underworld Tales*. I wanted to be able to say I'd read everything your dad published, but it wasn't easy finding a copy, so it was the last Rouhl book I read."

"Anyway, you were right. The 'boxed manuscript' he talks about in the book is clearly our book of hours."

Harriet gave Carly a high five, then placed her hands flat on Carly's desk. "What I got from talking with you is that A.L. uses real people and situations as a starting point. He then embroiders the facts into wonderfully textured stories. Bottom line, I think that the Wood character is real.

"This pastiche," Harriet went on, "this medieval manuscript, must have been assembled from fragments by a skilled craftsman knowledgeable about sixteenth-century England—someone with talent but a loose sense of ethics. Someone who had a real workshop going. Above all, it has to be someone your father knew about, because one way or another, the manuscript wound up in your dad's possession. So there you have it: this Wood person is real, and he's out there." She ended with a shiver.

"It did occur to me that Wood might not even exist," Carly said, "but no, I get it. You have to be right. Dad had a lot of friends with money and a taste for art and clearly one of them brought Wood to Dad's attention."

Harriet had a small mouth, but her lipstick glistened and her teeth were a dazzling white somewhere at the top of an artist's value scale. She idolized A.L. Rouhl, and the notion that she had been drawn into one of the master's tales lit up her face.

"So, what if one of those friends, this Gill character, bought the manuscript in good faith—or at least on speculation about it being authentic—and your dad had exposed Wood as a forger?"

"Well, that's what it says in the book, but I can't help wondering how Dad would recognize a forgery in the first place. He was no expert. A.L. wasn't a highly educated man—not in the standard sense. He learned everything by reading."

"But you said he had great instincts."

Carly twined her fingers behind her head. "Why does it always come back to his instincts? Dad believed he had a kind of psychic gift. He even claimed to have glimpsed the future. He said so in the 'Questions' file he left me on his laptop." She groaned. "I can't believe I brought this case to Eilert Weiss when it's hanging on that kind of thread."

"Okay, but forget about the psychic stuff for a moment," Harriet said. "Doesn't it make sense that the manuscript was a gift, a sort of trophy for your dad exposing Wood? Why else would your dad have it in his collection of mementos?"

"Well, that's the story he wrote, anyway. The truth is we'll probably never know how the manuscript got on his shelves."

Harriet folded her arms. "We know practically everything in your dad's office was related to the stories he told. The manuscript is no different. Face it, Car. That box there belonged to the murdered man. I'm sure of it."

"Well, what do I do now? Dad's office is a sort of literary memorial, like Lucy Maud Montgomery's house up in Uxbridge or Mazo de la Roche's in Newmarket. I suppose I'll have to put the manuscript box back on the shelf there and forget about it."

"You could get an honest price for it as a pastiche, especially with the Rouhl provenance."

"I don't know. I'd feel I was exploiting Dad's name."

"I guess. So anyway, is the mystery over for you then?"

Carly considered that. "Any mystery is over when you lose interest in it. I'll get your copy of *Underground Tales* back from Eilert. I don't see him wasting a lot of time on my flimsy speculation. I wish I hadn't bothered him in the first place. By the way, I know I have a copy of *Underground Tales* at my house somewhere, but all his books are in his office on those packed shelves. I suppose I'll come across it eventually."

After a short lunch down Brant Street at The Queen's Head, Carly and Harriet went back to their desks at the magazine. Carly had made a point of staying out of the magazine's business, so the text open on her personal laptop this time was her own writing. Looking up from her screen, Carly watched with an odd sadness as Harriet worked. In a way, she was watching herself back in the days when she'd built up the quarterly from nothing, but Carly knew that this had to happen if she was to relinquish day-to-day operations of the magazine.

Harriet was doing fine. She had taken over much of what Peggy Goss had done and Harriet had begun to build the kind of loyalty that was needed to make the string of writers and photographers a coherent team. People—the advertisers, the employees, the contract people—needed to have faith in the stability of the magazine, and Harriet had the charm and reliability that demanded.

Around 2:15, Carly's phone chirped. It was the first time she'd had a call that day, a drought that long being a novel experience for her. Almost sadly, Carly directed the caller to Harriet's business number and then she laid her phone on the desktop and stared out at the parking lot of the small plaza and the people going in and out of the Lee Valley store. She could almost feel the pace of her life slowing, but at the same time, she couldn't shake the peculiar sensation that once again her father's stories and real life were coming together. When the phone rang a second time, she jumped a little. Odd that. Ringing phones had been her life until recently.

"Carly? Eilert Weiss here."

"Oh, Eilert. Listen, about the schoolhouse thing, I shouldn't have—"

"We found the schoolhouse. It's up near Milton at a place called the Halton Street Railway Museum."

"Oh, uh…"

"How are you, Carly? Is everything okay—I mean the magazine, your writing…"

"Yes, of course," she said, wondering what prompted that.

"There was a murder, a cold and savage killing about ten years ago."

"My God. Dad was right."

Weiss said, "And so were you. I was wondering, how

invested are you in this story? The murder. Emotionally, I mean."

"What? Me? Well, it's shocking, of course."

Weiss tried again. "I'm not putting this well. What I want to know is how close you are to this business. Is it personal? The victim was an Economics professor by the name of Cecil Warden. Does that mean anything to you?"

Carly took a second, uncertain. "No, nothing comes to mind. Was he a friend of Dad's, the way it said in his book?"

"I was hoping you could tell me. I'm trying to get a handle on how all this relates to you. You're the reason we're going over this ground again."

Carly wanted to groan. She suddenly saw herself as taking advantage of a fundamentally kind man. How in God's name had she had the nerve?

"Eilert," she said, squeezing her eyes shut in embarrassment. She wanted to apologize, but instead, she asked, "Is there a little girl connected to the case somehow?"

There was a puzzled silence on the line for a second or two. "No, I don't think so. Can you tell me anything more about that?"

"It may be nothing. Just a feeling, but you were asking about my emotions, and the thought of that girl was the only thing that made me feel pity. All the rest? Well, it's just Dad telling a story again. I've lived with that all my life."

"This little girl, who is she? Is she alive?"

Carly winced at her brazenness. "I don't know her name." But she felt like she was following the rules: if she had something to give to Weiss, she had to say it. This was a two-way street. "And no," she said, "I don't think she's alive."

Carly's father used to say, "In for a penny; in for a pound."

It was several minutes before Harriet could break away and come back to the desk where Carly had been making a show of tapping away at her laptop.

Harriet indicated Carly's laptop and smiled, rolling a chair over. "Something for us?"

"Actually, no. I'm writing another story. Maybe this is the one I can spin into a novel. I got the idea from our manuscript—the book of hours thing."

"So, how does that work? You just incorporate the characters from your dad's story and then see where it takes you?"

"Of course, I don't want it to be plagiarism or a rehash of Dad's work, so I'm making up fresh stuff: motivations, visual details, new characters. I'd forgotten how scary it is to rely on nothing but your imagination. I have to forget all the discipline of journalism and keep writing, hoping it will all come to me from—"

"From your imagination."

"Exactly. Weird thing about the imagination. It's what we had as children, but most people have it educated or embarrassed out of them by adulthood. We're taught, or we get the impression, that it's a waste of time and unprofitable. I guess there's enough truth there to discourage most people. Let's face it—I wouldn't be able to indulge my imagination if it hadn't been for Dad's estate."

Carly remembered how insensitive she had been taking Harriet out to a romantic restaurant for business, and she turned her attention to Harriet. "Did you ever want to write fiction?"

Harriet seemed surprised. "Me? No. I thought you knew me. I'm a groupie, not a rocker."

"I don't know—you're rockin' this place. Everything's humming along just fine." Carly's eyes ranged out across the scatter of monitors and printers poured over by staff, then she stopped and looked directly at Harriet. "I wanted to tell you..." Carly hesitated, her mouth half-open. "Detective Weiss—he just called. They found the schoolhouse. It still exists."

“Omigod! I can’t believe this. I think it’s great that you and the detective are collaborating again.”

“Is that what we do? I guess you’re right. It helps for a fiction writer to have sources, like a reporter. The difference is, I take what he gives me and make up stories about it. It’s nice not being accountable for your fantasies.” Carly lowered the screen of her laptop and swivelled to face Harriet. “Is that selfish of me?”

“That depends. What are you giving the detective in return?”

The question made Carly gape. “I’m not sure.”

“What’s the matter, Car?”

It seemed safer to change the subject. “I’ve been thinking about visiting the schoolhouse myself,” Carly said. “I mean, I could use it as research for my story.”

“You can do that? The place where the guy was actually murdered?”

“According to Eilert, the victim’s real name was Warden and, yes, the police think he was murdered there. Seems the old schoolhouse has been moved all the way to a sort of railway museum up Milton way.” Carly stretched back in her task chair, making it wobble and creak. “How about coming with me? It would be sort of fun, wouldn’t it?”

“Cool! History and murder and an A.L. Rouhl tie-in. I’m there. When can we go?”

“I don’t know. You’re the one with a steady job.”

“How about Wednesday? That’ll be a slow day. Practically everybody will be out of office.”

Carly grinned. “I’ll pick you up at your apartment around ten a.m. Wednesday, then.”

CHAPTER EIGHTEEN

Keith Blair hadn't earned his own office yet, which meant he was in a corner of the reception area tucked in behind the admin assistant and her noisy, flickering phone. The partners were always walking through with clients or heading out to expensive lunches, and today he felt more exposed than ever with his precious laptop forming an inadequate shield in front of him. He had phone calls to make, appointments to firm up, but he wasn't getting much done. He was supposed to be blitzing teachers, retired or nearing retirement, because they had nice pensions to invest and generous benefits to embolden them.

The last thing he needed was a visit from the cops right here in his workplace. He had thought the nightmare of old Professor Warden's death was finally in his past, but now here he was, staring at the glass door, expecting a couple of Halton detectives to show up. He didn't want anyone seeing this: the junior associate with little or no tenure being grilled about an unsolved murder, so he had been on guard ever since Weiss's phone call, ready to leap up and intercept him in the parking lot.

Eventually, he gave up the pretence of getting any work done and began hanging around the door, staring out at the BMWs and Mercedes parked beside his Camry. The pretty admin assistant was staring at him; soon, her phone would stop lighting up, and she'd want to talk. He made a show out of getting his coat off the bentwood rack, winding a blue scarf around his neck. He'd say he was expecting clients, which was unusual for him at the office, but plausible.

He didn't have to keep up the act long.

Financial Life occupied a unit in an industrial strip mall off Fairview Avenue. Behind the narrow strip of the plaza parking, the GO train tracks stretched, forming the top of a capital T, and as Weiss and Joshi pulled nose-first into the glass doors of Unit 8, a double-decker train was clattering by in a blur of silver and green.

Joshi had almost reached the door with the company name and unit number painted on the glass when it opened and a man in a black winter coat and a blue cashmere scarf stepped out.

"Are you Weiss?"

Joshi stopped and nodded towards Weiss. "Him."

"Sorry about this, but I thought about it and decided I didn't want a couple of detectives coming into my workplace asking questions. It looks bad. You understand. Would it be all right if we walked?"

Weiss was closing the door of the unmarked cruiser. "We could sit in our car."

"They're watching. Let's just..." and Blair began walking in the direction of the GO tracks. "I thought I'd finally left Cecil Warden behind, but here you are—ten years later with more questions." He said Warden's name slowly as though it was a heartfelt curse word. "I'm a financial planner, and that means people have to have confidence in me. You've no idea what a blight Warden's death has been on my life, and I did nothing but help an old man with his misguided renovation. A couple of weekends—that's all."

Weiss moved up until he was walking slowly at Blair's side. Weiss calculated the man's age and decided Blair, with his greying comb-over, had gotten old quickly. He could have been taken for middle-aged, though he couldn't have been more than thirty-five. He was still straight-backed and broad-shouldered though, and as tall as Weiss—easily strong enough to overpower an old man.

The three of them reached a chain-link fence and stood against it, looking up at the oiled gravel of the railway trackbed.

Weiss said, "Sounds as though you thought Professor Warden made an unwise investment in the old schoolhouse."

"I'm an investment consultant now. If I knew then what I know now, I would have told him he was biting off more than he could chew. I mean, he was a college professor, working past his retirement age. What possessed him to buy an old ruin? He should have known there would be a lot of work to do. I could have suggested a dozen better investments…in retrospect."

"But you were only a student then," Weiss reminded him.

"And desperate for a little extra cash," Blair agreed. "I was working three jobs, trying to save for an engagement ring that summer."

"And are you married now?"

"No. For the rest of the month, that bloody investigation hung over my head. I figure it was one of the reasons my girl lost interest in me."

Weiss raised an eyebrow. "Because she thought you might be guilty of the murder?"

"No, it wasn't that. She was the one who picked me up that afternoon—at three o'clock. I didn't have a car, so she offered to come for me when I was finished with the schoolhouse. Except Warden kept me late with stuff that could have waited, so she had to stand outside looking at the fields and getting steamed until I managed to get away."

"You told the investigators that you didn't have a particularly friendly relationship with Warden."

Blair shifted his weight, gripping and re-gripping the tubular top of the fence in discomfort. "I had the quaint idea that telling the police the truth about our relationship was the best course. Frankly, Warden was buying my expertise cheap. He'd heard about my craft work."

"Yes; you made what, furniture?"

"Mostly end tables back then. I had a simple pattern, and I was knocking them out to make a little money on the side."

"You're too modest. Detective Sutton noted in the file that they were nicely finished. Scrollwork, pie crust edging—that takes a gifted carpenter."

"I've always been good with tools, and I do love the fine work."

"How about artwork? Ever painted or worked with inks?"

Blair put his arms up on the fence and stared at Weiss. "They never asked me that. Why are you asking me about art?"

"So, you do draw?"

"I was the one who made the pattern, designed the tables. So what?"

"It would be a shame to give up on a talent like that. You must still work at your craft from time to time."

Turning, resting his back on the fence so he could glance back at Joshi, Blair narrowed his eyes. "The odd repair or refinishing job. They've got low toxicity stains now. No fumes. It's a hobby." Blair frowned. "Do you know what it means to live under suspicion, Detective Weiss? They never found the killer, so I'm stuck in a police file with a question mark beside my name. I thought maybe I was getting past all that at last, but here you are, and now I'm wondering if I'll go to my grave under suspicion. It's so hellishly unfair."

Weiss tried to look sympathetic, but Blair was prickly, off-putting. "Best thing for you would be if we finally found the killer. You left Professor Warden alive and well. Your girlfriend says you came out to her car in a bad mood, but she thought she heard movement in the schoolhouse after you reached her. And then, what, you went home?"

"I had an essay to write. It was an incredibly stressful time, holding down part-time jobs, helping Warden, and working on my tables. If you lay graduate economics on top of that, you've got a recipe for an emotional breakdown. It was a low point in my life."

"But you didn't break down, did you? Even with the strain of the investigation. You went on to finish your degree and make a career for yourself. Strikes me you're a pretty tough guy. Tenacious."

"Is that a detective thing? You somehow make every compliment sound as if you're checking off boxes against me. Warden wasn't interested in my artistic side; he wanted me to check the foundations and repair the porch steps. Why are you so interested in my skills?"

"Honestly, I was wondering if you shared an interest in antiques with Professor Warden. Did you know that he was a collector?"

"Antiques? I knew he was interested in history, but we never discussed antiques."

"Hmm. Fair enough."

Joshi asked a few questions about Blair's class schedule that term, but there was no point in rehashing what was in the file, so he looked at Weiss, thanked Blair, and the three of them started to walk back towards the cruiser.

Weiss followed Blair to his unit and watched him go inside. Weiss and Joshi held back, making an effort to keep out of sight from the doorway.

If Blair was innocent, he was a very unlucky man. Weiss

remembered with pain how his wife had cleverly ruined his own reputation with his bank and with the force. It had taken years to rebuild his credit rating. Innocence seemed a fragile defence at the time. Only the dire diagnosis from his wife's psych examiners had saved him. Once the depth of her insanity was established, Weiss was able to expose the intricacy of her sabotage of his life and work. It had taken all his skill as a detective.

Joshi waited for Weiss to find his keys and unlock the cruiser. "I see where you're going with the craft stuff. You're still thinking Blair may be connected to Warden through the antiquities market."

"It's possible, I suppose. These days, Blair would have to have a workshop in his basement or yard. I checked his house on Google Earth and he has a small outbuilding. Kind of interesting that he has a bungalow now and he's not married."

"He's an investor," Joshi offered. "A house in Burlington is a hell of an asset."

"Anyway, he was living with his parents and commuting to classes back then. He was making side tables, but all he had was a corner of a basement. I can't see him working with vellum. Still, he's got a solid frame. Even then, he would have been big enough to smother Warden, and he did mention furniture repair."

Joshi closed one eye in thought and opened the car door. It wasn't until he was sitting in the passenger seat doing up his belt that he suddenly said, "Fabric repair sheets."

Weiss lay one hand on the wheel. "If you're doing fine invisible repair of, say, a seat cushion, you would cut a patch and apply it to the back of the material, being careful to reconstruct the tear or puncture on the visible side."

Joshi sniffed and angled the seatback to his taste. "He didn't say he was doing repairs back then. It's all kind of weak." Joshi waited for Weiss to get moving. "Just an impression," he added. "But I don't think Keith Blair is doing so well these days."

"Suspicious of unmarried men, are we?"

Joshi ignored this fresh attack on his cherished prejudices. "The man's as nervous as a cat. I'm thinking he's not secure in his job which, judging by his office, isn't much for a guy with a graduate degree in business. Maybe what he's been living with is guilt or fear of discovery. He's sure not happy that we're looking at the Warden case again."

Weiss started the engine. "The business about the girlfriend hearing motion inside the schoolhouse as they were leaving. That's soft, too. If Warden *was* lying on the floor dead, a clever guy could have arranged for a desk to fall over."

"Oh, yeah? Show me that trick sometime, will you?"

"Why? What have you got planned?"

"Hah. You haven't a freakin' clue how it could be done, have you!"

CHAPTER NINETEEN

Carly pulled into the gravel parking area beside the visitors centre at the Halton Street Railway Museum.

The main building had the appearance of an old-fashioned station, probably relocated to the site, and it anchored the whole sprawling operation. A sign under the eaves identified the station as Rockwood. Some distance across the tracks from the station on the loop that led back into the forest was the work area, an industrial-looking structure with big hanger-style doors. One of the doors was open and you could tell from the figures in overalls milling about the antique rolling stock inside that this was where the restoration and maintenance of the carriages and streetcars were carried out.

Harriet, who always seemed amped up to a higher degree of enthusiasm and vivacity than Carly, led the way up onto the platform. Above a green slatted bench, an old-fashioned chalkboard divided up into neat columns offered the date, the number of the car, and its departure times. Carly read that streetcar number 327 was leaving on the hour. Car 2894 would enter service at 11:00. She looked at her smartphone. They had twenty minutes to kill before the next trip into the forest.

Carly said, "I found out that they've got the schoolhouse set up back in the bush, so we're going for a ride."

The interior of the station itself was an echoing, barn-sized concourse defined by a bowed window and vertical tongue-and-groove panelling that was warmed by decades of varnish. There were racks of tourist pamphlets and large antique railway posters protected by plexiglass. A glass case filled with dozens of toy carriages and Lionel Train boxes reminded everyone of the type of middle-aged-to-retired (mostly) men who had built this site amid the farmland and forest and kept it alive as a publicly funded fantasy.

Harriet was particularly drawn to an old-style French memo board, which was crisscrossed with black ribbons pinned to a cushioned surface. The ribbons held a scatter of letters and postcards artfully displayed to create the illusion of casualness. In a way, it mirrored the whole place. Someone had tried to make it look old, turn of the twentieth century perhaps—the Belle Epoque—and the letters were handwritten. The postcards were sepia-toned and postmarked: street scenes of old Toronto, antique cars. But like the station itself, the board was a bit too solid, a bit too clean.

Carly knew she shouldn't touch the displays, but she couldn't help brushing her fingertips over the painted wooden frame of the memo board. With a start, she withdrew her fingers, holding them up so she could see what was bothering her.

Harriet peered over her shoulder. "What's up? Prick your finger?"

"I don't think so."

With a smile that seemed to flash, Harriet moved on, continuing her own tourist thing.

Carly wiped her hands together, frowning. She wasn't up to explaining the peculiar wave of unease that had just passed through her. She scowled at the memo board for another minute and followed Harriet.

Harriet was absorbed in a cross between a wheelbarrow and baggage cart that had been permanently decorated with early twentieth-century luggage: steamer trunks and travel wardrobes with leather handles and riveted metal corners. These weren't reconstructions; every case was worn and abraded with the beige scuff marks of real leather.

One wall was covered in simple block letter names—stops along the old Toronto run: Carlton, Church, Parliament, Exhibition...

The ticket window, which was framed in metal bars, actually disclosed a large office with wooden desks and old rolling chairs, and the desks were cluttered with the authentic apparatus of days gone by: hurricane lamps, ledgers, and an ancient typewriter. On the far wall, mounted between two tall windows was a big, wooden-framed wall phone, its two brass bells glinting in the light from a period ceiling fixture. Outside the window, a damp Ontario flag with its Union Jack heraldry hung limp and twisted.

Carly approached the young female volunteer who was handling ticket sales. Her reporter's instinct had made her crafty and her approach oblique. "I called ahead and spoke to someone," she said, "and explained that I was assisting with a police investigation. I don't want to make a big deal out of it because it's deep background stuff, but I wanted access to the schoolhouse you have on the property."

"The schoolhouse isn't open to the public yet," the young woman said. "There isn't even a platform there. It's just an old empty building in the bush."

"Not *quite* empty. I gathered from our Detective Weiss the furnishings were brought here along with the structure. He told me the plan was to use the furnishings in the restoration."

"Oh, I didn't know that. Most of us haven't even been inside. It hasn't been signed off by the building inspector, you see."

"Yes. I thought there might be problems, but I have this letter," Carly held up a folded computer printout, "that Detective Weiss was kind enough to email me of this map of the site. See—there's my name. And there's his."

The email, sent from Weiss's office computer, was innocent enough, but as a matter of course, it had Weiss's name and rank in the footer and a Halton Police Services logo at the top. The young woman frowned in curiosity but seemed satisfied.

"Right. Okay. I suppose all you need to do is show your correspondence to the conductor and he'll have the driver stop at the schoolhouse for you."

"Thank you. Who is the actual CEO around here?"

"There's not one single boss, but our Mr. Sylvester kind of does everything around here, and he's responsible for a lot of the details you see around you, like that memo board. Some of the stuff had to be built from scratch based on old photographs." The girl gestured at the calendars, mail sorters, and wooden pigeon holes built in around her.

Carly glanced around admiringly. "Thank you. I want to make a donation to the museum from my bank card. Can you handle that for me?"

"Of course. That's very generous of you. We depend on donations from local government and enthusiasts to keep us up and running."

Carly worked the card reader while Harriet came up behind her.

"Thank you so much," the ticket seller said. "The conductor's name is Ed. Driver is Vern. They'll take care of dropping you off and picking you up. Enjoy your trip. I wish the weather was better for you."

Carly looked out at the overcast. There was blue sky visible here and there, but clouds hung dark and low, marching steadily to the east.

The vintage Toronto Transit Authority streetcar number 237 was pulled up alongside the wooden platform and a few tourists were already mounting its iron steps up into the motorman's cab. Harriet, with her usual youthful excitement, was the first up the steps, and she stood grinning as Carly swung up and past the middle-aged driver with his beaked pillbox hat and black uniform jacket. His sleeves were banded with Toronto Transit maroon, and he wore a chained pocket watch, apparently a badge of honour around here.

A conductor wearing a leather lap bag was punching tickets, being careful to catch the confetti in his bag. Carly waited until she could get his attention, then showed him Weiss's email.

"Ah, yes, Detective Weiss. No problem. I'll tell Vern to make a special stop. It'll be an hour before we get back to pick you up, I'm afraid. Will that work for you?"

"Perfect. Thanks."

"It's a bit of a gloomy mess, you know, but Detective Weiss said we wouldn't be held liable, so just be careful getting around all the junk."

"Is there lighting?"

"The guys ran a temporary line in from a junction box, but it's just an industrial extension cord; enough for a couple of power tools and work lights. That's all. There's no plumbing, so don't try to use the toilets."

"Got it. That will be fine."

Harriet laughed at Carly's pained expression. "I hope you're right. We should have worn Depends."

"There's always the bush." But Carly made a mock shiver at the thought.

A watery light fell through the last of the autumn leaves, throwing a grid of window shadows across the streetcar's brown deck. The floors were as implausibly clean as volunteer enthusiasts could make them, and Carly was reminded that these streetcars were cherished museum pieces, not commercial vehicles.

The two women swung along the horizontal handrail towards the back. There was a long bench down one side of the car and double leather seats down the other, each with its convenient hand bar across the back.

With Carly in the lead for once, they went all the way to the rear. She made an expansive gesture at the back seat. "I did some research. They used to call the old Guelph to Toronto run the corkscrew line or the seasick railway because it went through so many twists and turns, and this," Carly spread her arms, "is the thrill seat."

"The back seat?"

"Yup. From what I read, the ladies with their shopping sat here and gossiped while the tail end of the car would swing out at every turn. Get cozy." Carly twisted around on a vertical handrail, sprawling theatrically onto the curved bench. She was having fun. "Of course, we won't get as much of an effect on this little curve through the forest, but the tracks actually do incorporate a little bit of the Guelph to Toronto track. I'm going to enjoy myself. Come on."

Harriet gave a laugh that was like tinkling wind chimes and sat beside Carly, so close their hips touched.

There were a dozen others on the streetcar, three on the long side bench, the rest pressed against the windows on the seat side. There was a husband and wife with a baby, men wearing baseball hats, and a teenage couple.

Harriet pointed to the line of show cards that ran above the length of the windows. "Check out the ads. 'Every woman will eventually vote—for Sunshine Krispy Crackers!' How's that for period accuracy?"

The old streetcar lurched into motion, driven by an electric motor run off the overhead power line. It rumbled along, clacking over the joints in the track. It was a pleasant sound, redolent of a quieter time when the pace of life was still governed by nineteenth-century rolling stock: a seemly time when rails had seams.

They passed a siding where an old street railway carriage had been adapted as a narrow cafe advertising ice cream. It had closed for the season, as would the rest of the museum property in a week or so. The big maintenance building would house the bulk of the collection through the freezing days of winter behind those big industrial doors, where a few hardy souls would work getting ready for a spring opening day.

Vern, the driver, who preferred the term "motorman," took his time, glancing at his watch to stay on schedule, and the streetcar curved around back towards the forest from which it had come.

"Look! We're heading into the trees," Harriet enthused.

The trees, red-leafed maples and blue-grey spruces, began drifting past the windows on each side as though the trees were the ones grinding by on steel wheels. The sound was curiously soporific; steady, hoarse and hollow, more of a calm sea lapping a sandy shore than steel on steel.

Carly subsided with a sigh, letting her head loll back on the seat. Her breath steadied too, and she smiled up at Harriet, who was grinning down at her, seated straight-backed beside Carly. Somehow the prim hands-on-lap attitude suited Harriet.

It's the way she looks in the office, Carly thought—alert, keen, remorselessly awake. Harriet was a force of nature, but her keenness could wear you down sometimes.

Carly let her mind roam. Her eyes closed, and when they did, she found that the complex lines and decorations of that gorgeous fake frontispiece—the one from the manuscript—were blooming in her memory. She must have been tired because even the warmth of Harriet's hip against hers faded into a dream of delicate brushstrokes and gold filigree. And then there was that drone and click of the rails...

It wasn't a long circuit, but at this leisurely pace, it would take the passengers exactly an hour to get back to the visitors centre. There was a scheduled stop of five minutes at a rural platform where the guests could dismount and take in the fresh forest.

There was a pleasing sameness to the sounds and sights as they moved, even when the sound ebbed a little as they began to move closer to the schoolhouse.

"Poor thing," Carly said quietly, and Harriet frowned down at her in surprise.

"Carly?"

Carly smiled in her waking dream: the weave of the manuscript illumination had dissolved in her mind to a homespun blanket and a pretty little girl stirring beneath it. It was time for school to end, a time for everything to end. Carly groaned but couldn't help grieving for the child's weak innocence. Her breath came in ragged gasps, like someone drowning in their sleep.

"Poor thing," Carly breathed, so low that Harriet had to lean down to make it out. Carly's eyes fluttered but remained closed.

Harriet glanced quickly at the passengers. Everyone was absorbed in the view out the front window. The conductor had taken a seat near the driver. When she looked back down, Carly's head was slumping gently to one side, her hair touching Harriet's arm.

Harriet thought she had never seen anything so beautiful. Carly's lips were repeating the strange phrase in a benediction, but this time only her breath came from her slightly pursed mouth, dreamy and intimate.

"Poor thing," Harriet repeated, hoping that she was the suffering soul weighing on Carly's heart.

It was impulsive and foolish. Harriet knew it even as she

closed the few inches to Carly's lips, but she knew that the long-standing passion had taken over and she couldn't deny it. It felt like a kind of soft suicide, but a splendid romantic suicide that ended everything: the longing, the dreaming...

Then she kissed Carly gently in the moving leaf shadow. The gentle touch of Carly's lips might have been a slow needle into Harriet's jugular because she could feel it from her belly all the way to her toes. Carly didn't pull away or stir. Instead, she spoke in a voice that was somehow intimate and far away at once.

"I have to pick Dora up after school," she breathed. "She'll be lonely if someone isn't there to be with her. So lonely."

Harriet drew back breathlessly and tried to make sense of what was happening. Was Carly dreaming? Had Harriet kissed a sleeping lover? Or had she just betrayed a friend? Harriet pressed her own lips, wondering if she had smeared her lipstick, and saw with sudden horror that she'd left a tiny patch of her plummy gloss on Carly's lower lip. Carly might never notice it, but Harriet would see it.

A minute passed and then Harriet looked up to see Ed, the conductor, approaching them. He looked content and in the moment—a guy playing with his electric train set on the carpet on Christmas morning. Ed hung onto an overhead rail as the streetcar entered a curve.

"We're coming up to the schoolhouse. Vern's going to stop and let you off. I'll be obliged if you wait by the tracks at exactly," he checked his pocket watch, "11:20. You got that?"

Harriet glanced down at Carly, but her friend was still deep in some inscrutable dream, so Harriet smiled up at the conductor. "We'll be there on time, watching for you."

The conductor smiled back. "Anywhere along the track. There's no platform there yet, so we'll just stop, give you time to climb up." He nodded and returned back up the carriage.

"Carly. Carly?"

Carly stirred, squeezed her eyes shut and straightened as

though she'd been slouched there for hours. Her eyes popped open when the tram came to a creaking stop. Up front, the motorman turned in his seat.

"This is the schoolhouse," he said.

The other passengers crowded the windows to see the pale structure of the schoolhouse with its distinctive bell tower stuck in the centre of a muddy clearing.

Carly was on her feet in an instant. "Yes, thank you. We're coming."

Harriet stayed put for a second, and Carly looked down. "Coming?"

Harriet stirred, but all she could think to say was, "Who's Dora?"

"Dora?" Carly blinked. "Hey! We have to get off. Come on."

Harriet got to her feet a trifle unsteady and followed Carly up the carriage to the open folding door.

Ed, the conductor, looked professionally concerned. "Can you manage? We haven't built a platform here, so you'll have to jump down. Be careful. It's gravel below right now."

When the two women were both out on the oily sloping gravel, the motorman shouted down. "I'll be back in an hour. Don't forget." He grinned down at them, then levered the door shut and engaged the electric motor.

Carly and Harriet waved at the passengers in the windows and the streetcar sparked and jerked forward into a steady rumble. It took only a minute for the curve to take it out of sight.

Harriet turned to the forest. "My God," she breathed. "There it is. I read about it in an A.L. Rouhl book, and bingo! Here it is. Amazing."

Carly pulled her collar together against the damp cold. "Yeah. There is something amazing about this. In fact, bloody creepy. I'm glad you're here with me."

Harriet stared at the back of Carly's head as the taller

woman started down to the clearing. "Yeah. Me, too."

There was no path or landscaping yet. It was as if the schoolhouse had been dropped unceremoniously on a grassy, partially bulldozed patch of ground, but as they got closer, Carly was relieved to see that the steps up to the front porch had been propped up for the work crews, and they had no difficulty getting up to the front door.

"Have you got a key?" Harriet asked.

"Eilert told me they never bothered with a key. The original's missing and they didn't want to drill into the old door frame."

"Yeah. Who'd bother to come all the way in here to steal an inkwell or two?"

The door gave with a firm nudge from Carly's shoulder and they stepped into the gloom of the front annex. Carly pointed to the washrooms to her left. "You can't use the facilities, but there is electricity."

She found an antique stem and knob switch on the wall wired into an orange extension cable with plastic twist caps and snapped it downward. The annex room around them was gloomy, but a feeble light came on in the main schoolroom, defining the slope-shouldered archway into the classroom.

They walked through into the schoolroom proper, which loomed large around them, stepping carefully in the gloom.

There was a caged light hanging on its electrical cord from a crossbeam that spanned the ceiling vault. The ceiling was high, and the way the light was shaded threw the upper panelling of the room into a looming shadow. The brightness of the bulb pooled in a soft circle on the bare floor tiles at the centre of the room.

Harriet gulped. "Wow. Needs a lot of work."

"Yeah. I gather that the building has been used for nothing more than community events ever since they closed the school. Truth is, it's been empty for most of the last two decades."

The big black stove was offset to one side in front of the teacher's desk, its thick pipe a rusty column to the roof. The big desk was on a raised platform about six inches above the main floor and on the edge of the lighted area. Behind it, a chalk dusty blackboard rose in deep shadow. There was an ancient union jack hanging from a slanted flagpole in one corner.

Harriet was at Carly's shoulder, glancing back and forth from the desolate room to Carly's profile. "Here we are," she said with heavily ironic cheerfulness. "And once again, I'm wondering what you hope to find."

"Nothing," Carly said. "Nothing specific, I mean. I just need to visualize the place, you know—for my story. Funny though. Now that I'm here, I have this odd *déja vu* feeling."

"Know what I think? I think you're still counting on this creative imagination thing. You think you can 'pick up' something here; whatever that means."

"Well, you know, I've got this theory. It has to do with the way Dad could always whip up a complex yarn from next to no research. It always bugged the hell out of me."

"Lay it on me. I happen to find myself at loose ends right now."

Carly hugged her forearms to her chest, feeling the chill in the room. "Okay, so...what if I'm a sort of detective, like Eilert Weiss, only I'm not consciously amassing evidence—not *consciously*, see? But I'm a great observer. I always have been. A lot of journalists develop keen observation skills. So—here's the good part—what if I'm collecting information, you know, at a subconscious level? Okay, and then—still subconsciously, mind you—I put it all together. Suddenly, I know something, but I can't tell you how I got there. See what I mean?"

"So you're kind of a savant?"

"Maybe. Huh. Savant. That's clever."

"As a friend, I gotta tell you, it's borderline flakey."

Carly sagged. "Yeah. But it's better than goddamned clairvoyance." She shuffled sheepishly, disturbing the cobwebs that the sweepers missed. "Look, just let me wander for a few minutes. We're stuck here until 11:20 anyway. That's the better part of an hour."

"Knock yourself out. I've got my phone."

Harriet wandered in the direction of the archway until she found a student desk that hadn't been stacked. She dusted it off with a tissue and slid her thin body onto the seat. It was a child's desk, but it seemed to fit her perfectly, and she laid her smartphone on the sloping part of the desktop. It was dark back there, but she didn't need light to read a screen.

Carly watched her for a moment, then stepped up on the dais, brushing the teacher's desk with her fingertips. Up close, even in the gloom, she could see that the blackboard had writing on it—not lesson outlines or anything; that would have been creepy. It seemed that the blackboard had been used to post prices, probably for some auction or flea market, and even those recent notations were smeared and partially erased.

She remembered what she had learned from handling the manuscript. "Stop thinking, goddamnit."

"What?" Harriet called.

"Nothing, sorry."

Carly turned and looked in the direction of the big iron stove. In its time, the bulky wood and coal burner would have been the only warmth for students and teachers through the freezing temperatures of a southern Ontario winter. She found herself stepping down into shadow, her fingers this time tracing the dusty stovetop. She rubbed her fingertips, shaking the dust off them, but something made her turn back to the iron plating of the stovetop.

Resting her palm flat on one of the removable circular plates built into the stovetop, she frowned. Was that warmth? The room was cold. Shouldn't the blackened iron stovetop be cold?

Why should that bother her? The room was so quiet she

could hear a pulsing hiss in her ears. Carly, who read everything, knew about the discovery of gravity waves that pulsed through space-time like ripples. In her mind, the air of the room had a gentle throb to it.

A moving shadow made her glance up, and there was Harriet in the opposite corner of the room, the light of her phone making her face look pale and tiny.

"Harriet?" Carly said, loud enough to be heard, and Harriet looked up at her, her expression empty.

Except it wasn't Harriet. It was a girl much younger, with tousled cornsilk hair and a crumpled linen skirt with a bib and shoulder straps over a blouse.

"Harriet?"

Then suddenly, a pulsing warmth filled the room with radiance, and there were others—around twenty of them, all fresh-faced and squirming with energy. Desks were aligned neatly and the light was suffused with shafts of winter sun, and the atmosphere was filled with the sweet smell of woodsmoke. The dust and cobwebs were gone, replaced with motes of chalk dust, a stirring of freshly printed book pages and spots of spilled blue ink.

Carly took in the room in an instant, and, just as quickly, she picked out the little girl in the back with a single pigtail and straight bangs down to her eyebrows. She wore a plain linen dress with shoulder straps over a shirtwaist. And Carly somehow knew that her name was Dora.

Another pulse of air and time, and the room was a cold, gloomy place, and Harriet was lit by her screen. "Hmm?" Harriet said. "Everything okay? You look weird."

Carly was suddenly aware of a sharp pain on her palm, and she snatched it up where she could see it. It was hard to tell in the shadows, but as she shook her fingers, she knew that her palm had been burned. She looked down at the woodstove, but its rusted black surface was nothing more than a profoundly dark shape surrounded by velvet shadows.

Harriet unfolded herself out of the desk and hurried over. "What's the matter? What happened to your hand?"

"It's okay. It's not bad. I think I kind of burned it a little."

"What are you talking about? It's freezing in here."

Carly squinted down at the black iron panel. "My hand was on the stove."

"Maybe the workers have been using it," Harriet said. They both touched the black surface, running their fingertips here and there. "Feels cold to me."

Carly wanted to explain. Wanted to tell Harriet about waves in space-time, pulses, and the warmth of a classroom filled with children, but that would have taxed even Harriet's sympathies.

Instead, she asked, "Do you have any moisturizer in your purse?"

Harriet swung a small shoulder bag around and poked her phone into it. She rummaged for a second and came up with a hotel-sized bottle of hand cream. "Here."

Out in the daylight, Carly's right palm looked a little red, but the pain wasn't bad. They kicked stones and worked their phones until Harriet decided to ask once more. "So, who's Dora?"

Carly looked at Harriet and then up at the schoolhouse's bell tower. The first time Harriet had asked the question, it meant nothing. This time, Carly trusted her imagination. "I think—I think that Cece Warden wasn't the only person to die in that schoolhouse."

Harriet wanted to frame a follow-up question, but before she could speak, she noticed that the daylight had disclosed the tiniest smear of plum lipstick on Carly's lower lip. She was still wondering what to do when the streetcar rattled and creaked out of the trees and began to slow beside them.

CHAPTER TWENTY

Weiss and Joshi pulled into the circular driveway of Brenda Warden's house around ten a.m. A slightly stooped woman with smooth, grey-blond hair and frameless glasses came out onto the front porch as they were getting out of the car, stepping down with the awkwardness of poor eyesight and balance onto stamped concrete that had the appearance of coloured paving stones. She was fine-boned and short. She and the lanky Cecil must have made an odd pair.

Weiss looked up from the cruiser's door and met Brenda's eyes. It was odd the way Brenda seemed to simultaneously hold welcome and anxiety in her expression. By the time Weiss reached her, she'd been joined by a taller, younger woman whose entire aspect was a youthful variation of Brenda's own oval, narrow-chinned face.

"Detectives Weiss and," Brenda looked at Weiss's partner, "Joshi, is it? Please come in out of the cold. I have coffee ready." Inside she said, "This is my daughter, Corey. She'll get the cups. Please have a seat."

The younger woman left, her angled ebony bob swaying with every movement. She moved with a grace and confidence that made Weiss realize that Brenda must have been striking in her youth.

The room was spacious but full of fabric warmth and the expensive-looking trophies of money well managed and carefully spent. The layout was dominated by a window seat that curved out into a bottle-paned bay. A white cat with the same velvety nap as the cushions frowned back at them. Bookshelves, built into the clean lines of the room, demanded attention because they were designed to display rather than warehouse books.

Weiss quickly scanned a shelf before accepting a comfortable place on the couch: political, economic, social, nonfiction, mixed with the odd, worn leather binding of a bibliophile's prize find. The coffee table was a glass-topped display covering a gaudy majolica bowl.

Brenda Warden picked up on Weiss's darting glances.

"My husband was the collector. I've kept the things I care for and passed the rest off to my daughter, Corey. She's the best judge of what's valuable."

Corey returned from the kitchen and settled a tray onto a serving cart. "I've sold some of Dad's collection," she said, pouring coffee. "He had a few valuable things, but I've also donated some pieces of interest to the university's rare books room. And of course, there are a handful of art objects that I treasure myself. Dad's taste was refined but pretty personal. My own tastes are a bit different."

Weiss looked at Joshi. The detectives had barely spoken a word. This wasn't beginning the way he had expected. He hadn't asked a thing about Cece Warden yet, far less his hobbies.

"I'm wondering why we're talking about Professor Warden's collection. He was a professor at the DeGroote School of Business, right? That's MacMaster University. Was collecting such a big part of his life?"

"Oh, uh, he was pretty much what he appeared: a teacher of

Economics at the Ron Joyce Centre here in Burlington. That's part of DeGroote. Rather middle-of-the-road liberal in his tastes and not much of a socializer. He was dedicated to his job, but, well… He lived his life indulging his love of history and the little artefacts that brought it to life for him. Collecting is one of the few things that could get him worked up. Hobbies are often like that. Me? I'm a gardener."

"Worked up?"

"Well, you know, he'd get excited by something he spotted that had value. Annoyed when he lost a bid; that kind of thing. I never saw him get that way about world trade or bank mergers."

Corey, the daughter, cut in. "Has something new come up? Are you reopening his case?"

"Something small. Maybe inconsequential, but if you don't mind, I want to ask you about a single manuscript that has turned up. Naturally, I've reviewed all the questions the police asked you—potential enemies, who knew about his movements, the schoolhouse—that sort of thing, but this caught our attention recently." Weiss held up his phone, which was glowing with a picture of the beautiful frontispiece. "It's an antique hand-lettered book on vellum which is contained in its own case."

Brenda moved to take it in, but looked blank and shook her head. "Show Corey. I never took much of an interest in his books."

Corey got up and walked over. Weiss stood to show her the phone. "Oh. Wait a minute," Corey said. "Maybe." She looked at her mother. "That was one of the last pieces he bought. I remember that one page. It's beautiful."

Brenda shrugged. "If you say so. Did you give the book to the university?"

"No. It was Dad who gave it away. I remember. That's right. It turned out to be a fake. Dad was so angry about that."

"Did he say he lost a lot of money on it?" Weiss asked.

"Maybe as much as two thousand. I'm not sure, but it wasn't

the money. Dad hated cheats and frauds. Got that from his study of capitalism. I think he was a bit of a closet socialist, and it got him upset when people exploited others. More than that, he hated the fact that he'd been taken in. I got the impression from overhearing Dad that the guy who sold it to him was clever in an oily sort of way. Everything the dealer said about the manuscript was crouched in reservations and qualifications. Dad said it made him think of dealing with a crooked car salesman. The dealer weighted his pitch so that you felt the book was worth taking the gamble."

"And this salesman, did either of you meet him?"

"Oh, uh. No, sorry."

Weiss persisted. "Do you recall his name?"

Corey was offering Joshi sugar. "If Dad ever mentioned it, I can't remember. Dad would go pretty far afield on his collecting trips. He got that book up in Peterborough, I think."

Weiss raised his brow. "Peterborough? Why Peterborough?"

"The manuscript was offered for sale online. Dad had to go there to check it out at the seller's place. He obviously was satisfied because he brought it home."

"I think your father might have threatened to sue or expose this fraud," Weiss said.

"Dad could get pretty worked up over things, but I don't think he ever sued anybody." A flicker of realization passed across her face. "You think this fraud guy could be the murderer?"

"Murder over something worth two thousand dollars is kind of rare, but your father threatening to destroy an antique dealer's reputation? It's worth looking into."

"Oh, my God. I see."

"It's a pity you don't remember the dealer's name."

Brenda was bewildered, but Corey understood the gravity of the question. She looked a little sick. "I think everything was done using one of those online pseudonyms, but there's no way I would remember even that. I wasn't involved."

"Don't feel bad. That might have only given us a website, anyway. I don't suppose the name Wood means anything to you?"

Corey looked at her mother. "No, I don't think so."

Weiss pointed to his phone. "This manuscript turned up in the library of A.L. Rouhl, the famous writer. Is that who your dad gave the book to?"

Both women reacted with surprise, but it was Brenda who seemed the most excited. "Good heavens. Cece and Alistair were friends. There was one moment—it's coming back to me now. A.L. and his wife were here in the house, and Cece was showing off his collectables. Alistair took an interest in one of them. I mean, here we had this famous author in our home, and he's suddenly all excited by a book. A.L. got a sort of faraway look in his eyes and then he thumped the book and started huddling with Cece. I couldn't hear what they were saying; anyway, I was more interested in talking to Jean—that's Alistair's wife. I don't remember the rest, but Cece looked at the book differently after that."

Weiss sat forward in his seat. "You knew A.L.'s wife? Carly's mother?"

"Oh, my, yes. It was Jean and me who were old friends. A.L. just sort of came along, and he got to know Cecil that way. A.L. wasn't much of a socializer on his own, but Jean used to drag him out to see people. My husband was the same."

Corey added, "If I'm remembering correctly, Dad had the manuscript assessed at the university and I guess A.L. must have been right because Dad wanted to destroy it after that. He was embarrassed that he had been taken in and didn't want the thing on the market to fool others. I don't know why A.L. would want it."

Weiss turned off his phone and tapped it against his palm.

"I'm guessing that A. L. was more interested in human nature than historical relics. He probably promised your father he would hold onto the manuscript. He was something of a hoarder. A.L. loved a good story, and—" Weiss sagged a little, looking penitent. "Forgive me if this sounds crass, but for A.L., the story must have got more dramatic when Cece was murdered. It seems he got around to writing about the manuscript after Professor Warden passed."

Corey blanched. "My God! What did he say?"

"Well, if we're right, and the passage in A.L.'s book refers to this manuscript, then A.L. implied your father died because of it."

Brenda put her cup down in a clatter of porcelain. "But…but the damn thing was a trifle. What did you say, Corey? Two thousand dollars? Cecil was a wealthy man, Detective."

Weiss shrugged. "You're right. It seems implausible. Some people say A.L.'s so-called 'travel writing' was fiction. He would take a real person and situation as a starting point and embroider it into a fanciful yarn. The thing is," Weiss rubbed his forehead slowly, "in this case, his yarn amounts to a theory that's as good as any the police were able to come up with, so we thought it might be worth following up."

Corey was staring at Weiss, open-mouthed. "Does Carly know about this?"

Weiss was taken aback by the question. He was still trying to come to grips with the fact Carly appeared to know nothing about the Warden connection, but it was Joshi who asked, "You know Carly Rouhl, Ms. Warden?"

Corey looked around as though dazed. "Well, we're acquainted. My folks have known the Rouhls, it seems, forever. Carly and I used to see each other now and then in college." She stared up at the ceiling, thinking. "Last time I saw Carly, we went with some other friends to a Barenaked Ladies concert at a hockey arena in Baysville."

Corey chuckled at the memory. "She won't forget that trip! We got caught in a hailstorm coming home and had to pull off at a roadhouse. We ran from the car to the door with our coats over our heads with the hail coming down in bullets. Carly was worried that her dad's car would get all dinged up. We laughed about it afterward, but it scared us out of our wits at the time. What a racket! It was like having someone dump marbles on the roof. Turns out there was a tornado up in Barrie that was on the news that night."

Weiss seemed to have run out of questions, but there was more after that, with Joshi, warmed by the excellent coffee, carrying the rest of the conversation. Weiss was subdued, puzzled by the way Carly seemed to be woven into this case more intimately than she knew herself.

He listened though, and Joshi was good; feigning an admiration for A.L. Rouhl's writing, Joshi teased out details of the relationship between the two families. It became clear that it was the bond between Brenda and A.L.'s wife that kept the families in touch. That didn't surprise Weiss. A.L. and Cece came across as introverts with little in common. After the death of A.L.'s wife, the connection withered.

Weiss realized that Carly had never mentioned her mother Jean in their conversations. As he thought about it, he came to the conclusion that it was Carly's mother who would have been horror-struck at her old friend's husband being murdered.

Apparently, Joshi noticed Corey wasn't wearing a ring. It seemed casual enough when, with flattering disbelief, he said to her, "You're not married, Ms. Warden?"

To her credit, Corey smiled and, without hesitation, said, "Just never met the right woman."

Joshi returned her smile and went back to enjoying his coffee.

Joshi was driving when they turned out of the Warden's driveway. It had grown dark while they were inside, the days getting shorter. The Wardens lived in a pretty gated community that was settling now into the deepening autumn gloom, and they could see that Brenda's neighbours had taken advantage of the last of the mild weather to put up early Christmas decorations: sleighs, reindeer, and the odd Grinch.

Weiss said, "I can see why Sutton eliminated the wife as a suspect."

"Because she wouldn't have benefitted much from Cece's death?"

"No—because she's too small."

Joshi thought for a moment. "Disposing of the body, you mean?"

"Yeah. The killer thought he had to dump the body. He was wrong, by the way. Nothing was gained by rolling Warden into a ditch except a couple of day's delay of the autopsy. Anyway, Brenda Warden is too small to have manhandled her husband's body into and out of a car."

Joshi pouted. "A fabric repair patch; you could—I mean, a politically insensitive guy could—think of it as a woman's weapon."

"Not really, because it would require brute strength to pull it off."

"True. And it's an amateur's weapon, so Brenda didn't hire a pro to murder her husband either." Joshi glanced at Weiss's reflection. "Okay, so what's bothering you?"

Weiss was frowning at the windshield. "Carly," he said. His eyes wandered to Joshi's fingers on the steering wheel. "Carly doesn't know! She never made the connection between the book and the Wardens. They were family friends! How could she not know? Corey remembers *her*."

"Why does that surprise you so much? To Carly, the damn book was just another one of her dad's trinkets."

"No—and that's the point. Think about it, Prem. She picked it off the old man's shelf from all that other stuff, the ashtrays and photo albums and baskets. Chose to bring it to me. Why? Why that manuscript?" Weiss paused, and lost in thought, he glanced at Joshi.

Joshi waited, then, "Come on, Eilert. Why is this getting to you?"

Weiss turned his gaze back to the palatial houses moving past the windows, their stone and brick facades picked out in the rose-coloured light from floods hidden in the bushes and rockeries.

"I was just thinking," he said at last. "I've started to buy into the idea that Carly has some impossible gift—that she can see things others can't. It's jarring to find out she can miss the obvious."

Giving Carly credit for special insight made no sense of course, just as Clendenning's peculiar career as the seer of Peterborough had made no sense to Weiss.

Peterborough. Where Warden got the manuscript. Huh. God, how Weiss hated co-incidences.

After a few seconds, as though resolving something in his mind, Weiss said, "You're right."

Joshi, having no idea what his partner was talking about, said, "What, right again?" and grinned.

"Carly's blindspot about the manuscript. I suppose it's perfectly natural. The Wardens were her parent's friends, not hers."

Joshi, who had come to view the Rouhl woman as an oddity, wasn't so sure.

CHAPTER TWENTY-ONE

Joshi chugged up the stairs from the cafeteria carrying a large paper cup of coffee and another of tea, the paper tea bag label hanging from the lid. As soon as he reached the second floor, he saw Weiss standing outside their office in the corridor, leaning against the door.

He handed Weiss the tea, looking wary. "What's up?"

Weiss thanked him and fiddled with the little flap on top of the lid.

Joshi nodded at the office door with their names lettered in black. "What's the matter? Somebody using the pencil?"

Weiss stared at his cup. If it was getting too strong with the bag in there, he didn't seem to mind. "So we're back to Blair."

"Why are we back to him?"

"Because it appears the manuscript dealer lived in Peterborough."

"That doesn't eliminate the dealer entirely."

Weiss let that ride and said, "You called the fabric patch a woman's weapon."

"Oh, oh. Are you going to go all politically correct on me now?"

"No, it's not the 'woman' part. It's that I wasn't thinking of the patch as a *weapon*—it's too unusual; of course, in this case, that's *exactly* what it is. So let's ask the traditional question: how did the murderer dispose of it?"

Joshi worked the lid off his cup. "The killer threw the patch in the garbage somewhere—anywhere but the schoolhouse; you can forget about recovering it."

Weiss closed one eye. "Right. He couldn't leave it at the schoolhouse, so he would have had to take it away with him. That's no problem because it's just a sheet of paper, right? Fold it up. Put it in your back pocket. If it was Blair, his girlfriend would never see it."

"I guess," Joshi nodded, "and it would be easy to bring it to the scene, too, if the killer knew what he was about to do. Same thing: Fold and pocket."

Weiss said, "It was a warm summer's day. Blair was wearing jeans. In the afternoon, he was sweaty as though he'd been doing something strenuous."

"Like smothering an uncooperative economics professor."

"And he was wearing a sort of golf shirt with no pockets."

CRASH!

Joshi jumped, spilling coffee on his fingers. He switched hands and did a half spin, shaking his right hand. He came to rest in a feral crouch, staring at the closed office door.

"What the f..."—a sentiment that was stifled by another shake of his hand.

Weiss reacted with alarm almost as quickly, reaching to save Joshi's coffee. "Ah, Prem! I'm sorry. I didn't think about your coffee. Is your hand okay?"

"I'll live." Joshi's eyes slipped from the office door to Weiss. Slowly, his shock turned into a scowl. "You *didn't.*"

"I just wanted to see if it could be done."

Weiss switched hands, holding the teacup in his left as he took the office doorknob and turned it. The door swung aside, and they stepped into the narrow space between their desks. Weiss's wheeled office chair was lying on its back, scattered with books and paper.

"I used a ruler weighted on one end with books," he said. "It took me a while to get it all balanced just right, and I wasn't sure how long it would take for the books to slip off the ruler that was supporting the chair back. I tried to only use things that might be found at the schoolhouse. It was an experiment."

Joshi stared at the chair. "You're lucky I didn't shoot a hole through the door. Man, imagine trying to explain *that* to the super." He looked up at the window. "The shot probably would have taken out the window glass. I would have become office folklore—the day Joshi shot up the second floor."

Weiss made a calming gesture. "All's well. And now we know that Keith Blair's alibi is soft. He could have rigged that noise his girlfriend heard after they were together in her car."

They were still picking up books and file folders when Joshi's phone chirped. He spoke into it for a moment and then looked up. "It's Liana. We've got to go by her shop."

Prem Joshi's wife, Liana—a small, fiercely intelligent, raven-haired woman—ran an eye clinic in the Longo's plaza off Walker's Line. A prominent optician, she had a staff of two women, one a receptionist who sat behind a high, built-in counter, and a technician who did field tests and sold frames from the wall of samples. When the detectives got there, Liana was in her consulting room with a client, so it was Michelle, the tech, who greeted them.

"She'll be a few minutes, Prem. Can I get you a coffee? How are your computer glasses working out?"

"Honestly, I hardly ever use them. Too lazy to get them out, I guess."

"Or too vain," Weiss offered.

"No thanks on the coffee. I just had a cup." Joshi shot a resentful glance at Weiss. "Well, I had three-quarters of a cup, anyway."

They sat in the reception area watching the TV beside two waiting customers and Weiss resorted to finding Waldo in a kids' book. A few minutes later, Liana came out talking to an elderly woman wearing glasses attached to a gold chain. Liana managed to give Prem a glancing hug without dropping a line of her conversation with the client.

Liana smiled at Weiss, who did his gentlemanly shuffle and nodded cheerfully. "Prem says you're coming to the rescue of our schoolhouse case."

"Always bailing out my hubby. Prem's been telling me about the murder."

"She browbeats it out of me," Joshi said defensively. "She thinks I'm a reality TV show. This case got her fascinated."

Liana's smile was brilliant against her dark, creamy complexion. "That's because I can help. Just another gumshoe on the job with you guys. Can I have the file folder, Hilly?"

The receptionist seemed to know exactly what Liana was referring to, drawing a manila folder from a vertical plastic organizer. "We've been talking about this all morning," Hilly said. "It's brutal!" She spoke with such relish that Weiss wondered if every customer who had come in that morning had heard the story.

Joshi reached for the folder, but Liana held it against her white lab coat. "I just want you to know how much trouble I went through to get this. I had to go through three levels of networking to find someone who had this stuff on hand. Turns out Jane Gilchrist took a course in upholstery last year. You know Jane, Prem. She's..."

But Joshi had deftly worked the folder loose from Liana's grasp and was ceremoniously opening it for Weiss to take in.

"Voila!" Liana grinned. "Your murder weapon."

Weiss stared. He'd seen images on the web, but this wasn't quite what he expected. The fabric patch had slightly rounded corners and it was thicker than he'd imagined. As big as a sheet of printing paper, it had a brown vinyl side and a paper side—strong parchment paper that would be peeled off to expose the adhesive.

"I bet Sutton didn't have an enterprising wife on the case with him." Weiss grinned.

"Yeah. He was content with slapping a sheet of paper on his partner's face." Joshi smiled at his wife in pride.

Weiss carefully folded the vinyl sheet in half. "Look at this, Prem."

He was suddenly aware that the secretary, technician, and even the lady with chained glasses were crowding in for a look. They had all been primed by Joshi's tale about the murder. Weiss made a note to use this indiscretion the next time Joshi needled him about speaking to a reporter like Carly Rouhl.

"Oh, yeah," Joshi said, not wanting to admit that he saw nothing of significance about the vinyl pad.

"Look how thick it is. It doesn't fold neatly like a piece of paper." Weiss tried folding the sheet again into quarters. "It looks more of a Big Mac than folded paper." Weiss was exaggerating, but the vinyl resisted being folded to a neat edge and had more bulk than he had pictured. "If you tried to stuff this in the pocket of your jeans, it would show."

Joshi nodded. Avoiding names, he said, "The girlfriend would have noticed."

Liana was beaming. "By the way, I gave Jane five bucks for that patch. They come in a package of three for $14.95."

Joshi hugged his wife in silent thanks and then, embarrassed at how much his affection showed, he hurried Weiss out into the parking lot, leaving an excited true crime seminar in full swing behind them.

They went through the motions of unlocking the dark grey cruiser, but Weiss's mind was somewhere else.

"Does this change anything?" Joshi asked as they stood looking across the roof of the cruiser.

Weiss rested his elbow above the driver's side window, still examining the patch on the roof of the car, watching the way the protective parchment was beginning to separate from the adhesive layer at the fold lines.

"For me, it does. Maybe Blair's girlfriend wouldn't remember a bulky back pocket in his jeans when Blair was leaving the schoolhouse, but Blair had to bring this thing with him in the morning, too. I just don't think a guy planning murder would sit in a car with so conspicuous a thing in his hand or folded up getting crushed on his ass."

Joshi hung on the passenger's side car door for a moment. "You're back to saying you don't think Blair did it." He sighed. "But if we don't have Blair, we've got nothing."

"Not quite," Weiss said. "We've still got Peterborough."

"Peterborough?"

"In A.L. Rouhl's book—the one that got Carly interested in the schoolhouse murder—the killer was a guy who faked antiques as a sideline. Fine, so we've been thinking that could be Blair. He's got some skills as a carpenter and he knew Warden was interested in history. Fact is, though, anyone could have come to the schoolhouse after Blair left. The only other scrap of information we have relating to Rouhl's book is that Warden met the antiquities guy in Peterborough. That's what the daughter Corey said, remember?"

Joshi hung his head and rubbed the back of his neck. "So now we're relying on a work of quasi-fiction and Warden's daughter."

"I know this is hard, Prem. Rouhl's books were written to entertain, and it's impossible to tell what's real in them. We know the names aren't real because he had to protect himself from lawsuits, but the impression I got from reading the file Rouhl left on his laptop for Carly, and from talking to Carly herself, is that Rouhl made up as little as possible. He'd use real places and times, details from his travels, relationships; all of that. Then he'd fill in the rest from his imagination somehow."

"Yeah. Anything for a story."

"The point I'm trying to make is that if the antiquities dealer does figure into this in some way, then so does Peterborough."

Joshi closed his eyes and sagged against the car door. "Now I'm the one who's feeling nostalgic. Remember when we used to solve crimes by using unambiguous facts?" He swung into the passenger seat and waited while Weiss got behind the wheel and did up his seat belt. "So where do we look next? Peterborough? It's, what, four hundred miles away?"

Weiss slumped in defeat. "I was thinking more of a web search: book shops, small-time furniture stores."

Joshi scowled his skepticism.

"Well," Weiss grumbled, "the only other thing we have going for us is the schoolhouse."

"The wandering murder scene."

"Right."

Weiss touched the key but didn't start the engine. Instead, he gazed through the windshield at the car's grill reflected in the optician's window. This went on for a moment: Weiss staring, Joshi quietly thoughtful. The silence didn't feel odd. They were doing their job, evaluating whatever it was they had learned.

Then Liana came to the glass door and looked out. She was still talking to her colleagues and clients inside, but she was wide-eyed in curiosity at the two detectives doing a whole lot of nothing outside her door. Joshi shifted uncomfortably, seeing the situation through his wife's eyes.

Unable to take it anymore, Joshi looked across at Weiss. "Say it, Eilert. Use your words." For Liana's benefit, he was trying not to move his lips, so he came across as a bad ventriloquist.

Weiss screwed one eye shut and said, "I was thinking what a strange idea it is to move an old schoolhouse to a streetcar museum."

"Yeah, so? Sylvester said all those volunteer guys were time travellers. Trying to gather the past together in one place so they could all play there."

"Yeah, so they go and get themselves a schoolhouse." Weiss was gripping the wheel, working it like an exercise machine. "Aaron Sylvester said it was *his* idea to get the old building trucked up to the museum site. I mean, I get that the museum people had a vision—"

"A kind of mid-century pioneer village built around a railway," Joshi shrugged.

"Yeah, yeah, but a schoolhouse? It's still, I don't know, quirky?" Weiss moved his hand to the passenger's headrest behind Joshi and looked across at him. "I remember at the museum, the woman at the ticket cage saying Sylvester had *made* some of the period reconstructions around the visitors centre." Weiss's eyes went wide. "Prem! Did you know that Sylvester means woodman? It's Latin or something—you know—Pennsylvania, Transylvania? It would be just like a smart-ass writer to make a hidden allusion in the name."

Joshi shifted in his seat, affecting cool, trying to hide his excitement. "Okay, interesting, but if Sylvester was the guy who arranged for the school to be moved, why would he preserve the scene of the crime so that people could go snooping around it? Wouldn't he want it demolished?"

Weiss's eyes were darting. "Yeah, okay, but there are two ways a killer could go with that: he could hope someone would demolish the murder scene, protecting his ass, or... Well, you know, Prem: the type of psycho who wants to *preserve* the scene?"

Joshi was nodding slowly. "Yeah. The trophy taker, you

mean? The guy who shows up at the victim's funeral. The guy who wants to revisit the scene of his crime—*that* guy."

"There's no evidence in the schoolhouse; Sylvester knows that. The forensics team found nothing there. But think about Sylvester: he's obsessed with the past and he's an illusionist trying to recreate it. So, maybe he's attached to the scene of his greatest deceit. What if the schoolhouse isn't a monument to the twenties or the thirties; what if it's a monument to *him?* To his cleverness in getting away with murder."

"Damn it." Joshi's head went back and his eyes closed. "I think there's something there, but it's still speculation—all of it. We don't have enough to bring Sylvester in, but we could give him a visit, see if we can shake him up a bit."

"I think we've got enough cause for a warrant to search. He *is* personally responsible for moving our damn murder scene, after all. I could take care of that today and be ready to look at his home tomorrow."

Joshi breathed out noisily. "Okay, but it's important that Sylvester doesn't know we're coming. We can't let him dispose of any evidence he has at his home."

"Like vinyl repair patches."

Joshi turned his mind to procedure, something he was comfortable with. "I'm going to get someone at the station to call the museum. We don't want anyone knowing it's the police calling. We can find out if Sylvester is going to be there volunteering tomorrow, or at home."

"Yeah. We can't just break into his place, so he's got to be at home." Weiss was sitting bolt upright now. "If he is going to be at the museum, we'll find him there, take him home, and execute the search while he watches; that way we can make sure he doesn't warn anyone else about what we're doing."

"Do you know where he lives? House? Apartment?"

"No, but we'll work backward from his phone number. Shouldn't be hard. If this hunch is correct, it'll be a detached house. He needs a private place to make stuff: a workshop of some kind."

Joshi rubbed his hands together. "We'll need a couple of uniforms for the search."

"Okay. I'm hearing a plan. Let's go."

CHAPTER TWENTY-TWO

Back at the Halton District Three Police Station, Weiss and Joshi took the stairs to their second-floor office. The office looked less bare than it had been when they first moved into the new building a couple of years ago. Apart from the filing cabinets and accumulating clutter, there were now a few of Weiss's plants, desert succulents that didn't require a lot of attention and bloomed once a year near Christmas, and Joshi's photos of a bewilderingly large extended family.

"Prem, you're taking care of having someone call the museum. Have them say they're a delivery service and they need Sylvester's signature. We need to know whether Sylvester will be on-site at the museum tomorrow. It'll take some fast talking; if he's not there, make sure no one calls him at his number and gives him time to think about what he's going to tell us. It's important that we surprise him."

"Where are you going?

"Just out here in the hall for a minute. There's a call I have to make. There's something that's bothering me about Carly Rouhl and the Wardens."

Joshi narrowed his eyes and swivelled slowly to his desk, his face expressionless. The kind of calls made in the corridor was personal. Besides, any mention of Carly Rouhl made Joshi uncomfortable.

Weiss ambled to the end of the corridor, working his phone. He turned to rest his back against the end window and listened to the line purr. His call to Carly went straight to voicemail, but she returned the call before he could leave a message.

She sounded cheerful—grateful for his call. Weiss, on the other hand, felt clumsy, like a teenage boy not sure what the girl thought of him. Weiss had been drawn in by a beguiling woman once before, his wife, only to find out he'd misjudged her motives. The "free spirit" he married quickly turned into a spiteful harpy. It had been a life-scarring lesson.

"Carly," he said, once the strained greetings were over, "how well do you know Brenda Warden?"

"Who? Am I supposed to know her?"

"Brenda Warden—wife of Cecil Warden."

"Sorry, I'm drawing a blank here."

Weiss felt strangely off-balance. This had the feel of catching a suspect in a lie, but he couldn't believe that of Carly. "How about Corey Warden?" he said.

There was a brief silence on the line. It didn't last long, but it was the kind of stalling silence Weiss was familiar with when a criminal sees his statement doesn't hold water and decides to change his story.

At last, Carly said, "Oh-kay, come to think of it, I did know a Corey. Wow! There's a name from the past. How on earth did you come up with that?"

Or maybe it was the kind of silence that happens when a memory comes winging in from left field, leaving you dazed.

Weiss was thinking, so Carly went on. "Are you referring to a girl I knew in college? Goth, went in for really short hair, didn't say much, kind of hung out on the fringes of our lunchtime crowd."

"I'm talking about the daughter of Cecil Warden, the man who died in the schoolhouse ten years ago."

"Whoa! Unbelievable. Are you saying she's the same Corey? I would have had a hard time even remembering her last name if you hadn't told me."

"But...Corey told me you took a road trip together up to Baysville."

"What?" A pause. "Omigod, that's true. She came along as a friend of a friend. Sat in the back and hardly said a word. I remember now. We saw the Barenaked Ladies at the local arena."

"What about her father, Cecil? Cecil Warden. He's the man who was murdered in the schoolhouse."

There was another stunned silence. Then, "Cece. Dad's friend, Cece—I do remember a Cece. Omigod! Cece is Gill Watters?"

"And you never made the connection?"

"What? No! You know how it is, Eilert. Your parents talk about their friends, you hear the names, but... Well, I was a self-absorbed teenager, and then I was away at the university for so long. I lived in a student residence on Charles Street, near Yonge and Bloor, right in the heart of Toronto, and my life was a buzz of excitement being in the big city. The last thing on my mind was my parents' friends. Then I went away to the States, to Cornell for journalism. If Cece is our murder victim, he must have died just after Mum passed away. After that, Dad was never an outgoing person; he became reclusive, and then his health failed. We never saw anybody."

"I understand, but you're saying when you came to me with this schoolhouse murder, you had no idea it involved the Wardens, friends of your parents."

"Absolutely. Hadn't a clue."

"So, then you're saying, what? That the manuscript just happened to catch your eye?"

Weiss cupped the phone to his ear and rested his elbow on the window ledge, looking out at the houses of the Headon Forest community, mid-level homes built in the nineties. He didn't say anything for a moment.

Carly listened to the rustle of the phone against Weiss's cheek. When he put it that way, it did sound odd—one of those coincidences that make police officers suspicious. Confused, she felt she had to fill the silence. "You sound doubtful. Honestly, I had no idea."

"I believe you, of course. It's just that it must have been difficult for you to come to me with nothing but your father's largely forgotten book."

"It was the manuscript I found in Dad's office—the one with the lovely frontispiece. It was a fake, but there seemed to be a story to it."

"Go on."

"What do you want me to say? I don't understand."

"I'm trying to follow the chain of events that brought you to me with a murder case. I'm considering bringing a man named Aaron Sylvester in for questioning and frankly, I'm kind of uncertain how I got to where I am with all this. I'm used to following a sequence of logical connections. Your intuition—I'd be embarrassed to admit that's all I had to go on."

"You're thinking I've made trouble for you."

"No, no!" Weiss pressed his hand to his brow, glancing around to see if anyone was spying on his discomfort. "It's not that at all, Carly. I'm just wondering… Your uncanny instincts have…they've guided me before, but they also leave me bewildered. You're telling me you had no emotional motive to avenge your father's friend, that you were drawn to and intrigued by that one piece of clutter on those overcrowded shelves."

Carly was slow to answer. "I—uh—I guess that's right. I was with Harriet and we just…noticed…"

"The Wardens were your *mother's* friends, really, weren't they?"

"Oh, absolutely. Mum was the sociable one."

"You've never mentioned your mother."

"She passed when I was away in Ithaca. You know—at Cornell."

"So, no lingering feeling of obligation to your mother?"

"I told you…" Carly stopped short as though she was re-evaluating. "My God, Eilert, you're confusing the hell out of me. When Harriet found a reference to the manuscript in Dad's book, that's when it felt sort of personal. Dad said in the book that this Gill Watters character was a friend."

Weiss thrust his free hand in his pocket, hiding his balled fist. He couldn't have put it into words, but this woman whom he trusted was either lying to him or she had a blind spot about the manuscript. He wondered if she was lying to herself. He was prepared to go ahead with the case, following his own instincts, but he had trouble accepting this random act of curiosity on her part. He'd spent time in A.L.'s office surrounded by his packed shelves and he wanted to know why this murder case had come tumbling out of that chaos to wind up in his hands.

Carly was picking up on Weiss's discomfort. "Eilert? Are we okay? I'm really not sure."

"Yes. We're okay." He quickly changed the subject. "I'm going to go into the streetcar museum tomorrow and talk to someone named Sylvester. We're thinking he may be our forger."

"Tomorrow."

"Yes, I'll let you know how it goes. Don't tell Prem I told you, or anybody for that matter. We're hoping to catch Sylvester off guard."

"Eilert, Dad said that this forger didn't know how strange he was." There was a sudden edge of panic in Carly's voice. Her curiosity was about to put Weiss in danger. "He wrote that this Wood guy had a kind of split personality—even used the word monster. 'Monsters walk among us.' What I'm saying is, this Sylvester guy could be dangerous."

"Yes, I remember the reference."

Carly gave a fleeting, humourless laugh. "Suddenly, I feel I'm responsible for all this." Her tone darkened. "If Sylvester is the one, don't be fooled by his charm. Dad said that the forger sent a side of his personality to that schoolhouse that was perfectly prepared to use violence, to commit murder."

"Prem and I, we'll keep that in mind. Please don't worry, Carly."

Neither one of them said goodbye. There was just a pause that seemed to be filled with tender concern, then a gentle, fatalistic click on Carly's end.

Weiss straightened, had one last look at the overcast sky, and began walking back to his office.

Joshi looked up from his laptop as Weiss came in. "You're going to want to see this."

Weiss sat on his chair, but his mind was elsewhere.

"Hey! Eilert. Wakey wakey. I need you to see this. What's the matter?"

"Carly and Brenda Warden. Carly didn't know where this was going, that the Wardens were her parents' friends. Funny, huh?"

"A riot. Now, I'm going to make a titanic effort to forget that Rouhl woman is behind all this and drag you back to solid police work."

Weiss closed his eyes in a slow blink and sighed. "What have you got?"

Joshi jerked a thumb at his screen. "I've got goddam Peterborough, that's what I've got. Before he moved to Burlington, Aaron Sylvester worked on the Trent Severn Waterway—specifically as an engineer on the lift locks in Peterborough."

Weiss slapped his hand on Joshi's shoulder. "My God, Prem! It has to be him!"

Joshi shifted his head from side to side. "The only way this works is if Sylvester came all the way from Peterborough to hunt Cecil Warden down like an animal. This is serious premeditation."

"Bizarre, isn't it?" Weiss said. "Sylvester comes across as this jolly train buff, but for him to have done this, he must have become a cold-blooded hunter, driving around the streets of Oakville and Burlington, stalking his prey. It must have taken him a while to find out about the schoolhouse. Then what? Was he sitting in his car in the heat, across the fields, watching the schoolhouse? Did he watch Blair and his girlfriend drive away, see his opportunity and move in?"

Joshi grimaced at the thought. "His opportunity to surprise Warden and smother him to death, you mean?" With an expression of disgust, he closed his eyes. "The creep must have enjoyed himself. Now he lives here."

CHAPTER TWENTY-THREE

They were in the car, squinting into the rising sunlight, following the GPS to Aaron Sylvester's house. The morning had been busy, checking out the cruisers, briefing the two uniformed officers in the second vehicle. It was the first time Weiss and Joshi had a chance to talk. Weiss was driving.

"So, we're sure Sylvester is at home?" he asked.

"We can't be sure without phoning him and blowing the surprise, of course, but the desk at the railway museum says he's not on the duty roster today."

"That's enough to go ahead on. I was right, by the way; his house is a detached two-story up the road in Waterdown. I've got the warrant to search the place, but there needs to be someone there to let us in."

Joshi shifted in the passenger seat, his excitement obvious. "You saw what I got on Sylvester from the web, right? He got a civic award from the City of Burlington Council two years ago for his volunteering. There was mention of him working on public utilities as an engineer in his younger days, whatever that means, but he's been retired from his day job for years."

"Public utilities? You mean water and electricity?"

"Or it could be roads and bridges and stuff. It makes sense that he wound up on the lift locks. He would have been drawn to the nineteenth-century engineering of it all."

Of the two cruisers, one was unmarked; the other, carrying the two officers, had the low visibility markings of a traffic control car. Together, they pulled to the curb in front of a tidy house on a quiet residential street. The hardscaping was stark and symmetrical, and there were few bushes or plantings, as though the owner had other things on his mind besides gardening. There was a single garage that was closed, and no car in the driveway.

The four of them approached the front door and Weiss let one of the cops, a lean, tawny-skinned woman full of rookie enthusiasm, ring the doorbell. At first, there was no answer and Joshi stepped down to check out the garage, but then a face appeared at the bay window. The woman at the window recognized the uniforms and seconds later the door opened a crack.

"Yes?"

"I have a warrant to search these premises. Would Mr. Sylvester be home?"

"No, he's not here. Could you come back this afternoon?"

Weiss recognized the delay tactic. Sylvester might be inside destroying evidence right now. "I'm sorry, but we need to come in. Please read the warrant so you know what your rights are."

With that, a female cop shouldered her way past the woman in the doorway and they all went inside. Joshi knew what he was looking for and went off to check for a basement workshop. The two uniformed officers began a room to room, looking to see if Sylvester was home. Weiss went quickly to a window overlooking the backyard in case Sylvester had gone out the back. He saw a simple square lawn with a single maple tree and a prefab tool shed. There was a high, tightly planked fence with a lattice top and nowhere to run.

Weiss returned to the woman who was cowering in a white

terrycloth robe. She had dyed blond hair, high cheekbones, and full lips, but the worn-out look of an alcoholic or drug user.

"And you are?"

"A friend," she said with a slight accent.

"Are you in a relationship with Mr. Sylvester?"

She snorted derision. "Sometimes." Weiss waited, conveying impatience. "He calls up when he needs company."

Weiss nodded. They might need more later, but for now, he figured the woman was working for tax-free income. She might have been a professional once, but older now, he figured she was just grateful for Sylvester's calls.

"Where is he?"

"He volunteers at a railroad thing up in Milton."

"They say he isn't scheduled to work today."

"Damn right. We were supposed to go out to the mall this morning, but he got this call last night, and after that…" She rolled her eyes.

"After that, what?"

"He got all worried and was like, 'I've got to go into the site tomorrow.'"

"Do you know who he talked to on the phone?"

"Aaron, he can be closed-mouthed. All he wants to talk about is old shit. History'n stuff like that. Gets kinda weird with it sometimes."

Joshi was back. He held up a long roll of material. "No fabric patches, but this is brown vinyl, and he's got every damn type of duct tape and glue you can think of. There's a padlocked cupboard. We'd need a bolt cutter. I'm not sure if our warrant covers that."

"It does, but we've got to get to the museum. I don't know how, but I think somebody's tipped Sylvester off." Weiss looked at the roll of vinyl for a moment. "Look, Prem, you stay with the uniforms and get that cupboard open; you know the profile we're trying to match to Sylvester. See what he's got locked up in there. I'll go on ahead to find out what's going on up at the site. Bring the officers with you and join me as soon as you can. I don't plan on doing anything until you get there, but I want to make sure Sylvester doesn't run."

Joshi started to object, but Weiss was already heading out the front door to the cruiser. Joshi stood there, turning his attention to Sylvester's worried-looking companion.

"Why don't you have a seat, ma'am." Then he glanced at the roll of vinyl in his hand and made his way back towards the basement door.

CHAPTER TWENTY-FOUR

Weiss pulled into the lot behind the visitors centre and half-ran to the front of the building. On the platform at the main door, he paused, his hand on the door handle. He didn't want to create the impression he was bursting in, so he took a breath and straightened.

It was early and there were no tourists yet, so his elaborately casual entrance still met with some interest from the three staffers setting up for the day. Weiss made a show of examining one of the posters on the wall and then sauntered to the desk with its caged ticket window.

"Would, uh, Mr. Sylvester be here? I don't see him around."

The young woman seated on a rolling stool behind the cage said, "He's here at the site, but he told everyone he was taking an eight o'clock ride."

"On the streetcar, you mean?"

"Yeah. It's unscheduled, but the streetcar's due back any minute now. He'd be coming back on that, I guess."

Weiss considered what he had been told. Something was wrong. The park didn't even open until nine-thirty. "What do you mean, he told everyone?"

The ticket clerk blinked. "Oh, I just mean that he made a point of informing several of us here at the reception centre. Maybe he wanted to let us know he was available to work, or maybe he wanted to make sure he didn't miss you."

"Miss me?" Weiss looked around suspiciously. "I never told him I was coming."

The young woman appeared confused, glancing at the other volunteers. Another woman, older, heavyset, carrying a broom, sidled over.

"You *are* Mr. Weiss, aren't you?"

"Yes, uh..." he was going to add 'Detective Weiss,' but suddenly, he felt he was playing some sort of game. Had Sylvester not wanted them to know this was a police matter?

"That's what I figured," the older woman said. "Aaron said he was expecting you, but wasn't sure exactly when you'd come, so he was going to get some work done in the meantime."

"Expecting me..."

"Sure. Even said you'd be alone."

Weiss was stunned and didn't know what to say. He couldn't imagine any scenario in which Sylvester could know he'd be here, let alone by himself. He walked back to the door, stumbling slightly in an absent-minded way. Outside, he could see the broad sweep of the railroad tracks curving past the corrugated steel barn of the maintenance building before plunging into a gap in the wall of trees—the oily black of the sleepers, the dusty crumble of the aggregate.

When he got out onto the wooden platform, he walked the length of the visitors centre's facade. The sun was playing hide-and-seek behind the rain clouds, but the temperature had gone up a degree or two, so there was a low mist that turned the forest into a distant mountain range with blue-grey peaks.

Weiss became aware of the conductor, seated placidly on a bench, enjoying the mellow autumn weather.

"Morning," Weiss said. "I saw you working with Vern the motorman and Aaron Sylvester."

"Yup. I remember you. I'm Ed." He tipped his peaked pillbox hat. "And you're Detective Weiss."

"Hello, Ed. A bit early for you folk, isn't it?"

"Tell you the truth, I'm grateful for the excuse to get up in the morning. If it wasn't for this place, this time, I swear I'd be vegging in front of a goddamned breakfast show on TV, watchin' some skinny Minnie pointin' to weather maps instead of lookin' at them storm clouds in person. This?" He waved his hand at the tracks. "This is a meaningful job, only there's no pressure."

Weiss leaned against a post supporting the overhang. "You have your schedules to keep, though."

"Ah, yeah. That's lovely too, you see. A planned day. Six hourly runs through the forest. Plenty of time for coffee and sandwiches. It makes me happy."

"But there's been a run already. I was told Aaron Sylvester had gone round at eight."

"That's right. Aaron does as Aaron pleases around here," Ed said, and he jerked his thumb at the forest. "Vern rode him to the schoolhouse to drop'm off. Didn't need a conductor for that. It's Aaron's day off, but he just had an itch to do some work on the schoolhouse and the streetcar's the easiest way of getting there."

"I guess Aaron's like you," Weiss said, "prefers to live in the past."

Ed looked up, in the mood to talk. "Well now, Aaron's a bit different from most of us folks."

"How's that?"

"Most of us old-timers—honestly, I think we're clinging to our youth. The younger ones here, they have a kind of nostalgia for the time their folks lived in. They use words like quaint and steampunk, whatever the hell that is."

"And Aaron?"

"Well, he sure don't belong in the here and now, that's for sure. He's a reader, and he's got a lot more clicks on his time machine than the rest of us."

"Excuse me?"

"With Aaron, it's not just this turn of the century stuff." Ed gestured to the building behind him. "No, Aaron'll tell you stories about witch burnings and old plagues. You wanna know what an oubliette is? Ask Aaron. He's your man."

Weiss chuckled. "Okay, I give up. What's an oubliette?"

"See, I didn't know either till Aaron brought it up. It's a hole in the deep dark bottom of a castle where they throw you and forget about you. Gave me the creeps, that one."

Weiss cupped his chin and closed his eyes. For perhaps the first time since Carly had drawn him into this case, he felt a tinge of certainty about the murder of Cecil Warden.

There was a chime from his jacket pocket and Weiss took out his phone. He took a few steps away from Ed.

Joshi's voice, excited: "Bingo! Sylvester's cupboard is a freaking chamber of horrors. You wouldn't believe the psycho shit he's got in there. Better than that: he's got an open package of those sticky pads and the package looks old. Not exactly the murder weapon, but ammunition of a sort. It's kind of like matching the bullet."

"Not quite, but he's starting to fit the profile of a killer—he's got some sort of psychotic side to his personality." Weiss cradled the phone, thinking. "Prem, you've got to get over here and bring the uniforms. It's pretty clear somebody tipped Sylvester off that we were coming. In fact, he seemed to know I'd show up at the museum alone; he's tracking us somehow."

"Don't go paranoid on me, Eilert. There's no way he could know that. And don't try to arrest him until we get there. Just—I don't know, keep an eye on him if you can."

"It's not that simple, Prem. I'm at the visitors centre right now and Sylvester's gone off by himself over to the schoolhouse."

"The schoolhouse? Why would he go there?"

"That's the thing—if he knows we're coming for him, I'm thinking two possibilities: he's going to lose himself in the woods, come out on one of the rural side roads around here. Or..."

"I can think of a dozen better ways to evade arrest than bolting through the woods, most of them involving a car."

"That's true, but he's improvising, and the people around here, they *think* differently. Maybe Sylvester wants to flee...to the past."

"That would be very poetic if it wasn't also total bullshit."

"Okay, but there is one way he could actually make that work—vanishing into the past, I mean."

"I'm listening, but just so's you know, I'm also rolling my eyes."

Weiss pinched his temples. "This has the feel of an endgame to me, Prem. I don't know how, but I think Sylvester knows that we want him for murder. And if he knows that it's over... We've seen this before."

There was a disturbance on the line, Joshi breathing out in exasperation. "I see where you're going. The bugger's going to kill himself."

"In the woods," Weiss said, "at the schoolhouse, where it's quiet and where he's surrounded by days gone by."

"Okay, enough with the friggin' poetry. We're on our way. I have to seal the house and drop the woman off at District Three, but we shouldn't be more than a half-hour getting to you. Go look at some pamphlets or something."

Joshi ended the call. Weiss put his back against the wooden wall and, besides a sandwich board sign, he melted into the long morning shadows to think. Weiss wondered how much Ed, the conductor, had heard, but the bench beside him was empty now, and he could see that Ed was down the platform. He had a lunch box hanging from his hand—the old kind: black metal, arched at the top to hold a flask. It was as in-character as his striped suspenders.

A rumbling rose to the level of cresting surf and number 367 rolled out of a gap in the forest. It ran smoothly along its iron rails, the odd spark popping from the power cable above it. It approached them and pulled alongside the platform in a great sighing of brakes and suspension coils. The front access door folded open.

Weiss arched off the wall and sauntered along the platform to where Ed was looking up at the footplate of the streetcar. The driver, his elbow resting on the accelerator lever, was talking to Ed. The morning's topic: the strange behaviour of Aaron Sylvester.

"Just asked me to drop'm off," Vern was saying.

"Did he say when he'd be coming back?" Ed wanted to know.

The driver tipped his hat so he could scratch his bald scalp. "Said he'd flag down one of the regular circuits."

Weiss moved beside Ed. "Was Aaron carrying anything? Tools? A lunch bag?"

The driver narrowed his eyes in thought. "He did have a bag. A paper sack all sealed up like a sack o'flour. 'Cept it was plain brown paper."

"Did it have a label?" Weiss asked.

"Nah. I figured it was nails or tacks or somethin' from a hardware store." The driver swivelled in his chair. "He wasn't very good company this morning. Not his usual self. Is Aaron in trouble or somethin'?"

Weiss shrugged, his hands in his coat pockets. "When's your next circuit?"

The driver looked back at the seating. A dozen visitors had

already climbed aboard and were lounging against the windows. "Our first scheduled run of the day is in five minutes."

Weiss turned away, stood staring at the wooden planking for a minute, then began pacing. It was an aimless, maddening shuffle, getting him nowhere. If Sylvester were planning suicide, how would he do it? A gun? Something more macabre? Something that required solitude? He thought about the plain paper sack.

He stood there weighing possibilities until suddenly the bell on the streetcar clanged and the door unfolded into the closed position. Weiss blinked once and jumped to the door. He knocked furiously until the driver levered the door open again.

"I'm coming along," Weiss said, swinging up inside and onto the front bench.

The driver, surprised, looked back at Ed, who was standing halfway down the carriage, holding onto a handrail. Ed was wide-eyed, but he nodded, and the doors levered shut once more.

The driver swung his accelerator arm and the old streetcar jerked and clattered forward into a steady roll.

Weiss sat forward in his seat behind the driver. "If Aaron wanted to strike off into the woods, is there a short way out of the park?"

The streetcar was juddering around a corner past the maintenance building, beginning its run back towards the forest.

"Well, I suppose he'd have to walk south, but it's a hell of a trek through the bush, and there's a gully just this side of the fence. But, holy shit, he wouldn't do that."

"Sorry. I need to get to the schoolhouse. You can drop me off." Weiss was already showing his warrant card. "And then I need you to return to the visitors centre and wait for my partner. There'll be uniformed officers, too. Do you understand?"

"Holy... Yeah."

The streetcar was rumbling along at a leisurely pace for the benefit of the tourists, but the forest was now spreading out ahead. And then they were surrounded by the canopy, thinned of leaves but skeletally dense all the same. The power line looped overhead from tower to tower beneath a narrow sliver of grey sky, the track curving slightly, and the forest was closing in behind them.

CHAPTER TWENTY-FIVE

After twenty minutes or so, the driver slowed at the straight section of track in front of the schoolhouse and Weiss got ready to dismount. He summoned Ed and grabbed his arm.

"So you guys go straight back to the visitors centre and wait for my partner. Got it? This trolley is commandeered until we tell you otherwise. Sorry, but that's what we need."

"I'll have to go right 'round the circuit, you know," the driver said. "This rig doesn't back up—not without a mechanic, anyway. What will I tell the on-duty site manager?"

"Tell him Aaron Sylvester is helping us with our inquiries."

"Christ on a cracker! Shouldn't I just wait?"

"I'd prefer to have my partner here for this. I would have waited, but I need to know if Sylvester's here or if he's struck out into the forest. If he *is* at the schoolhouse, I need to know what he's up to. I'm not planning on doing anything until I get some backup."

The door clunked open. Dropping from the iron step to the crushed stone of the trackbed, Weiss turned and shuffled down to the weedy path. It was cool and the mist made the forest feel close. He felt a single raindrop on his cheek. Weiss waited with his cell phone in hand until the streetcar rattled noisily down the track, then he touched Joshi's number.

Joshi came on the line and Weiss could hear the rush of a car in traffic. "Where are you?" Joshi barked.

"Listen, Prem, I'm at the schoolhouse—approaching it from the path."

"What the hell? Why didn't you wait for me?"

"I had to make a snap decision. I think Sylvester's going to do something theatrical, burn down the schoolhouse, blow himself up; I don't know, but he had a brown paper package with him."

"Okay, you've got me worried, Eilert."

"I'm going to keep my distance. I just need to know what we're dealing with. The streetcar will be waiting for you and I've told them you're coming."

Weiss rang off, leaving Joshi tongue-tied and breathing noisily as he walked along the weedy path. The schoolhouse with its lofty bell tower loomed up behind a veil of mist. In the silence, Weiss could hear the crunch of his shoes on the strewn aggregate thrown down amongst the weeds by the work crew.

He mounted the deck to the front door and listened. It was faint, but Weiss had the sense of someone moving around inside, so he gripped the doorknob and turned it. The door opened, sagging a bit in its distorted frame.

Weiss went inside slowly, picking his way through the darkness of the cloakroom. He moved to the square-shouldered arch opening onto the main schoolroom—and there was Sylvester standing up on the dais behind the woodstove. Weiss thought about remaining there in the shadows, but Sylvester looked up and it was obvious that he had been watching for Weiss, waiting for him to appear.

"Good morning, Detective Weiss."

Sylvester had clearly just risen from the big teacher's chair as if in politeness. He sounded weary, saddened. The room was pleasantly warm and Weiss realized that Sylvester had stoked up the old wood stove. He smelled the burning wood and heard the faint crackle of glowing embers.

Weiss knew he had to keep things easy and conversational to bide his time until Joshi arrived. If he had to, he'd just sit on one of the old desks and watch what Sylvester was up to. He took a few stiff-legged steps into the room, looking around. Most of the floor space was still clear, the old furnishings piled against the walls as before, but there were a couple of the ancient one-piece school desks with their cramped seats placed near the raised dais as though they had been used by workmen for eating their lunches or resting tools on.

Weiss expected Sylvester to ask him what he was doing there, so he waited.

Sylvester spoke first, but all he said was, "Come up near the stove and get warm, Detective Weiss. It's wretchedly cold and damp out there, isn't it?"

"Hello, Mr. Sylvester." Weiss ambled forward, affecting casualness while taking in every detail of the room, watching for weapons or combustibles. In the corner of his eye, he saw some crumpled brown paper discarded on the floor: the empty sack. The heat radiating from the big iron stove drew his attention next, until Weiss found himself standing below Sylvester, about where the first two rows of desks would have been back when the school was used for teaching. "Firing up the woodstove; were you planning on staying?"

Sylvester smiled sadly, profoundly incurious at the detective's arrival. "One of the joys in what I do," he said, "is imagining the past coming alive again. Warming the room with the old stove—that's another way of doing just that. We're volunteers here, Detective. Amateurs in the old sense of the word. That means we work for the love of reliving the past. Come and see, if you like. Enjoy the warmth. Come feel what those young learners felt on a cold autumn morning as they set about their day's study."

Sylvester moved slowly, bending and lifting an old iron bucket from the floor beside him. It looked heavy.

Weiss was instantly wary. "What's that? What's in the bucket?"

Before Weiss could say another word, Sylvester gently rested the bucket on the stovetop. "Well now, a bucket was kept here by the teacher's desk as a safety precaution back in the day, in case the stove overheated—filled with water, you see?"

Weiss kept his voice even. "Fine, well, I want you to leave the bucket there and step away from the stove, please. Why don't we talk—about the past. I gather you've educated yourself well on the subject."

Sylvester held his ground. "I would enjoy talking with you too, but I find people today don't understand. The poet, W. H. Auden, once said that the past is a strange country where strange people live. Our lives today are so layered with civilization, fashion, and far too much information that we're out of touch with the vulgarity and brutality of our ancestors."

Weiss caught a passing flicker of light on Sylvester's face. Being lower than Sylvester, he couldn't see it, but Weiss realized that one of the stove's circular plates must have been removed. When he looked back, he noticed Sylvester's hand was on the bucket.

Weiss drew his coat and jacket aside, exposing his belt holster. "Step away. Now!" His tone had shifted to a barked command.

Sylvester's eyes widened, not in fear but excitement. "Are you going to shoot me, Detective? Maybe I'm wrong. Maybe you *would* understand how men of violence thought back then." Sylvester looked down at his hand. "This bucket? You're right. It's not water. Actually, it has crystallized ammonium hydride in it. Do you know your chemistry? In the eighteenth century, the scientist Joseph Priestly used iron filings soaked in nitric acid to achieve the same effect, but that would be a bit, uh, hit and miss." His fingers closed on the bucket's handle. "I'm going to pour the chemical on the fire. Watch."

Weiss took a step back, brought his pistol up into his two hands and aimed at Sylvester's chest. "Stop! Now! You don't have to die here, Sylvester, but by God, you're forcing my hand."

Sylvester sniffed peevishly. "Oh, fine. Whatever you say." He left the bucket on the hot stove, but now he was pulling a black bundle of fabric from the drawer of the teacher's desk. "I've been here since dawn getting things ready. You want to talk about the past? One of the things I enjoy doing is historical costumes. I even made armour for a television show once. Can I at least show you this?"

Weiss wanted to stall until Joshi arrived. One way of doing that was to keep Sylvester talking. He let his hands drop until his gun was pointing at the floor.

"Sure. What is it?"

"It's called a plague hood," Sylvester said, sorting out the bundle in his hands. "Medieval doctors wore them when treating plague victims. This alarming-looking beak was filled with aromatic herbs that the poor physicians believed protected them from the disease. They were wrong, of course. Terrible thing, the plague. You would break out in sores and boils and die in torment. A quarter of the population of Europe died that way. Just think of that."

Holding the black material up like a magician so Weiss could see, Sylvester slipped the hood over his head, and as it settled on his shoulders, it resolved itself into a mask with a long, drooping beak. It was a chilling sight.

Sylvester had become a predatory bird—a raven or a crow. Only his eyes glinted through holes in the heavy material. Weiss swallowed, feeling vaguely sick. He flexed his fingers on his gun, but still, it pointed at the floor.

As soon as the hood was in place, Sylvester laid his right hand on the bucket. Weiss jacked the pistol up, aimed for the centre of Sylvester's chest the way he had been trained, and stood there, the only sensation in his world at that moment the cold solidity of the trigger.

"Sylvester, goddamn it, *stop*! You're about to die."

It's all very well to threaten someone with a gun, but shooting someone dead for gripping a bucket is another matter. Weiss hesitated. What was really going on here? Was this attempted suicide by cop? Did Sylvester want him to shoot? Or were they both about to be blown to pieces in the shrapnel of the stove?

Sylvester paused, the hooded eyes staring at the gun without a hint of fear, then, calling Weiss's bluff, he quickly upended the bucket into the stove.

There was a sudden *whoosh* that enveloped Sylvester in a pale haze. It billowed down off the dais in a fog bank, rolling around Weiss, and Weiss strained through the haze to see what Sylvester was up to. He had expected an explosion, but this?

"What in God's name are you doing, Sylvester? I just came to talk."

Sylvester's voice came through the cloud, muffled by the hood. "There's no need for pretence, Weiss. I knew you were coming..." There was wonderment in Sylvester's voice as though he hardly believed what he was saying. "...and I know why. It's bloody wonderful, isn't it?"

Weiss's breath came quickly as he tried to follow Sylvester's slow movements. "This is madness. You've got no reason to think—" The cloud smelled vaguely sweet with a raw metallic edge. Weiss stopped, trying to catch up, but his mind was a ball of wool. "What do you mean, you knew? Someone told you I was coming?"

"It's amazing, isn't it? Someone tells you what's going to

happen, and then, it does! He's a detective, like you, you know, but still, how *could* he know?"

"A detective?"

Weiss struggled to frame a question, but it was as if his thoughts were whirling in the cloud above his head, spinning off into the dark recesses of the room. Was Sylvester talking about someone in his own department? Only Joshi knew where this investigation was going—Joshi and the two uniformed officers. Sutton over in Oakville had never even heard of Sylvester.

Sylvester went on talking, not gloating, but genuinely amazed at what was happening. "Well, he *claims* he's a detective. No one I called up knows for sure. I try to keep a low profile, Detective Weiss, but this guy? He bloody well *knew* me. He knew about my antiques business. God knows how. So, this detective guy, he calls me up and says he can save my ass. He knows what I did, and then he describes it to me as though he was there watching! You hearing me? Like he was standing there watching me while I snuffed old Cecil Warden. I'm on my phone listening to him, totally stunned, and his voice says, 'For a thousand bucks, I'll tell you what to watch out for.'" Sylvester was still on the raised dais, but he was out from behind the stove now, and Weiss felt numb.

"A thousand!" The black snouted hood gave a muffled laugh. "Not much of a shakedown as these things go, was it? Funny thing is, though, I recognize the business model. You demand a small enough sum that the mark decides he can afford to play along. Ask for too much and it doesn't work. You see, this guy is a small-time operator. He knows that if you play the racket often enough, and if you're careful with your money, the profits can start to add up."

Sylvester was taking his time, waiting for Weiss to inhale nitrous oxide and drop, and with every breath, the detective's consciousness was slipping away.

The voice, muffled by the black hood, went on "The phone

call really shook me up, so I decide I'm going to drop off the money where he says. And, what do you know, after that, he phones back and delivers on the deal—even tells me your name. 'Watch out for a Halton detective named Weiss,' he says. Just like that. 'And a nosy bitch called Carly Rouhl—the writer's daughter.'"

Carly's name seemed to drop out of nowhere, but Weiss was beyond reasoning now.

"So when you called me on the phone that very first time," Sylvester was saying, "sure, I was shocked, but I was also prepared. I thought that having been warned, I could deflect you somehow. I still don't know how you followed this back to me. I thought the case was dead."

A figure moved in the noxious cloud, one hand held up as though he were balancing a tray of drinks. "Then the guy on the phone calls me back, tells me that you'll come for me alone, and he even tells me *when*. I wondered about that; he had his money, didn't ask for more. I think he actually wanted me to eliminate you."

"What…are you…talking about?" Weiss's voice came out slurred and weak.

"I'm not much of a criminal," Sylvester moaned. "I'll admit it. I'd be a hell of a lot richer if I was. But even I have contacts—people who've heard of this detective and his game. The word is, he reaches out to felons, murderers, even petty frauds like me, and demands payment—a bribe—either for his silence or for information about the police. He didn't ask for a fortune, 'cause he knew I wouldn't have it, but if you pull off the con often enough—well, it adds up, you see? That was my philosophy, too—stay below the radar. Don't give in to the temptation to go for the big score.

"Listen, Weiss, I'm not one of those serial murderers you read about. I'm just desperate. I don't even own a gun—imagine that. So, I had to improvise. When the guy was right about you calling me, I figured I could trust what he was saying. And then, when he told me that you'd come to the schoolhouse alone, that gave me hope."

Weiss felt his knees failing. He dropped to all fours, the grit on the floor tiles pressing into his hands, his fingers loosening on the gun.

Sylvester moved nearer. "I almost bungled old Cecil. He was a weak, old, spindly guy, but he managed to bang me up a bit before he stopped fighting. It's the adrenaline, you see. I learned from that. Now, you? You're bigger, stronger. I knew I had to have you immobilized before I could do to you what I did to old Cece."

Weiss had a sense of Sylvester stepping to his side, but his head was spinning, the room distorting and filling with an unearthly light. He could feel his elbows weakening.

"It's a pathetic murder weapon, isn't it?" Sylvester was saying. "But at least I know all about adhesives. I use them in my work all the time. Good with my hands, that's me. That'd be perfect for my tombstone, don't you think? And that's not a joke, by the way. I've been saving for an impressive monument. I mean, what the hell else can I do with my money?

"And there's no one else who'll make the arrangements. Price of being a loner, I guess. You see, I don't have any illusions about getting away with all this. Not for long, anyway. I'm just buying time. I'm an improviser, and believe me, if there was a way of letting you live, I'd go for it. Probably. At least there won't be any blood, and it shouldn't be too hard to get rid of you out here in the forest. Sorry. That's pretty boastful. I'm just a stupid screw-up improvising as I go along. Pathetic, huh?"

Sylvester was kneeling too now, the deadened voice inches from Weiss's ear. Even as he sank to his elbows, Weiss understood that what Sylvester was holding wasn't paper, but he wasn't even aware of his service pistol clattering on the floor tiles in front of him.

He wasn't fully aware of the attack when it came, either.

Somewhere in a flowing miasma of semi-consciousness, Weiss just knew that he could no longer breathe. Struggling through pure instinct, he clawed at his face. He was caught up in a surreal nightmare in which his fingers and some unseen gloved hand were doing battle. He had the idiotic delusion that someone was trying to pull his beard out by the roots.

When it was all over and he began to think clearly again, he understood two things. Improbably, he wasn't dead, and he was now seated. His face was stinging as though it had been scorched with a burst of flame, and his arms and hands ached from exertion. He couldn't move them, and now that the dizziness began to clear, he could see Sylvester's head, still enclosed in the black hood, as he was binding Weiss's ankles to the chair with silver tape.

When he was done, Sylvester stood and pulled off the cloth hood. Beneath it, he was wearing a tight rubber gas mask. When Sylvester stripped the webbing of the gas mask off, casting it aside on the desktop, Weiss saw that Sylvester was as flushed and out of breath as he was.

"That didn't go well." Sylvester panted, staggering a little. "The gas dissipated too quickly. I hoped I could dispatch you in your sleep, but the nitrous oxide didn't stop you from struggling. That damn beard of yours is the only reason you're still alive. I can see the only way this is going to work is if your hands aren't free."

Weiss shook his head, trying to get the sick sleepiness out of his mind. The smell of the gas had almost gone. Weiss could see that Sylvester's lower lip was trembling. He appeared on the edge of tears, but with a fatalistic sniff, Sylvester picked at the corner of a second adhesive sheet and began peeling back the protective layer of parchment to expose fresh glue. He took another step, looking frightened this time, and being careful.

Sylvester was thinking it through: Weiss had managed to

deform the vinyl sheet and tear an air passage because his hands were free. This time, he would only be able to move his shoulders and head. If Sylvester could stand behind Weiss and pull the vinyl sheet back, forcing Weiss's head back against his chest, he would succeed.

Sylvester stood there, his eyes wide with loathing, trying to find the cold centre that would carry him through the next few minutes of agonized struggle. The detective wasn't powerfully built, but he was wiry and there was a grim fierceness to him. Would Weiss die that way, trying to scream curses into the vinyl as it adhered to his cheeks and brow? Would his death throes be violent enough to tear the tape on his arms? Weiss might manage to topple the chair, but that wouldn't matter, would it? Sylvester could still reach down and press.

Press. He remembered. That's all it took—just enough pressure so that Weiss couldn't work an air passage to his mouth. This time, the adhesive would do most of the work for him. Even so, the thought of those few minutes—three? Four? Five? —of brutal struggle made him tremble.

Another step and Sylvester was within reaching distance of Weiss's face. Sylvester heard the chair creak as Weiss strained against it. It was a heavy wooden armchair, but the joints were dry and loose.

Weiss tried to mirror Sylvester's dispirited tone. "There's no point to this, Sylvester. Where are you going to go? All this buys you is a nightmare of stumbling around in the woods."

"I'm counting off my freedom in hours, Weiss. Not days. It's all about time, isn't it?"

Weiss managed to arch his back violently and the chair tipped away from Sylvester's outstretched hand. But instead of tumbling backward, the chair jammed against the blackboard with a sickening scraping sound. Weiss's feet were off the ground now and the chair was wedged in place. Weiss realized this was it. He was about to die, and his thoughts were trying to flee his body to a place of comfort and solace.

He was surprised to see his wife there—he had loved her once, after all. And there was Carly Rouhl. There was Prem Joshi, who would carry the burden of Weiss's death to his own grave. And there was... Toni Beal. Only *she* stayed there, swimming in his vision as Weiss waited to take his last breath.

It was while Sylvester was standing there, the pad flat on his right hand, that Weiss heard it—the rumble of the streetcar. He'd heard it often enough to recognize the click and rattle of its old steel wheels and coiled springs. Weiss's eyes darted to the windows and the archway, then back to Sylvester's hand. Sylvester had paused, distracted.

His mind beginning to work, Weiss said, "That's right, Sylvester. Someone's coming. This isn't going to work."

Sylvester looked down at his hand, calculating.

"Do you see?" Weiss went on, trying to measure his tone. "Now it's all about optics: do you allow yourself to be caught threatening a police officer, or do you let me go and surrender to me? That's what we'll call it, okay? You surrendered to police. It's just a phrase, but it'll sound good in court. Might make a difference in your sentence—maybe a big difference."

Sylvester hesitated, listening to the sound of the rails, the adhesive pad balanced on his outstretched fingers. He had to do that, keeping the patch open, or the damn thing would stick to itself and his improvised murder weapon wouldn't work.

Weiss was rigid against the tape binding his wrists and ankles, and he could hear the chair squeak against the blackboard with his futile stretching. Maybe this wasn't deliverance. The schoolhouse wasn't a regular stop on the circuit. Maybe the sound of the old Toronto streetcar would grind up and then roll away into the mist, heading back to the visitors centre. Was it possible Prem hadn't made it in time for this circuit? Had old Vern and Ed got it disastrously wrong?

Weiss and Sylvester waited. That steady rumble was keeping Weiss alive from second to second. Coming, coming.

Weiss saw Sylvester straighten as the streetcar rattled alongside the schoolhouse pathway. He only needed a few minutes to kill Weiss, then he could run out into the mist and try to disappear. The vinyl bounced a little on his outstretched palm as though he was a baseball pitcher readying to throw a "Blue Bayou"—the ball batters feared—the one that blew by you, the one that struck you out.

Then Weiss released his breath, the deep quavering breath that might have been his last; the streetcar was stopping. Sylvester seemed to deflate, his hand sagging. Weiss watched with unspeakable relief as the vinyl closed in his hand, sticking to itself. Sylvester had lost his nerve.

The metallic grinding stopped, and they waited in the fleeting silence. After a few interminable seconds, the sound of hurried steps came from the cloakroom—light clicks on ancient linoleum. Weiss closed his eyes in an agony of suspense; it didn't have the shuffling gait of Joshi's rubber-soled boots.

But Sylvester didn't know that. With an air of desolation, he lifted a box cutter from the desk and came at Weiss.

There was a second of hesitation and then he sliced the tape from Weiss's right wrist. Weiss ripped his arm free and snatched the box cutter from Sylvester. Weiss slit the tape on his left wrist, grinding his teeth as the blade snagged and bit into his coat sleeve. His arms were both free and, as Sylvester watched with flat eyes, Weiss dipped down to cut his right ankle free. He was aware of Sylvester stepping away in dejection.

Weiss jerked forward in the chair, making it bang down to its front legs. He looked across the desktop to see Sylvester staring out into the gloom with a look of astonishment.

A sharp, high-pitched cry of alarm that was almost a scream filled the schoolroom. "Eilert!"

Weiss stood, the chair still dragging on his left ankle. The tangle of school desks was shrouded in shadow, but the tall thin silhouette amid the clutter wasn't Prem Joshi.

"Carly?" Weiss gaped in surprise.

Sylvester staggered. "Carly? Carly *Rouhl*? You were the other one the guy on the phone warned me about."

The dynamic in the room suddenly shifted, and Weiss jerked his gaze back to Sylvester. The forger was looking about, desperately searching the shadows, and Weiss remembered that he no longer had his service weapon in his belt holster—and that Sylvester must know where it was.

Carly moved closer, emerging into the light, and the grim tension in Sylvester flooded back. Weiss saw why. The police issue pistol was lying within reach on the student desk in front of him. Weiss jerked forward, but the armchair clattered behind him, hanging from a thread of tape.

Sylvester made his move, his shoulder coming forward. He was counting his chances in microseconds and millimetres. Carly was closer to the gun than Sylvester was now—but she hadn't realized it yet. She followed Sylvester's gaze. The pistol couldn't have been more than a shadow on the desktop, but Carly committed and lunged at it at the same time as Sylvester. They thudded shoulders and spun apart as Weiss stood watching helplessly. Weiss calculated the possibilities even as he struggled to rip away the last of the tape on his ankle: Carly wouldn't know how to handle the pistol, and Sylvester could easily overpower her.

Carly staggered a few steps back from the collision, and her hand came up in a nervous, awkward way.

There she was, wobbling on her heels, a strand of dark hair coiled across her face—pointing Weiss's gun.

Sylvester glanced at the gun and then at the doorway, considering a run toward it. Carly fumbled with the gun, wondering if it had some kind of safety catch. Sylvester didn't know any more about guns than Carly, but getting shot in the back didn't align well with his wish to play for time, so he stood his ground, sullen and quiet.

The teacher's armchair rattled free on the dais with a loud clatter. Weiss raised the boxcutter and ratcheted the blade out another inch. "Aaron Sylvester, I'm arresting you for forcible confinement and attempted murder."

That was enough for now. The murder charge could wait.

Sylvester blinked and sagged back against the wall. An old Union Jack flag in the corner toppled from its stand and fell to the floor.

Weiss stepped down. "Carly, where's Prem? Did you see him?"

"Oh, God! I'm sorry, Eilert. I let the motorman think I was your partner. He remembered me from when I came with Harriet."

Weiss blinked. "You impersonated a police officer?"

"Well, I didn't *say* I was a detective or anything. I just said I was here to help you. Besides, I knew there wasn't time to wait for Prem or anyone else. The streetcar was there waiting beside the platform." She wanted to babble on, running on sheer nerves, tears starting in her eyes.

Weiss reached gently for Carly's shaking wrist and made a show of flipping the safety on the pistol to the off position. But he left the safety on. He didn't want any accidents. "Please keep this pointed at Mr. Sylvester if you would." He retrieved the silver tape from the big desktop. Still frowning in dismay, Weiss managed a quick smile—the kind that made his moustache bristle and cracked pond ice out of his eyes. "And thank you."

He ripped off a length of tape and seized Sylvester's wrist, twisting it behind him.

With Sylvester's hands bound, Weiss took his elbow and pulled him toward the doorway. Carly started to follow, shuffling like someone in a dream, the pistol dangling now. She stopped, and Weiss frowned back at her.

"Carly?"

Carly blinked, still confused about what had just happened, and terrified at what *might* have happened if she'd been slower on the uptake, but the effects of shock caused her thoughts to wander in an unexpected direction.

She looked down, thinking she understood why she felt compelled to stop on that exact spot, but even as she took in the empty floor tiles where Cecil Warden had died, she wasn't sure. Two words crossed her mind.

"Poor thing," she muttered, and even as she said it, it seemed an odd thing to say about old Cecil Warden. Then she had the oddest sense of being surrounded by small, silent people—timid, wary, lonely.

She felt a slight friction against her sleeve as though fingers as insubstantial as wafting air were imploring her to stay and take her place up on the dais—up behind the desk.

"It's all right," she whispered. "I'm not afraid," and she turned back to the schoolroom to look.

But the imploring fingers were from another time, a time worn away by wave after wave of gravity. There were pressing matters for Carly in the here and now, and the room was empty.

Carly sensed the figures retreating back into the shadows to resume their eternal game, their hands clapping like the rhythm of wind-blown rain on the roof. *Miss Mary, Mac, Mac, Mac. Silver buttons up and down her back, back, back...*

At last, she nodded at Weiss's questioning gaze and followed him out through the annex to the trackside. The streetcar was there where she had asked the motorman to remain. "Wait for us," she had said with just the right tone of command. She hadn't *exactly* been impersonating a police officer, but she thought, with satisfaction, that she'd nailed the Humphrey Bogart snarl. Well, Lauren Bacall anyway.

Weiss settled Sylvester on the back seat while a dozen tourists stared and whispered along the aisle. The conductor approached Sylvester and said, "Aaron?" but Sylvester turned his face away and stared stonily at the forest. Old Ed backed off, slighted by a friend.

Without taking his eyes off his prisoner, Weiss used his cell phone to contact the police dispatcher. When the call was over, he turned to Carly, who was on the side bench watching him.

"I was calling for backup, but dispatch said they sent another car twenty minutes ago. I guess my partner's here and he called in another unit as a precaution. Seems there's a small army waiting for us at the visitors centre. Prem's more cautious than I am—I guess because he has family. Lots of it."

CHAPTER TWENTY-SIX

Joshi was waiting on the platform when the streetcar rolled to a stop at the visitors centre. He had his hand resting angrily on his waist holster when Sylvester stepped down, followed by Weiss. Sylvester's hands were secured behind his back, and Weiss had to help him to the platform.

There were now four uniformed police officers on hand, and a couple moved in on Sylvester. They took him off in the direction of the parking lot while a gathering of five or six volunteers filed out of the centre to look after them in disbelief. The rookie woman cop put her arms up to contain the group as though directing traffic. She'd caught on that Sylvester was dangerous.

Joshi scrubbed his face in exasperation. "Judas Priest, Eilert!"

"I know, Prem. It didn't work out the way I intended. When I got here, I felt my hand was forced because I was afraid Sylvester would either make a run for it or kill himself. I'm not the world's greatest field operative; I can't understand how I keep getting us into all these messy situations. I'm much happier at my desk, you know."

Joshi fumed quietly for a moment. It was hard to dump on Weiss. He always made himself a soft target. Joshi had less sympathy for Carly Rouhl, though. She was tough and could stand up for herself.

He rounded on her as she stepped down onto the platform. "You made it impossible for me to be there to help my partner, Ms. Rouhl. This could have ended badly for both of you."

Carly gripped her collar as if against a freezing wind. "I'm sorry, Detective Joshi. I really am, but I knew that you would be too late to help Eilert. I'm probably guilty of something, but—"

She brushed a strand of hair out of her eyes and tried for the umpteenth time to think it through. If she hadn't arrived when she did, Sylvester might have...

Weiss put a protective hand on her shoulder. "Seems it was Carly's time to save me, Prem, but consider yourself on deck for next time, okay? God knows I need you."

Joshi tried to speak, his mouth opening and closing, then he grabbed Weiss's elbow, hauling him away from Carly's side.

"Next time? *Next* time? Has it occurred to you that this thing with you and Carly Rouhl isn't the most wholesome relationship in the world? I know it's not just me. My last partner retired without so much as a scratch; last I heard, he was into rug hooking. We were just going to bring Sylvester in for questioning, and you go out there and face him alone. What the hell went on in that...that schoolhouse, anyway?"

Weiss seemed at a loss for words. It wasn't Carly's Rouhl's fault that last winter he had nearly died of exposure on Marcella Cole's property, and it wasn't Carly's fault that he and Joshi had come close to tumbling down the escarpment on the Noah Goodwyn case. But he kind of saw Prem's point. These last three cases had made him wonder if he was even going to make it through to retirement. Fortunately, he knew how to distract his partner.

"Prem, listen to this: Sylvester said to me he was tipped off by a detective. He claimed that this detective knew I was coming for him. At first, I thought he must mean someone in the department. I've been stewing about it all the way back from the schoolhouse, and I think I know who Sylvester was talking about. It was *Clendenning*! Harry goddamn Clendenning has been manipulating this whole thing from the beginning."

Joshi did a double-take that was almost comic, disbelief written all over his face.

"Prem, he's not the quiet clean-up man I thought he was, and he's not the great consulting detective from Peterborough you heard rumours about either. Harry Clendenning's been using his contacts and his 'gift,' whatever that is, to pad his retirement fund—and to stay in the shadows."

"Clendenning? What the hell has he got to do with this?"

"Prem, you were the one to tell me about these people, cops who take the impossible cases and somehow make sense of them in a way the rest of us can't. Well, fine, you mentioned two of them—Mac in Orillia, and Clendenning in Peterborough—so I checked into them. Mac passed away a couple of years ago. That left Harry Clendenning, the Peterborough cop who consulted here and there around Southern Ontario, including here in Halton. Last week, I tracked him down to a retirement residence up in Parry Sound. A nice place; maybe too nice for a guy on a police pension.

"Even while I was there talking to him, I got the sense of a cynical, embittered cop who was all about playing the game. I didn't get a pleasant vibe from him even then, but I figured, you know, Clendenning did what I had done with the Marcella Cole case and the business with Noah Goodwyn—he would bend the evidence just enough to satisfy his superiors. You know how much it bothered me when I was forced to do it; selectively ignoring evidence and turning a blind eye to protect people. But at least I could tell myself I'd saved the innocent from endless persecution."

Weiss glanced around, making sure none of the tourists could hear. "I think Clendenning has been doing something completely different. He's been settling cases, but he's been protecting the guilty, and taking a kickback for himself in exchange for his silence."

Joshi stared. "My God. Blackmail? Can you prove any of this?"

Weiss slumped against the vertical siding of the visitors centre, his eyes ranging over the curve of tracks towards the maintenance building. "Well, here we are again, Prem. All I have is the word of Aaron Sylvester, the man we're arresting. He's going down for attacking me, and maybe for the murder of Cecil Warden. Clendenning is just a voice on the phone according to Sylvester, but Prem—I *know* it's him."

CHAPTER TWENTY-SEVEN

From the top of the five-story spiral parking lot, Harriet got a pretty expansive view of Lake Ontario across the narrow sweep of Spencer Smith Park. She walked down the ramp to the fifth-floor elevator, pressed the button, and waited. She wasn't sure why Carly had asked her to come here after work, but it was a short drive from the magazine and Harriet had a feeling that there was more to be said about A.L. Rouhl and the old schoolhouse.

The elevator took her to the street-level floor of the building and a small concourse with tables and chairs. To her right was the tourist board desk strewn with pamphlets; to her left, the opening to a Pane Fresco coffee shop. There was seating in the little coffee and patisserie shop, but the dinner crowd spilled out to the concourse tables, and seated against the street-side windows was Carly Rouhl, nursing a large coffee and an iPad.

"Busy day?" Carly smiled as Harriet slid in opposite her. "I got you a coffee. I hope it's still hot."

Harriet took a sip; warm foam and sugar. Exactly what she would order.

"What is this place? I've been by a dozen times but I've never bothered to come in."

Carly gestured to the nearby stairway. "Second floor is the Downtown Business Association; floor above that, The Halton Archives Project, which is why I'm here. In fact, I've been up there all day."

"Is it a sort of library?"

"It's an ongoing initiative. They're bringing archival material from all over the Halton Region—Milton, Halton Hills, Oakville—and digitizing it. They've got birth and death records, property deeds and town council minutes. All sorts of stuff. I wouldn't have a hope of finding what I need unless it was filed and organized in their database. You'll probably wind up using the archive for the magazine someday."

Harriet nodded. "Research. I figured as much. Your journalistic training again. Do you need some background for the story you're writing about the schoolhouse?"

"I guess you could say that's part of it." Carly folded her tablet closed and sat up straight. "Harriet, when we were on the streetcar, I remember you asking me a question."

Harriet shifted uncomfortably and sipped her coffee. She wasn't sure how much her friend remembered and it made her nervous. She thought about being evasive, but instead said, "You mean when I asked, 'Who's Dora?'"

Carly nodded slowly. "I never answered you. We were kind of rushed at the time, but the truth is at that moment, I didn't know the answer. I couldn't have told you. I'm pretty sure I do know now, though. I've known ever since..." She looked down at her palm. The redness had gone. "...ever since I burned my hand on the stovetop."

Harriet couldn't help herself; she felt relieved. Either Carly never felt her stolen kiss, or she had chosen to ignore it. Harriet had survived her slow-motion suicide because Carly was fixated on the name. It took Harriet a moment to offer the obvious follow-up question.

"So, who is she? Who is Dora?"

"I believe she's a little girl who died in the schoolhouse."

"But you don't know?"

"How could I know? It's just a name that popped into my head. The girl is all mixed up in my imaginings about the murder in the schoolhouse. You've no idea how maddening it is to believe something is true and be unable to tell anyone how you know."

"And you came to the archives to try and verify things? What did you find out?"

"I found out that Dora was a popular name for children in the early twentieth century. There are thousands of them listed in births and deaths. I found out a lot about the 1918 pandemic, how hundreds of school-age kids in Oakville were taken by respiratory failure after catching the Spanish Flu. I even found records confirming that some schools were used as quarantine locations, which, given the health care of the day, meant they were used as places to warehouse the dying."

"It sounds to me that you're probably right about Dora then."

Carly squeezed her eyes shut in frustration. "Probably."

There was a long pause during which they both looked out at the cars passing, some of them entering the parking garage. A little further down the street, Carly could see Benny's, the restaurant where she had met Evan after her father's funeral.

"Do you want to get something to eat?" Carly said. "My tab."

"Sure. They have quiche and quesadillas at these places, don't they?"

They stacked their coats on their chairs and took their purses with them. There was a short line along the glass counter. Carly looked over the baked goods on display beneath the glass.

"Maybe," she said idly, "if I was the type of person who knew how to work the data, I might be able to narrow the search, but I was getting nowhere. I don't have the patience."

Harriet asked for a quiche and salad. While she was waiting, she turned back to Carly. "But then you happen to know someone like that, don't you? Someone with patience? A literary bean counter?"

Carly laughed. She ordered a BLT and stepped back. "You're serious, aren't you?"

"I'm just sayin'."

"Evan and I, we aren't... We didn't leave things in a very good place."

Harriet accepted her plate and moved on. "This looks yummy. See you back at the table."

Carly stood waiting at the cash desk for her order, her eyes focussed about three miles beyond the menu board. "Mm," she said to no one in particular.

CHAPTER TWENTY-EIGHT

Carly was just out of the shower when her phone rang. She did a quick twist around her wet hair with a towel and it stayed put. She opened her phone to hear Evan's voice.

"You know I'm glad you called me earlier," he said.

"You are?" Closing her robe over her damp body as she moved, Carly made it to her bedroom and sat on the coverlet. "I had a hell of a nerve laying that task on you after the way I spoke to you at your place. I wasn't sure if you'd agree to help me."

"The way I remember it, you told me to accept a great career opportunity. It was the right thing to do. The hosting gig is a lot of fun."

"I sounded as if it was what I wanted you to do, but the truth is, I hate you being so far away from me."

Evan was silent for a moment, and Carly thought he might be taking satisfaction in that little victory.

"I think I've met Dora," he said.

"What? What did you find?"

"I had to get a bit forensic to narrow the search. I tried focussing on the pandemic research and used the U of T Faculty of Medicine archive. I knew I was dealing with mortality lists, so I compiled a list of Doras of school age, limited it to villages and towns that have long since been incorporated into Oakville."

"Unbelievable. And you got a name out of all that?"

"I got more than a name, but I'm not sure you want it."

"Evan, I have to know. It's hard to explain, but I feel as though that little girl and I were together at the end. It turns out the Cecil Warden murder was closer to home than I imagined, and somehow it got all confused in my mind with poor Dora."

"Her name was Dora Anne Preston, and she had an older sister, Delores, who survived. The parents were Michael and Felicity Preston, a farming couple."

"Evan, that's great. You're amazing. I can't believe I gave you such a hard time about your skills."

"We organizational geeks do serious research now and then."

"Why did you say you weren't sure I wanted what you found?"

"Ah, yes." Evan rustled the phone against his cheek, stalling. "Because I probably should have stopped there. Instead, I got clever and wandered across campus to talk to some arts people. I won't bother you with the details, but a specialist in folk art directed me to a photo archive."

"Oh, my God. You found a photograph?"

"It's not what you think, Car. I've just been looking through a portrait collection organized by name. It was one of the hardest things I've ever had to look at. But yes, I found her."

"Can you send the photo to me?"

"God, I wish I'd never mentioned this. Listen, Car, I need to explain something to you. There was a tradition in the nineteenth century of itinerant artists painting posthumous portraits of newly deceased children. Mourning portraits they were called, and families would use them to remember the loved one."

"Yes, I think I've seen some reproductions. But you said you had a photograph..."

"When photography came along at the turn of the century, the tradition changed."

"My God. You found a posthumous photograph."

"You wouldn't believe what I've seen. They would pose the child as if it was sleeping. Sometimes they would even sit the corpse on the mother's knee."

Carly felt a chill and clutched her robe tight at the neck. "How awful is Dora's portrait?"

"Not bad as these things go, but that's not saying much. I've had a tour of hell. The photo was hand-tinted, but...her eyes are open, Car."

Carly sat on her bed, stunned, unable to speak. Evan waited. At last, Carly decided, her voice breaking. "Can you send it to me, Evan?"

"If you're sure."

"I'm sure."

The connection was broken, and Carly waited, holding her phone in her open palm. After a few seconds, there was a chirp telling her she'd just received an email. She opened it and there was Dora Anne Preston, looking back at Carly with dead eyes. Her cheeks had been rouged with watercolour and her best dress had been turned blue by the photographer.

It wasn't the dress she had been wearing that day at the schoolhouse when Carly burned her hand, but it was the same girl. Sitting at her desk near the back of the schoolroom, her face had looked fuller, her complexion fresh, but it was Dora. A tear ran down Carly's face and a wave of confused emotions made her rock gently on the bed. In life, Dora had been a beautiful child.

But that's all she ever got to be.

CHAPTER TWENTY-NINE

Carly stood in the dark at the back of the control room, watching Evan's daytime talk show on the bank of monitors. A switcher was popping buttons to select cameras and a director was calling the shots, casually waving a finger. On the screens, Evan looked poised, and his natural charisma brought life to the set. He was wrapping up, tossing loosely scripted banter back and forth with a woman in front of a blue screen.

In the control booth, the director spoke with the easy manner of long experience: "And…roll credits." He waited and then, "That's a wrap. Thanks, people. See you on Monday bright and early."

The bank of monitors showed abandoned cameras and random shots of the studio as the light in the control booth came up.

Carly walked out of the shadows towards the brightly lit studio floor. The floods and spots were being turned off one by one with an audible pop from the circuits, leaving the set with its glass desk and pivot chairs in a curious half-light.

Evan picked Carly out from the mic booms and cameras and then stepped around the desk and waited to see what she would do. Carly smiled at the floor as though carrying some kind of shame and started towards him.

"No fancy handwriting analysis," she said to him, "but the magic is still there. You're fantastic at what you do. This show is going to be a success, I'm sure of it."

"There's no future in graphology. Did you know they don't teach handwriting in the schools anymore?"

They were standing close now, and Carly could see that he had television makeup on. She'd taken some time on her own makeup this time, and she was wearing her favourite coat, a cream A-line with big collar buttons that looked cute against her throat. She knew she might only have one shot at this.

"Seems I'm not coping too well with you being away," she said.

"It's a long hike from Burlington. I've been thinking about you. Did you ever get to the bottom of that manuscript business?"

Carly sighed. "Ah, see now, that's good, because I want you thinking about me. A lot, in fact."

"I do that. The hard part is not being with you. I need you. I need to come home to you."

"And I want to make that work," Carly said. "Do you think maybe… I mean, I know you're a professional screen personality now, but do you think you could kiss me before I have an emotional collapse in front of all these tech people?"

Evan stepped toward her, bending her back with the force of his lips. She held on, squeezing his arms, wondering if her legs were still there below her.

From somewhere above Carly's head an amplified voice boomed, "Are you getting this on tape, Charlie?" There was a mic pop and a woman's laugh. "Just kidding, Evan. Carry on."

Carly and Evan were inches apart, caught up in the moment, and Carly knew she had a chance. "You quit early on Fridays," she said.

"It's a lunchtime show," Evan said. "The Friday show's over at one."

"So, long weekend then?" Carly said hopefully.

Evan nodded slowly. "Definitely. I don't want to spend it with my sister's family."

"Then you'll come back to Burlington with me? I've got a pretty interesting story to tell you."

He kissed her again and touched her face. Then, remembering the question, he said, "Oh, by the way, that would be a yes."

The amplified voice from the control room boomed overhead again. "Can we use any of this on the evening news?" Evan grinned. "Kidding, Evan," the voice said."

Then another voice, far from the mic, said, "He wishes."

The logistics after that were ugly. They both had cars, and it was rush hour. They could see the highway from the parking lot. It was pretty much always rush hour on the 401. Agreeing to meet at her house on the lakeshore, they pulled out of the CTV parking lot in separate cars and joined the weekend traffic.

Inching along in stop-and-go traffic past Yorkdale Mall and the Ford plant, the two hours in her green Mazda weren't so much a cold shower as a sexual pressure cooker, and she gripped the gearshift with profane intensity all the way to the QEW Niagara.

Evan got to her Burlington home fifteen minutes after Carly, so when she opened the door to him, she was fresh out of the shower with a white bathrobe tied at her waist. Her hair was a towel-dried mess and she had all the sophistication of a peasant grape picker. Mistaking the picker for the grape, Evan quickly nuzzled her ear and began walking her backwards towards the stairs, somehow managing to part her robe as he went. Not for the first time, Carly wished her bedroom was on the first floor.

CHAPTER THIRTY

They led Aaron Sylvester to the unassigned workspace at the District Three station, then he was seated on an office chair to wait, one wrist cuffed to an armrest, a uniformed officer standing over him.

The door opened again, and a detective walked in with a plastic document case. "Name's Joshi," the interrogator said. "We didn't get much of a chance to talk before. Thought it might be better if I did this interview. It'll give Detective Weiss a chance to cool down."

Joshi sat in an armchair and put the case on the table. "After all, Weiss was the one you attempted to murder in cold blood. Between you and me, I think he's a little pissed at you. Maybe I can bring a little more detachment to this. What do you think? Do you want to talk about your future, Aaron?"

"I'm thinking about a lawyer. How would that be for detachment?"

"Your option. We could wait for a lawyer. Thing is, lawyers aren't magicians. You were observed going about the business of trying to murder a cop. Oh, and the witness? A well-respected daughter of a literary hero: a smart, articulate, unimpeachable woman. Your goose, judicially speaking, is cooked. Let's not forget that you confessed to the murder of Cecil Warden—right there on the scene of his murder. I'll tell you, Aaron, you may not be much of a criminal, but you've got a flair for the dramatic."

"Okay, so I'm screwed. Why do I need to talk to you?"

"Well, the Q.C. is going to ask the judge if he'll be so kind as to lock you up for years."

"What's a Q.C.?"

"Queen's Counsel. We're in Ontario. The Queen has a strong interest in your case and you're going to be spending a long time in Her Majesty's care. Thing is, the prosecution might be inclined to reduce your sentence if I can tell them how much you helped the Crown."

"For God's sake, stop talking about the Queen."

"Oh, I thought you'd appreciate the historical context, you being interested in history and all. We've searched your basement workshop; you're not just interested in playing antique trains, are you, Aaron? You're kind of into the dark ages, wouldn't you agree? And I mean *dark*. Some of the shit you've got down there you could sell on a porn site."

"Some of my reconstructions have been used in the movies. Maybe some of them were porn, I don't know. It's not illegal."

"Good for you, but here's the key to this: we've got you. What we want is Harry Clendenning. Back when you were gloating to my partner about how clever you are, you said a detective warned you we were onto you. Let's talk about that."

"What do I get in return?"

"That's for your lawyer and the Crown to decide. The prosecution, if you prefer. Everything you say in here is being recorded. It'll all be going into evidence. So I'm listening."

Sylvester shifted his bulk on the chair. "I don't know names. This old guy calls me up. I can tell he's old because he's all wheezy and he coughs from deep in his chest. And he says he's been thinking about me."

"How did he get your name?"

"Damned if I know, but he knows about Weiss and he even knows about that Carly Rouhl woman. That got my attention because I'd heard of her and her magazine."

"What did this old guy offer you?"

"He was a slick bastard. He had his pitch down pat; a carrot and a stick."

"The stick—that was a threat, right? That he would tip Weiss off that you murdered Warden?"

"Right."

"So, what was the carrot?"

"He said he could tell me when Weiss was coming for me."

"Did he say how he would *know* something like that?"

"No, but he was right, wasn't he? He knew Weiss was coming to the schoolhouse, and he knew that he would come alone. When Weiss phoned me up that first time asking questions about the schoolhouse, I figured that the wheezy guy knew what he was talking about."

"Then it occurred to you that you could eliminate Weiss. If Clendenning was right, he was handing you Detective Weiss on a platter—alone and vulnerable. It gave you plenty of time to prepare."

"I figured I had nothing to lose. If I could stop the Warden investigation, I might have a chance."

"Why didn't you just run?"

"I thought I still had a shot at getting away with everything. I've been getting away with shit pretty much all my life. This might sound strange, but you know what else impressed me about the guy on the phone? He didn't ask for much. A thousand bucks in cash dropped off behind an arena in MacTier? Hell, you can't get a computer for that.

"And the funny thing is, I understand why he did that. He did it for the same reason that I never went for the big score—to keep a low profile. You don't ask for too much, see? But if you pull off the con often enough, it adds up over time. It's an income. Con men generally get caught because they're greedy. I don't know this Clendenning or whoever, never met him face to face. But he's not greedy. Whatever his sources were, it was obvious he had worked his pitch plenty of times."

Weiss was waiting in the next office in front of a small desk monitor, looking at a high-angle shot of Sylvester.

From the doorway, Joshi said, "We don't have Clendenning. You know that, right?"

Weiss said, "A cash dump behind an arena? Can you believe that? MacTier is a little town a half-hour south of Parry Sound. It's a railroad town with an old caboose on the main street—Clendenning's little joke on Sylvester, I suppose."

"The point is, we have the word of a murderer, and no positive I.D. Just a cough and a wheeze."

Weiss crushed his long crew cut with his hand. "It burns me up when I think about that smug bastard Clendenning looking down from his hill. And to think that I went to him for help!"

"Well, if you're right about him, all you did by visiting him was let him know you were aware of his activities. He probably didn't take well to that."

"I can't ask you to take any of this Clendenning connection seriously, Prem. You've been patient about it, but when it comes down to all of this psychic precognition crap, I'm playing in a whole 'nother field all by myself."

"You're forgetting I was trapped up on the escarpment with Noah Goodwyn's ghost, or whatever the hell that was. Being scared shitless makes you a bit more humble about this psychic stuff. I can't help noticing though, that this sort of thing started happening with old man Rouhl and his carefully staged suicide. Seems to me that somewhere along the line we've been drawn into the world of A.L. Rouhl and his creepy books."

Weiss creaked back in the office chair and wove his fingers over his three-button vest. "You're thinking about that manuscript; the one that Carly—"

"Yes. Carly. Carly Rouhl. Look, Eilert, I'm just saying, it might be a lot better for your health if you stayed away from Ms. Rouhl from now on."

Weiss looked into Joshi's large hooded eyes and read the concern there. He was grateful for that; there weren't many people in his life who gave a damn about his career, his future, or his happiness. He thought for a moment, remembering what Harry Clendenning had said about lightning rods, then, with pain lining his face, he said, "Prem, I'm sorry. I'm not sure I could do that."

CHAPTER THIRTY-ONE

Weiss didn't hesitate to flash his warrant card at the Bayview Retirement Home's concierge; this was as close to police business as a relaxed view of the law would allow. The young woman at the welcome desk informed him that she had seen Harry Clendenning passing through to the solarium minutes before. Weiss hadn't called ahead, but it was too much to expect to take Clendenning by surprise. Old Harry didn't want a scene, and that meant surrounding himself with as many bridge club ladies and Bobby Orr worshippers as possible.

They called it the solarium because it resembled a greenhouse for cultivating ladies with perms and necklaces, and it was an adjunct to the main tower of the Bayview Retirement building. The residents could sit here in palm court splendour eking out the weak rays of the autumn sun which were happily complemented by a forced-air heating system. There were a few spruce trees artfully placed outside to scatter shadows, softening the angular furnishings. The effect was reminiscent of a mid-century lifestyle ad in a glossy magazine.

And there, holding court with three elderly ladies in pastel pantsuits, was Harry. Weiss wondered how many times Clendenning had regaled book club women and true crime buffs with his stories, shocking them with his cynical toughness and charming them with his tales of cases solved and justice supposedly served.

Weiss walked up to the group arrayed on a red couch and two cushioned easy chairs. "Hello, Harry."

Clendenning didn't look at Weiss directly, as if showing off his gift for precognition. "Still on first name terms? Good. I was just telling the ladies you'd be coming." He made a polite show of rising to introduce the ladies. "This is Tilly; she was the CEO of a construction firm. Ada was a nurse practitioner and she's got a Ph.D. Melody is a jazz pianist. You should hear her on Saturday nights—magic."

Weiss ignored the boasting. "Things didn't work out the way you hoped down in Milton, did they? The way I see it, you were pretty much running the whole show."

"Wish I'd been there. I have the sense that it was a close thing."

Weiss forced a smile for the benefit of Clendenning's audience. "Do you think these impressive ladies would excuse us for a few minutes? We should talk."

"Officially?"

Weiss worked his jaw in frustration. Harry wasn't having visions of himself in jail because it would never happen. Maybe Aaron Sylvester's business model had broken down, but Clendenning's never would.

"Maybe this *should* be an official visit, but…no. Just you and me."

The seniors at Harry's side had fallen silent, sensing in his wide stance and stony stare, Weiss's anger. One of them picked up her purse from the floor and held it in her lap protectively. "Go ahead, Harry. We'll wait."

Clendenning hesitated, weighing his options, then started to move his feet with a slow effort. Weiss walked away to a thick square column built around the rebar that supported the heavy overhead glass panels and waited. Clendenning stopped and stood still for a moment; he wanted to disguise the effort it took him to get moving after sitting.

Weiss watched the sunshine over Georgian Bay for a few minutes, then heard Clendenning limping close. "Why'd you bother coming all this way, Weiss? We've got a classic stand-off here. Things would have been simpler for me if Aaron Sylvester had closed you down, but you haven't got anything on me you can use."

"Maybe I wanted to thank you."

"You lost me."

"You didn't go after Carly Rouhl. She's your equal, after all."

"She can't do a damn thing without you, Weiss. She's nothin' but a reporter. You were the one she needed to make trouble for me: a working cop. I knew you'd wind up coming after me that first time I shook your hand at the elevator."

Weiss made eye contact, his face grim. "You're right about one thing, I haven't anything I can use to put you behind bars where you belong. Having said that, and entirely off the record, of course, the reason you're still alive is that you didn't try to hurt her. If you ever do, I'll come up here and throw you off your bloody balcony."

"Easy, Weiss. Nobody's going to touch your lightning rod."

"I can't jail you, Harry, but I wanted you to know I'm shutting you down."

"What do you mean?"

"I can't arrest you, but maybe you can remember a little what it's like being a working cop in the computer age. I'm a hell of a writer myself, Harry. The Hemingway of paperwork, my partner calls me, and I'm going to make sure one or two honest cops in every jurisdiction in Ontario is on the lookout for your interference."

"You can't make unsubstantiated accusations about me, not even on the damn web. I'll sue."

"I said I was good—it's all about the wording, you know. Nuance and inference. But you're not a subtle guy, are you? Maybe you wouldn't understand that. You sure as hell understand networking—that's the way you built your reputation."

Clendenning was silent except for his heavy breathing, and Weiss had the feeling that Harry Clendenning was tired. He'd climbed his hill and he didn't have much fight left in him.

"Well," Weiss said, "I have a lady waiting, too. She's out in the car, so I can't stay. I expect your lady friends are wondering what all this is about. Why don't you tell them another true crime horror story? How about 'Murder by Patch?' Goodbye, Harry."

Weiss walked out of the solarium and across the lobby. When he got outside, he stopped on the easy access ramp and closed his eyes for a moment. He let the sun warm his face. The air was cold, but the sun was sending its slanting rays all the way back from the distant tropics, and it felt pretty damn satisfying.

CHAPTER THIRTY-TWO

Carly and Evan awoke to an early snow that lay in a thin but perfect dusting across the lakeside park. They had a breakfast that was celebratory and filling and then whiled away the morning lounging in the window seat, nursing orange juice and feeling the sunlight on their faces.

Before lunch, they got around to talking about the Sylvester case and Evan listened to Carly describe her lunge for the pistol, mirroring her remembered fear. Evan held her hand.

"Okay, kid. It's over and you're safe. Time to forget and move on."

But Carly's journalistic need to make sense of it all kept working while she began to load the dishwasher. Evan followed her into the kitchen.

"We could go up to the Dutch Mill and have their lunch buffet," he said. "It'd be nice looking out at the fields covered in new snow. They have a fantastic salad bar."

When Carly didn't answer, Evan moved behind her and rested his hands on her hips. "What's bothering you?"

"Telling you all that, about Weiss and Sylvester and everything… It's the first chance I've had to put it all together. I can't help thinking."

"Do you need to do this? You've been through a lot, and you have to let yourself heal emotionally."

"I know, but there's this part of me that, I don't know, seeks out patterns? It tells me that I'm still missing something."

"Has this got to do with your storytelling? The Rouhl curse?"

She twisted to look at him curiously. "You mean my crazy imagination?"

"I'm not putting it down, Car. I'm not. I could as easily have said it was a gift, but I think maybe it's both."

She nodded, her palms on his shirtfront. He cupped her hair, kissing her ear, but all the while Carly's eyes were darting, and when at last they separated, she found herself staring out to the hallway towards the door at the end.

"What is it?" Evan said, looking worried.

"Will you indulge me one more time? I think it's important."

She took his hand and walked slowly into the corridor that ended at A.L.'s office. Evan looked everywhere but at that door. Behind it was the memory of his own near-death experience. It was the room where Marcella Cole had pointed a gun at his chest.

But Carly was opening the door and drawing Evan in. She released his hand and made straight for the low-backed desk chair in which her father had died. Fearlessly, she plunked herself down and gripped the armrests.

"All right," she said, staring fiercely at the wall of books and nicknacks that were her father's physical legacy.

Evan waited, slouching in the doorway as though ready to pull her out of the cluttered room.

"So, Harriet and I were here…"

Suddenly, Evan moved his feet; Indy had followed them from the kitchen. The handsome Lab sat on his haunches in front of Evan and looked at Carly. He licked his mouth and settled on the rug. Carly knew that was Indy's spot. The place where he had always curled up while A.L. worked. The sun pooled there, warming him.

Frowning, Carly glanced left at Indy, and she pointed to the shelves opposite. "You know, it was Indy who drew our attention to that damn manuscript. Indy. A.L.'s constant companion."

Evan turned to look at her. "Easy, Car. This could get weird. You're saying your dog's possessed."

Carly laughed. "No, I don't think that. Indy may have a touch of doggie PTSD, but he's all right. I'm just saying, maybe he can hear things we don't, voices that we're starting to forget. I mean, think about it. Cece Warden was *A.L.'s* unfinished business—not mine. What if all of my so-called visions were my father's doing—his power working through me? Through this house, through this room?"

"Whoa! You don't buy into all that ghost stuff. I know you don't."

"Let me tell my story as it comes to me. We can talk about ghosts another time. I'm just wondering—what if it has been A.L. all along?"

Carly leaned forward, putting her elbows on the desktop. "My ego made it the story of Carly Rouhl and her instincts, but A. L. is the one who lost a friend and couldn't do anything about it. He was right about Marcella Cole being a murderer, and he was right about the antique dealer being Cecil Warden's killer. Did you know that Sylvester means woodman?"

Carly got up and turned to the window—the window that last year had somehow stopped the clock on a freezing cold Thursday in mid-winter, and stayed that way until Marcella Cole died. She gazed out, remembering the way everything had looked from where she stood: still—no birds, no traffic, no movement at all, as though that moment in time had frozen too.

"One of the last things A.L. said to me was that he thought ghosts inhabit the moment of their death, which happens to correspond with their place of death. Because death is the point at which time ceases to pass for us, you see? I once asked him what difference it made—time, place? He seemed to think it *did* matter. He said that the moment of a person's passing—the nanosecond of death—might be as spacious as—I think he said Aunt Matilda's parlour. Or," she gestured at the packed shelves, "it could be as roomy as his cherished office, his beloved house."

Evan shrugged. "So now this isn't a ghost story, it's science fiction. All this stuff about time is just pointless speculation."

Carly went on staring at the haze over the lake, remembering. "When I was standing in the schoolhouse, I had this… Call it a vision. I felt a series of pulses moving through the classroom, each pulse bringing with it a glimpse of children at their desks, warmed by ancient sunlight and an old stove." She looked down at the fading redness on her right palm where the stove had burned her, then at Evan. "It was a happy time for the children, you see—before the post-war pandemic that decimated the community and took away poor Dora.

"Dora was there in the classroom that day. It's as if I saw her there at the back of the room, reliving a happier time. Dora was one of the children who died of the Spanish flu that year. It would have been 1918. The schoolroom had been turned into a sort of field hospital with mattresses all over the floor, and poor Dora died there on that very floor of respiratory failure. That can happen when the virus attacks your lungs. So sad. And that just happened to be the same patch of floor where Cece Warden was smothered to death by Sylvester.

"I guess that's what happens when you start to think of time as fluid. Events can get kind of mixed up together; Warden's murder was on the very same spot as Dora's passing. Those two people—the child and the old man—were separated by the thing that's most inconsequential to a ghost—time." Carly glanced upward, her eyes searching the ceiling as she recited her father's words from memory, "Time is a mere tyranny imposed on the living."

"Come on out of here, Car. This isn't healthy for you."

"Funny. It feels healthy. Catharsis, remember? When you think about it, Sylvester's crime wasn't just treachery against A.L.'s friend. In A.L.'s broader perspective, it was a desecration of Dora's last resting place, too."

Evan straightened against the door frame and held his hand out towards her. "Your dad was god-like in his talent. You're a writer and it's natural that you revere him. But you're going to have to get past this, Car. It's *your* talent that matters now. Go on writing, and imagining, but I need you here...with me."

Indy got up and padded towards Carly. He nuzzled her knee as she reached down to scratch his ear. "It's all right, boy. We'll never forget him."

But then she walked past her father's dog and buried her face in Evan's shoulder, rubbing her face in his warmth. They stayed together for several minutes before Indy's priorities shifted to his food in the kitchen. He trotted off down the corridor. Carly and Evan closed the office door and followed.

CHAPTER THIRTY-THREE

Weiss was at home. He had a book on his lap, the massive coffee table hardcover of Judy Cutler's *Maxfield Parrish*. Weiss had been attempting to lose himself in Parrish's painterly imagination. There was something unreal and yet perfect about the early twentieth-century landscapes. Weiss knew that Parrish had simulated his lakes and hills on a tabletop mirror—so much for naturalism. So why was Weiss drawn to that classically formal world?

Parrish let his wife leave for the Caribbean while he lived with his pretty serving girl and model. That wouldn't have been so bad, perhaps, but when it came down to it, after this faithful servant had been everything to him—his live-in mistress, the pretty face that smiled out of his impossible landscapes and fantasy gardens—Parrish refused to marry her. A servant girl was beneath him, after all. As an old lady, she'd left him to marry another.

And yet, for Weiss, those beautiful neoclassical scenes full of reflecting pools and leafy swings were somewhere to go when the sordid reality of his job became too much to bear.

His phone rang on the coffee table and Weiss picked it up.

"Hello. Weiss here."

"Eilert..."

"Toni. What's up?"

"Can you meet me?"

"Sure. At the station?"

"No. You know the waterfall at Spencer Smith Park? The one across the street from the art gallery?"

"Of course. But why?"

"If you could meet me there in a half-hour that would really...help."

"Toni, what's the matter?"

"Half an hour. Can you make it?"

"I'm leaving right now," said Weiss, and he disconnected the call.

Weiss parked in the art gallery parking lot and took the dazzle painted crosswalk out front over to the lakeside. The great glass pavilion attached to Spencer's Restaurant pointed in the shape of a sightseeing ferry out towards the great expanse of Lake Ontario. The light was gone and the Skyway Bridge to Hamilton was a chain of amber lights to his right.

Toni Beal—tough, a meticulous detective, a patient friend—was standing there where the little reflecting pool beside the pavilion poured over pebbles into a meticulously combed waterfall. It burbled down into the park where a few couples were walking along the lakeside walkway with its massive chained seawall.

Weiss smiled at her, which came easily, but Toni didn't return the smile. Her face was cold and gave nothing away, but it had to be serious if she needed to meet him on neutral ground.

He stood at her side. "Talk to me, Toni."

"Thanks for coming. I hope I didn't sound too lost on the phone. I didn't realize how damn melodramatic it would sound until I hung up."

"I'd meet you anywhere for anything. You know that. Curious, though. Why here?"

"See over there?" Toni turned to the lake and nodded over at the children's swings and climbing bars. "You told me you got together with Carly Rouhl there, right? That's where you met her for...what did you call it?"

Weiss remembered standing with Carly, negotiating a story about her father's death—one that his superiors would accept. "Mutual deniability?" he said. "I didn't want anyone overhearing what we were saying. I was a bit paranoid then, thinking her place might have some sort of recording device hidden under the kitchen table or something. Seems silly now."

"Must have been nice sitting on the kids' swings, looking out at the lake. "

"The first time we met there, it was bloody cold and the swings were chained up."

Toni looked at his face, worried. "There was a second time?"

"Yes. Oh, and we did swing that time. I spoke to her just before I met you in my car at the station. It was milder then. Springtime. I suppose it would have been pleasant enough that time if I hadn't been desperately trying to make sense of the Goodwyn case."

Toni nodded slowly, then she turned to their right, looking up. "And there? Well, you took me to Spencer's for dinner once. Do you remember?"

Weiss grinned. "Or did you take me? As I recall, I was falling apart at the time. You were..." He touched her hand. "You were the one point of warmth in a bleak landscape. I'm not sure I would have made it through that year sane—or alive, for that matter—if it weren't for you."

Toni swiftly brushed his hand away, shaking her head, anger

knotting her shoulders. "I don't want to hear any more gratitude from you, Eilert! I got what I needed back then, too. My marriage was going through a rocky stretch and my husband and I were holding it together for the girls. My daughters are both away in residence at Queen's University now, way down in Kingston."

Weiss couldn't help thinking about the agony of that year. "Thank God my wife and I never had a child. She would have used it to destroy me."

"Probably. But she's gone, and you survived it, okay? The question for you is, what now?"

Weiss knew what she was getting at. His moody solitude was becoming a chronic condition. He thought Toni might be remembering his date with the pretty archivist at police headquarters.

"The thing with Heddy never went anywhere. I tried."

"I know. She's given up on you, and good for her. Smart lady."

"Too good for me."

"Shut up with that self-pitying crap. She was too devout for you—that's not the same thing at all."

Weiss blinked. "Whoa. Easy, Toni. I still need you on my side."

"I'm glad. That's a start. Now, what about Carly Rouhl?"

"What? What *about* her? You can't actually see me with her, can you? She's a young woman with her whole life ahead of her."

"You're not that old, Eilert. I need to know if you want her in your life." She waited. "Well? It's a simple question."

"What's the matter, Toni? What's happened?"

"Don't avoid the question, Eilert. Please! You owe me honesty here."

"Damn right I do, and a whole lot more. Okay, here it is: I like Carly, I think she's special, and I think she's going to be a great writer. I hope we stay friends and I hope I'm there to congratulate her when they make her writer in residence at U of T. I hope I'm still her friend when the world finds out how talented she is." He moved so close he could feel Toni's warm breath. "But that's it. Have you got that now? Do you believe me?"

"Yes, thank God. I believe I do."

"Fine, now what's all this about? You've always given me honesty too, so just say it."

"I've left my husband. Now that the girls are off on their own, we don't have to make it work anymore. I don't know who's more relieved—me or him. And…I couldn't help wondering if that would mean anything to you."

"Toni."

"It's all right, Eilert. Whatever you may think, you don't owe me anything. I just wanted you to know because we—"

"Toni."

"What?"

"Shh." Weiss gently removed her eyeglasses and folded them carefully into one hand.

He kissed her slowly and gently on the lips, half afraid that she would recoil. She didn't. He kissed her again, and this time the two of them got lost in the moment. The lake and the cold didn't exist, and the guilt had gone, too. For Weiss, it was as if the world stopped rolling by, unlived and unsatisfactory. A decade of pain ended in one intimate moment, and he had the sense of placing a foot on solid ground for the first time in maybe forever.

Toni laid her face against his neck so that she was whispering in his ear. "No more talk about gratitude?"

"I can still tell you I love you, right?"

"Feel free."

"You know? I do."

CHAPTER THIRTY-FOUR

The song played in Carly's mind again. *Miss Mary, Mac, Mac, Mac. Silver buttons up'n down 'er back, back, back.*

It was as if she could actually hear the rhythmic clapping of the children's hands, Dora's among them. Silent but echoing, it made the living room of her house feel cold and hollow. She was glad Evan was close, sitting across from her on a footstool.

"Funny thing, though," Carly said, as she tried to relax on the couch. "Dad wasn't the social one. He would have been content to kick back in his office and dream the day away, writing when the spirit moved him." She put down her book and stretched. "After Mum died, that's pretty much what he did. It was different when she was alive. Mum was always dragging Dad to some social event, connecting with friends. I don't know if I ever told you; Mum passed away when I was studying at Cornell. After she was gone, Dad let his friends slip away. Most of them were Mum's friends, anyway. Dad got Indy, and that was enough company for him."

Evan reached over, captured her toes, and began to massage the ball of her foot. "You're thinking of that Warden woman," he said.

Indy shifted on the rug, trying to get the hang of the new dynamic around the house.

"Brenda. Yes. I barely knew her, but she was one of Mum's oldest friends—all the way back to high school, I think. Mum was a bridesmaid at Brenda's wedding, and of course, Brenda was at Mum's funeral."

Evan seemed surprised. "So Brenda and your mother were close, then."

"Yes. They didn't see one another all that often, but Mum called Brenda a lot. Spent hours on the phone with her, I remember. When I think about it, she must have been pretty much Mum's closest friend." Carly sighed with pleasure and pulled her foot back, sliding the other into Evan's hands in its place. "At least Mum was spared seeing Brenda lose her husband in such a terrible way. That would have been hard for Mum, too. Come to think of it, Mum passed away just months before Cecil did, right here in the front bedroom." Carly looked down the hallway wistfully. "That door there to the right."

"Isn't it odd that you never made the connection to Brenda when Weiss came up with the name Cecil Warden?"

"It is, isn't it? Eilert thought so, too; it was what made him uncomfortable. Detectives look for a nice clear chain of cause and effect, and it bothered him that I chanced to pick out Cecil's manuscript from all the clutter in Dad's office. He wondered if it was deliberate, if I was emotionally involved with the Wardens, but I didn't make the connection at first.

"Honestly, how well do you know your parents' friends? Maybe if Eilert had said 'Brenda's husband was murdered' it might have clicked in my memory, but I think I only saw Cece once or twice, and even then it would have been brief. The Wardens as a couple weren't on my radar. Turns out I even met their daughter Corey at U of T, but there were so many people that I made acquaintance with there. The name came back to me when Eilert mentioned her. By the way, I'm going to make a point of looking Corey up. I haven't seen her in years, but I recall she was nice. Eilert tells me she's gay and unmarried. Maybe I'll fix her up with Harriet. Anyway, Mum would have been glad that Brenda got some closure. I'm relieved it all worked out in the end."

The chill was settling through Carly's shoulders, and the warmth of Evan's hands was a welcome distraction. She patted the couch beside her, inviting Evan to warm the rest of her.

Indy had been following the conversation, glancing up now and then to catch a laugh or a sudden gesture. Evan was shifting to sit next to Carly on the couch when Indy became alert, turning his attention toward the hallway.

The Lab got up and angled his head, listening, one ear cocked; neither Evan nor Carly paid much attention when he began trotting out of the room.

He walked the short corridor to the closed door at the end of the hall and stood looking at the crack under A.L.'s office door. He flopped down on the carpet, his nose pressed against the door, and listened. There were two distinct voices on the other side, as there had been many times before. One, the familiar low-pitched mutter of an elderly man that made Indy feel comfortable and at home.

The other, a woman's voice, he'd not heard in life. It was warm and affectionate, and hearing its softness, Indy stirred. His tail moved in a steady whisper across the hall carpet. For Indy, not knowing the words, one lovers' chat was as good as another.

The End

ABOUT THE AUTHOR

Doug Cockell was born in Edinburgh, Scotland and did graduate work in Literature with acclaimed novelist and playwright Robertson Davies at the University of Toronto. Doug has taught Literature, Art, and Media Studies in Oakville and Burlington and was awarded the McLuhan Distinguished Teacher Medal for showing the common visual language shared by illustration, the movies and computers. He has offered courses through The University of Toronto, Brock University, and The Art Gallery of Burlington. In addition to being an author, Doug is an accomplished artist who came to art through his love of the great Twentieth Century illustrators, delighted by their charm and whimsy as well as their skill.

Requiem For Mary Mac is the third novel in the Requiem Series. Remember to add this author to your watch list so you don't miss future mysteries.

Doug enjoys hearing from his readers and he'd love to know what you thought of Book 3 in the Requiem Series. You can reach him via email at douglascockell@gmail.com

Lightning Source UK Ltd.
Milton Keynes UK
UKHW012148260123
416041UK00018B/258/J

9 781990 469060